THE
PRINCE OF
PALOS VERDES

A NOVEL

BY

STEPHEN SMOKE

White Lighthouse Books
466 Mawman Ave
Lake Bluff, Illinois 60044

ISBN 0-9820782-1-8

Library of Congress Control Number: 2008906717

Printed in the United States of America

Cover Illustration by Lawrence Fletcher
www.zonesight.com

Book Design by Margaret K. Lam

<u>DEDICATION</u>

On the eighth day God realized
He needed a permanent address*
So He created Palos Verdes

*Apparently the U. S. Post Office considered
God's explanation that He lived everywhere
and in everything a little too vague.*

Chapter One

Sawyer Black got the call just after three. Calls in the middle of the night were never good news. Good news could always wait till morning.

By the time the caller finished his first sentence, Sawyer was wide awake. That kind of news sobered people up fast.

"I'll be right there," he said as he threw back the covers and got out of bed. "And don't say anything to anyone until I get there. I mean *nothing*, Justin. Do you understand?"

The caller mumbled something.

"Focus!" said Sawyer forcefully. "The next few minutes are the most important of your life. Don't say *anything* until I get there. Do you understand?" he repeated, this time more slowly and hitting each syllable hard.

"Yes."

"Have you called a lawyer?"

"Noah St. James is on his way over."

"Good. I'll be there in fifteen minutes," said Sawyer and hung up.

Palos Verdes was actually several small enclaves on a peninsula that jutted out into the Pacific as you drove west from Torrance to the ocean. It was about four miles uphill from the Pacific Coast Highway to the top of the mountain, then another couple of miles down to the ocean. Before he moved "up the hill" Sawyer had asked someone how to get to Palos

Verdes. The man had told him, "No problem. All you need is a car and two million dollars."

Sawyer, who had traveled extensively, believed Palos Verdes was one of the most beautiful places in the world. Ocean views of Catalina to the left and Malibu to the right. Air clean enough to see through, perfect weather, sea breezes, the sound of the occasional fog horn, and a slower pace. It was like living in Los Angeles without living in Los Angeles.

When Sawyer pulled up in front of Justin Wright's three-story Palos Verdes Estates mansion the gates of the semi-circular driveway were open. There were so many black-and-whites parked on the street that it reminded him of the parking garage downtown at Parker Center. The flashing lights were off, but it was still a circus. And the media clowns were practicing their lines before the lights came up.

Sawyer noticed there was an LAPD car among the Sheriff's vehicles. Normally, the Homicide Team from the Sheriff's department out of Lomita would handle the call. But this was Palos Verdes. *Murder* in Palos Verdes. And the murder of Justin Wright's wife warranted a call downtown. Special handling was written all over this job.

Sawyer ducked behind an LAPD cruiser, made his way through the phalanx of uniformed officers and got a free pass when the officer in charge recognized him as a former LAPD homicide detective and ushered him inside.

Justin Wright's white hair looked a little tousled and, for a moment, Sawyer couldn't figure out why the man seemed to look so different. Sawyer had seen Wright in all kinds of situations, both business and social; in two thousand dollar suits and Tommy Bahama shirts and shorts. By the time he reached Wright, Sawyer realized what made the old man appear so different: For the first time since Sawyer met the man he was not in charge of the situation. Wright was always the alpha dog and he made sure everyone knew it. His enemies feared him. His friends admired him and were recipients of his generosity, whether they wanted to be or not. And more than a few of his friends feared him too.

Not Sawyer. He was intimidated by very little. Certainly not money and certainly not Wright.

Sawyer first met Justin Wright the year he moved to Palos Verdes when his first book set in Palos Verdes had just hit the bookstores. A few days after an article about the book was published in a local newspaper, he had received a call from Wright, who asked Sawyer if he and his wife, Rebecca, would like to join him and Judy for dinner one night. At first, Sawyer tried to politely refuse, but Rebecca twisted his arm. Her real estate business depended on networking and money—the Hill's most influential social network originated with Wright and worked its way out from there; and it was rumored that if God needed money, he got it from Wright.

Sawyer and Rebecca went to dinner at the Wright's mansion. Sawyer had been in mansions before and, even though this was the biggest he'd ever been in—25,000 square feet, not including the underground parking garage—it took more than money to impress the ex-homicide detective.

Dinner was memorable. A sumptuous five-course meal was prepared by one of the South Bay's top chefs. A one-thousand-dollar-bottle of Bordeaux was uncorked and savored. Cuban cigars were smoked on the veranda overlooking the ocean. Judy and Rebecca talked real estate, while Sawyer and Justin talked politics and crime—not that there was any crime to speak of in Palos Verdes. Not then, anyhow.

Sawyer discovered that he actually liked Wright. He seemed like a regular guy. As regular as any billionaire could be. He talked about baseball, specifically the Angels, and constantly grumbled about the fact that Los Angeles didn't have a single NFL team.

When Sawyer told him that he was working on raising funds for a boxing center in San Pedro for underprivileged youth, Wright seemed genuinely interested, although he didn't take out his checkbook.

The night ended after they watched a movie in the Wright's custom-built home theater. There was a popcorn machine and a candy counter stocked with Dots, Black Crows and Milk Duds. Sawyer didn't ask how Wright got a DVD of the movie they watched—it had just opened city-wide the night before and people were lined up to see it. He figured there were a lot of perks that came with a ten-figure bank account.

The next week Sawyer received a call from a detective who ran the fundraising committee for the proposed youth boxing project. He said the project had been completely funded by an anonymous donor. Sawyer never asked Justin if he had been the donor. He didn't have to.

The center was opened less than a year later and Sawyer had invited Justin to sit on the stage with him. After the ceremony, Sawyer had turned to his friend and said, "Thanks."

Justin had simply smiled and said, "You're welcome."

Chapter Two

"Sawyer. Thank God you're here," said Wright, a forced smile on his face that looked broken, unnatural.

Sawyer reached out to shake Wright's hand, but Wright hugged him instead. Sawyer knew that Wright was not a hugger; he was a firm handshake man. But Sawyer knew this hug was not a greeting; it was something more desperate. Over Wright's shoulder Sawyer recognized Riley Gaines, the LAPD's top homicide cop and Police Chief Howard Jones' go-to guy for high-profile cases. Cases the department needed to wrap up extra tight in order to withstand attacks from high-priced lawyers.

"Go into the library, Justin. I'll be there in a minute," said Sawyer in such a way as to make Wright understand that it was more than a suggestion.

When Justin had disappeared into the library Sawyer walked over to Gaines, who was waiting for him. "Didn't know you still worked the graveyard shift," said Sawyer.

"Rich people getting murdered trumps my beauty sleep. Least that's the way Jones sees it."

"Really..." Sawyer gave nothing away, but he wanted Gaines to keep talking.

"Howard called me himself. So, you know this guy?"

"He's a friend."

"I'd get your friend a lawyer and a professional spokes-hole before the morning news programs start making this more ugly than it already is," he said, looking at his watch. "It's already 'morning show' time in New York."

"What exactly happened here?"

"I'll tell you what we know, but what happened 'exactly'...I got no fuckin' idea. Yet. Call came into the Lomita cop shop from 911 about three. Guy's hysterical and he's screaming that his wife's dead on the floor. Black and whites are here eight minutes later and they secure the area."

"Cause of death?"

"Because of the fifteen or twenty stab wounds I'd rule out natural causes and suicide," said Gaines with a straight face. "Fifty-one-year-old female—looks to me to be about ten years younger—dead in the foyer."

"You find the weapon?"

"No, but we're looking. Husband's got blood on him which he says is from holding his wife, trying to revive her."

"Could be."

"Yeah... And if a caboose had wings it *could* be an airplane."

"You like Wright for this."

"Hell if I know, Sawyer. But you and I both know these things are never as complicated as they make them out to be on TV. Real people just aren't as smart as they are on 'CSI.' And real cops aren't as stupid."

"Did he make any statements?"

"You mean anything a lawyer needs to paper over?"

"Did he?"

"No. He was on the phone when I walked in a few minutes ago with someone who advised him against it. My guess is that was you."

Just then Noah St. James walked through the door. Some of the cops didn't recognize him without his suit and tie. Some did. The ones who did turned away. St. James was an attorney to the rich and famous and was a frequent talking head on the cable channels. Sawyer knew St. James through mutual friends and mutual combat—when Sawyer was a cop, they were always adversaries.

The men saw each other and Sawyer tilted his head toward the library and the lawyer disappeared through the library's double doors, which he closed behind him. A moment later St. James emerged and motioned for Sawyer, who excused himself and walked over to the library entrance.

"What?"

"Justin wants you in on this."

"A conversation with a friend is not privileged," said Sawyer, stating the obvious.

St. James shrugged. "He's adamant. I think he thinks it makes him look more innocent to the cops if he's talking to you."

"I'm not a prop. This is serious."

"I know. I tried to talk him out of it."

"Most of the cops here think he's guilty, and me talking to him behind closed doors won't change that."

"He's not thinking clearly. But you know Justin. He's used to running the show. Don't worry. I won't let things go where I think they shouldn't."

"I don't know…"

"He won't talk till you're inside."

"What the hell."

Sawyer followed St. James into the library and closed the doors behind them. The walls on two sides were lined with books, eight shelves deep. Opposite the entry was a thirty-foot bay window overlooking the Pacific. In front of the window was a twelve-by-five burled walnut desk. It was clean except for a phone, a 21-inch flat screen monitor, and an oversized G4 Mac laptop. To the right of the desk was a sitting area that contained a large black leather couch and two matching chairs. Wright sat in one of the chairs drinking something amber over ice. If anything, he looked worse than when Sawyer saw him a few minutes ago.

"Thanks, Sawyer. Can I get you something to drink?"

He thought about saying no, but he was ready for something to take the edge off. "What are you drinking?"

"Bookers."

"Sounds good."

After St. James waved off a similar offer, Wright poured Sawyer a half-glass of bourbon over ice, handed it to his friend and returned to the chair. Sawyer nestled into a corner of the big couch, while St. James prowled the library like an animal looking to defend its territory.

"I don't want you answering questions about your innocence or guilt in front of Sawyer," said the lawyer, establishing the ground rules.

"That's bullshit, Noah." Wright looked Sawyer directly in the eye and said, "I didn't do this, Sawyer. I swear to God I didn't kill Judy!"

"Look, Justin, you don't have to—"

"What? I don't have to tell you if I killed Judy? Are you kidding me! That's the most important thing you both need to know. I didn't kill her, okay?" He paused for emphasis. "I didn't," he said softly, as though speaking to himself.

Sawyer and St. James were thinking that O.J. had said the same thing and had even added the world "absolutely." It didn't really make any difference whether or not Wright swore he didn't do it and, in fact, it really didn't matter to St. James whether or not Wright actually killed his wife. It was now the lawyer's job to defend Wright as vigorously as he could, which translated into just one thing: Keeping Wright out of jail. That could be accomplished by preventing his arrest in the first place or convincing a jury Wright was not guilty...beyond a reasonable doubt.

"That's fine, Justin," said St. James as though Wright had said something inconsequential. "What did you tell the police? Besides the fact that you didn't do it," added the lawyer quickly.

"Nothing really."

"What does that mean?"

"Nothing important."

"Let me be the judge of that."

"Okay."

"So, let's start at the beginning. What happened tonight?"

"Judy and I had some friends over—"

"Names."

"Danny Rosenberg, Tony Arquette, Robert Sanchez, and Jake Woodbridge."

"Did they bring their wives?"

"No. It was our poker night."

"You said 'Judy and I had some friends over.' Did she play with you?"

"No. Well, occasionally."

"Did she tonight?"

"Maybe a couple of hands. It's more like a guys' night out. Is it important whether she sat in for a hand or two?"

"Justin, we don't know what's important right now. But if you change your story later, the prosecutor can use it to cast doubt on your truthfulness."

"I'm not changing my story; it's such a minor detail."

"Trust me, if a good lawyer wants to make you look like a liar, no detail is too minor for the job. Anyhow, go on."

"The game broke up about midnight. Are you going to get these guys involved in this?"

"This is a murder investigation, Justin. Everybody you and Judy ever knew is involved. Certainly everyone you saw or spoke with last night."

"Oh, man," said Wright shaking his head. The enormity of the situation was starting to sink in. The shock still kept most of it out.

"You said the guys went home about midnight."

"Eleven-thirty or midnight, I guess."

"You guess?"

"I had a little too much to drink. I excused myself about eleven and went into the family room and fell asleep watching the news."

"While your guests were still here?"

"I'd had a bad night. I'd lost enough for one evening. Everyone else had money on the table and they wanted to go on."

"So you fell asleep..."

"Right."

"When did you wake up?"

"Around twelve-thirty—Jay Leno was shaking hands with his guests and the credits were rolling. I remember because he was shaking hands with a blues guitar player whose album I just bought—Kelsey Moore."

"You didn't call 911 till about three."

"I didn't discover... I mean I didn't know..."

"You didn't discover what had happened to Judy for another two and half hours?"

"I turned off the TV and went upstairs to bed about twelve-thirty. I was tired."

"When you got upstairs, you must have realized that Judy wasn't in bed. Didn't that raise a red flag?"

"This is a little...embarrassing."

"Get used to it."

"Sometimes Judy and I sleep in separate beds. Separate bedrooms."

"Sometimes?"

"It's a big house. I often work at odd hours and sometimes Judy stays up to paint—she was planning an exhibition of her paintings next week..." Wright's voice trailed off and his attention drifted to someplace dark and empty.

"So you don't always sleep in the same bedroom."

"That's right. I don't see anything strange about that," he said defensively. "We know several couples who do the same thing. It's really more a matter of being considerate of the other person."

"How often did you and your wife sleep apart? What percentage of the time?"

"Is that important?"

"Frankly, Justin, it's starting to sound important."

"I suppose, maybe fifty percent of the time. Something like that."

"So after the 'Tonight Show,' you went to bed, by yourself. What then?"

"I went to sleep."

"And you discovered your wife in the foyer a couple of hours later. What made you get up?"

"I heard something."

"What did you hear?"

"It's hard to say."

"Think."

Wright took a dose of Bookers, closed his eyes and tried to focus. After a moment he said, "I don't know. It sounded kind of like a thud."

"Like a door closing? A body hitting the floor?"

"I don't know. Is that what I'm supposed to say?"

St. James ignored the question. "How much did you have to drink last night?"

"A few glasses of Bookers."

"What's a few?"

"I don't know. Probably one an hour. Say five glasses, starting around seven."

"But you were able to remember watching the news. Do you remember any particular story on the news?"

Wright closed his eyes again. "I remember a story about a dog coming home after being lost for a year."

"Good. So you didn't pass out or black out. You were just tired from a long day and a few drinks and decided to call it a night. Basically, there wasn't any time during the evening that you don't recall—at least while you were awake."

"That's right."

"Okay. So when you heard the noise that woke you up, you were sleeping in your bedroom. What happened then?"

"I went downstairs and saw Judy lying on the floor."

"Tell me *exactly* what you did then."

"I could see her from the top of the stairs. I ran downstairs, calling her name several times as I went, but she didn't respond. I could see the blood..."

"Do you recall if blood was still coming out of the wound?"

"I'm not sure. I picked up her wrist, felt for a pulse and I didn't get one. I started giving her mouth-to-mouth—"

"Which is why you have blood on your shirt."

"Yes."

"About the shirt... Do you normally sleep in your shirt?"

"No."

"Why didn't you take off your shirt before you went to bed?"

"I don't know."

"It wasn't because you were so drunk you just passed out on your bed?"

"No."

"Then why sleep in your shirt?"

"Sometimes I do that. It was a sweatshirt, and it was a little chilly, so I kept it on."

"Did you keep your pants on?"

"No. Is this important?"

"What happened then?" said St. James, ignoring the question.

"I started giving her mouth-to-mouth, but she was gone. Her eyes were staring up at the ceiling. Then I called 911."

"Do you normally leave your wife alone with four of your drunken poker buddies?"

Wright seemed stunned by the question. "What in the hell are you implying, Noah?"

"I'm just trying to get you ready for the world you're in now, Justin. That will be one of the more polite questions the media will shout at you. The cops are going to be more direct. You need to be careful what you say. To *anyone* from now on. The best rule is to say nothing and let me do any talking that needs to be done. Do you understand?"

"I didn't do this," he said, shaking his head and taking another swig of Bookers.

"It doesn't matter anymore, Justin. It only matters what twelve men and women think."

"You really think I'll be arrested for this?" said Wright, looking first at his lawyer, then at Sawyer. Neither man spoke. Which was more of an answer than Wright wanted to hear.

"My god! I can't believe this is happening!"

Noah looked at his watch and said, "Look, I'm going to meet my PR people at the office in about an hour." He stood and walked over to where his client sat. "Say nothing. You won't be arrested tonight and, with any luck, you never will be. But we have to go on the assumption that you will be and that everything you say, to anyone, can be used against you. I need you to understand that, Justin. The police are not your friends. No matter what they say, you're their number one suspect and they're going to try and trip you up. They may try to make you feel guilty for not trying to help them catch your wife's murderer, but more than anything they're just trying to manipulate you into sitting down and talking with them for hours. They think you did it until someone else confesses."

Wright nodded.

"I'm going to tell Gaines that you're not saying anything without me there, which means that you're not saying anything. Period. They know me. My guess is that they won't waste their time taking you downtown until they have something more concrete."

The lawyer shook Wright's hand and left, giving Sawyer a knowing look on the way out, just before he closed the door.

"Thanks for coming, Sawyer."

"You're welcome. But I don't know how I can be of any real help."

"You used to be a homicide detective."

"I'm retired. All I do is write about it now."

"I know. But I feel better with you on my side. I'm scared. You've been through this hundreds of times. I need you. I want to hire you."

Sawyer coughed a tiny laugh and shook his head. "I'm not a private detective, Justin."

"Look, you know me. I have my faults, but one of my strengths is that I'm a good judge of people and I'm decisive. I look at a situation, collect data, analyze that data and make a decision. And then I execute. No dilly-dallying."

Sawyer knew that was true. Wright was rumored to be worth between two and four billion dollars, give or take a few hundred million. He had made his money the old fashioned way—he inherited it. But to his credit, he had taken a small company left to him by his late father and recognized how to leverage its value a thousand times over. He had also put a sizable chunk of his assets into the Internet in the middle 90s, gambling on a couple of computer geeks who had developed a search engine. Wright was a decisive man and his decisions usually made him and his friends lots of money.

"Yeah, I know Justin, but—"

Wright stood and waved off his friend. "More Bookers?"

Sawyer held out his glass as his host poured.

Wright resumed his seat and said, "Look, if I hired a PI, the guy would bleed me and he would have no loyalty to me. And even if the guy promised to keep his mouth shut, he'd probably sell me out to the highest-bidding publisher. Bottom line is that I could never hire anyone I trusted more than I trust you. Plus, there's Gregg."

Sawyer had surmised that this was at least part of the reason he had been summoned. Eric Gregg was Sawyer's former partner. When Sawyer moved to Palos Verdes he had alerted his friend to the Chief of Police vacancy in the sleepy South Bay town. The pay was all right, the benefits were fine and the physical risk, when compared with his job on the LAPD, was infinitesimal. He knew Gregg would occasionally miss the adrenaline rush, but he knew Gregg's wife, Penny, would convince him to take the job. It had really come down to two against one—Sawyer and Penny against Gregg, who never really stood a chance.

"Eric's probably not going to be handling this," said Sawyer. "At least not on a daily basis."

"But he can find out things."

"The sheriff's department out of Lomita's got a homicide team. They were the first on the scene. But, you being who you are, and Palos Verdes being what it is, LAPD was called in. My guess is that things are going to be run out of downtown from day one."

"But Eric has access."

"Some, I imagine. Yes."

"And so do you."

"Look, Justin—"

Wright knew what was coming—the speech about there was just so much he could do ethically—and he waved Sawyer off again. "I'm not asking you to feed me inside information to help me beat a murder rap. I just want to know what's going on. I didn't kill my wife and I want to know who did. I know that, as a suspect, they're going to purposely keep me in the dark and the media will come down hard on anyone who shows me special consideration. All I'm saying is that I'd appreciate anything you can tell me. Ethically."

"But you can't hire me."

"I can. I can hire you as private security, or a security consultant, and put you on the payroll. Nothing illegal about that. In fact, I regularly hired off-duty and retired cops as security for a building I had downtown a few years ago."

"Okay, but I don't come cheap."

"A bottle of Bookers a week?"

"Double it."

"Done."

Sawyer finished his bourbon and the two men shook hands. Wright had calmed down enough so that he was back to shaking hands instead of hugging. Sawyer figured that was a good thing.

Chapter Three

It was about an hour before dawn when Sawyer pulled away from Wright's house. Something was bothering him. After a few minutes he realized what it was. Within a matter of about two hours, the grieving husband had seemed to compose himself to the level of social politeness. As a detective, Sawyer viewed that as, at the very least, unusual. As a husband Sawyer viewed it as, at the very least, peculiar. Wright seemed to lack certain emotions that Sawyer would normally expect to see in a husband who had just discovered his wife's dead body.

On the other hand, some of Sawyer's speculation was tempered by what he knew of the man. Wright was always unemotional, even when wildly good or wildly bad things happened to him in business and personally. Sawyer believed that Wright had loved his wife, but he had never observed them touching, kissing or being overtly affectionate toward one another. That same observation could be made of many of Sawyer's acquaintances. Perhaps it could be said of his own marriage.

Sawyer knew that Wright was a no-nonsense guy who arrived quickly at a bottom line and moved forward from there. He finally decided that there might not be anything out of character in what he observed about Wright this morning. Still, such a demeanor would not work in his favor with the police, the media or the public.

Not with a jury either.

Sawyer pulled his 2007 Lexus LS 430 into the driveway and parked without pulling into the garage. He went inside and returned a moment later with a bottle of champagne.

He walked over to a four-foot-high wooden angel propped up by a metal pole in the yard just to the left of his long driveway, sat down and leaned against it. Sawyer's wife, Rebecca, had bought the angel three years ago when she was going through her "angel" period, during which she read books about angels, and bought calendars and day-planners that contained images of angels. Just before Christmas three years ago she bought two wooden angels. Since then they had put them out in the yard every year just after Thanksgiving.

He popped the champagne cork, careful to muffle its sound. It was nearly five a.m. None of the neighbors' lights were on and the guy who tossed the *LA Times* out of his Corolla hatchback wouldn't be there for forty-five minutes.

Sawyer sipped the champagne from the bottle and slumped against the wooden angel. Out of the corner of his eye he saw the other angel on the opposite side of the driveway and raised the bottle in a silent toast. A few strings of Christmas lights hung limply around nearby trees. The lights were off but the two angels' faces came into view as his eyes began to adjust to the darkness and the moonlight.

No one knew what someone else's marriage was really like, thought Sawyer. Most people were appropriate with friends and knew how not to make a scene in front of others. Almost everyone figured Sawyer's marriage was a good one. Sometimes he did, too. But most of the time he saw it for what it was.

He took another swig of champagne which, on top of the Bookers, was making for a potent sedative. One reason he hadn't pulled the car into the garage was because he didn't want to see the empty parking space. Didn't want to be reminded in yet another way that Rebecca was gone.

After a few more pulls on the champagne bottle the morning sun began to shed too much light on the shadows in which Sawyer was beginning to feel too comfortable. He stood, kissed the angel on its faded halo, walked into the house, closed the door and went into the master bedroom.

To a bed that had never looked so big.

Or so empty.

Chapter Four

Sawyer was not destined to sleep late. His phone started ringing at 7:30. He had been asleep since about 5:15. "Yeah," he said to the first caller, through a Bookers and champagne haze.

"Did you hear about your buddy?"

"Michael? Is that you?"

"Yeah. You awake?"

"Not yet."

"Sorry. I was just listening to the news while I was fixing breakfast and it's all about Justin Wright and his dead wife."

"I know. I just got back from his place a couple of hours ago."

"You up for lunch at Marmalade? My treat."

"I better turn on the Weather Channel."

"What?"

"I didn't know Hell froze over."

"Don't give me that shit. I pick up a check every now and then. Besides, you're rich."

"One o'clock. If something comes up and I can't make it, I'll call you." And with that Sawyer hung up and buried his head in the pillow. A moment later the phone rang.

"Yeah…"

"Sawyer?"

"Who's this?"

"Veronica."

Sawyer cleared his throat and said, "Let me guess why you're calling…"

"This is serious, Sawyer. National news, not just South Bay-cute-adopt-a-pet-at-the-end-of-the-show news. This is CNN. This is FOX."

"Oh, and by the way, I'm fine. How have you been?"

"Sorry."

Sawyer knew Veronica Mays. Better than she knew herself, he had told her more than once. He'd known her before he married Rebecca. She was a former model, which pretty much explained why she was in the TV news business, and the two of them had "enjoyed each other's company" on a number of occasions—*before* Sawyer was married. Mays was married at the time, but she had an interesting way of justifying her actions that Sawyer didn't totally understand. They liked each other and were attracted to each other. Those were the only two forms of ID she required.

Veronica was no longer married. And they still liked each other.

"So, you free for lunch?" she said, not certain if Sawyer had fallen back asleep.

"No."

"Dinner?"

"You buying?"

"That's not like you, Sawyer."

"I should get something out of this."

"I'm open for negotiations."

They always flirted with each other, but this was more than Sawyer wanted to deal with before eight in the morning. "Call me on my cell after one. I'll know my schedule more then."

"I'll keep dinner open."

"Your call," he said and hung up.

Sawyer perused the morning papers and there was nothing about Judy Wright's murder in it—it had happened after the papers went to press. So he checked the Sports section—always looking for any off-season Los Angeles Angels news. There was none. Then he did the Jumble and the Sudoku. He was hooked on Sudoku puzzles, as were many of his friends. He figured that if he ever needed money he could set up a Sudoku 12-step program.

Television and radio were all over the Wright story. In fact, when Sawyer turned on the TV, Channel 10 was running a tape of Veronica Mays standing outside Wright's black wrought iron entry gate. At this point it was all the-police-have-no-leads-at-this-time kind of stuff. But Veronica added that "Billionaire Justin Wright, the victim's husband, is sequestered in his mansion and refuses to speak with the media." Sawyer hit the "off" button on the remote.

Noah St. James called. "Just to touch bases." He wanted to know whether or not Justin had told Sawyer anything the lawyer needed to know about. Sawyer told him what Wright had said and St. James seemed satisfied. He told Sawyer he was preparing for a noon press conference. The lawyer would not be onscreen. He had arranged for a professional "family spokesperson" to tell the public what St. James wanted the public to know about Justin during his "tragic time of grief." It was too early to put a lawyer's face on things. To do so would create a negative public image.

The professional spokesperson, a woman with whom St. James had worked before, would provide sound bites the lawyer wanted out in the media. Nothing more. She would not answer questions he didn't want answered and she knew how to run the show. Her specialty was not so much answering questions but knowing how *not* to answer them.

St. James would not be within twenty miles of the press conference, but he pulled all the strings. Sawyer didn't like the man, but he knew that if he were ever in serious trouble, St. James would probably be his first call. As long as he had the money.

Sawyer knew that sometimes you don't really like the people you need.

Chapter Five

Marmalade was one of Sawyer's favorite restaurants on the Hill and he hosted lots of publishing meetings there. It was also a good place for a drink or a before-movie dinner. The mushroom soup was the best on the planet and his two favorite bartenders in the South Bay worked there—afternoon shift and night shift. So he was covered.

Michael Hall was one of the most interesting characters Sawyer knew. He first met Hall when Hall was playing guitar at a downtown coffeehouse Sawyer used to go to occasionally after work. Sawyer also played guitar and sometimes did a couple of songs on an open-microphone night. Over a period of a few months, and a number of cocktails, the two men became friends.

At the time, Hall was a trader for a large brokerage firm, making lots of money, and playing guitar for kicks at night. He made so much money, in fact, that he quit his job as a trader and went out on his own. That worked so well that Hall and his second wife bought a house in Palos Verdes in 1999. It was the biggest house in the development, a point his wife never tired of pointing out to friends and neighbors.

The marriage went south at about the same time the Nasdaq did and Hall was forced to sell his house. But he didn't lose everything. Instead, he simplified his life and redefined himself. He lived in a two-bedroom condo on Highridge, not far from Sawyer's home. These days he generated income in a variety of creative ways, all of which, he told Sawyer, he enjoyed. First, he still did the occasional trade. Second, he played guitar at various venues around the South Bay, including The Admiral Risty in Palos Verdes and a couple of coffeehouses in San Pedro and Redondo Beach.

His third source income was probably the most creative job Sawyer had ever heard of—Hall taught a Tantric Yoga class at a local adult learning center. Hall had explained to Sawyer that Tantric Yoga was a type of yoga that provided students with specific exercises to channel their sexual energy in positive, creative and healing ways.

Sawyer believed that allowing Hall to teach Tantric Yoga in Palos Verdes was like giving Bonny and Clyde keys to the bank.

Hall had confided to Sawyer that he would not only have taught the class for free, but actually would have been willing to pay to be the sexual authority figure looked up to by the dozen or so women taking each class. Palos Verdes wasn't exactly "Desperate Housewives," but there were a lot of attractive "mature" women who spent time, effort, and money to make themselves look good. And they did. Hall had explained to Sawyer—sometimes in too much detail—that sex with women in Palos Verdes was incredible. He said they weren't so much "horny" as they were unwilling to part with an aspect of themselves that they had once found fulfilling. They enjoyed the lead-up to sex, the dance, the romance of being in love with someone and knowing that someone was in love with them, romantically. Again.

Sawyer had found Hall's explanation interesting because it was not given in a cynical way. He honestly enjoyed the company of these women, admired them and, Sawyer knew— even if Hall did not—that the romances Hall dabbled in filled an emptiness in his own heart that he also filled in theirs.

"I hear you're working for Wright," said Hall as he sprinkled some Tabasco on his potatoes.

Sawyer had ordered a bowl of mushroom soup and glass of Blackstone Merlot. He sipped a spoonful of soup and said, "Wright said he didn't do it." It was not a betrayal of trust and the former homicide detective weighed his words carefully. In fact, this was the message that Wright and St. James wanted out in the public: Wright is innocent.

"Yeah, well, what did you expect him to say?"

"I expect him to tell the truth," said Sawyer.

"Really?"

"Really."

"Look Sawyer, I didn't ask you to lunch so you could give me a scoop. I don't talk to the press. You have my word that I won't tell anyone anything you and I discuss regarding Judy's murder. Okay?"

"Okay." Sawyer believed his friend.

"So, what's your take?"

"I don't think he did it," said Sawyer without hesitation.

"Why?"

"He comes across as…" Sawyer was going to say innocent, but over the years he knew that few people were really completely innocent and portraying them as such often backfired, so he rarely used the word. "I just get a strong sense that he didn't do it."

"So who do you think did?"

"Don't have a clue." Sawyer left out the part about the four poker buddies. He knew that where there was serious money, serious enemies were never far away.

"I hope he didn't do it," said Hall.

Sawyer could tell that the man was sincere.

"I don't know him as well as you do, but I've been to a few of his parties over the years and he's always treated me well. Last year he and his wife came down to Admiral Risty. He left me a twenty-dollar tip. I was never sure whether he did it because he remembered me as your friend, because he liked the music, or because he felt sorry for someone my age playing in some bar for his amusement."

"It doesn't matter. The twenty dollars still spends the same way."

"Are you busy tonight?"

"I don't know. Things are pretty fluid right now."

"Why don't you and Rebecca come down to Admiral Risty tonight? Bring your guitar."

Sawyer had not told his friend about his problems with Rebecca and he wouldn't tell him now. "Maybe. What time?"

"Anytime after about eight would be good. I told Carrie you'd be coming by."

"Carrie?"

"She's gorgeous!"

"Asian, of course."

"Of course. Early fifties, but looks about late thirties. Trim enough to wear low-riders. Plucks her pubic hair. Very spiritual character."

"Sounds *very* spiritual. How did you meet her?"

"She's in one of my Tantric classes."

"So she thinks you're an expert on sex." Sawyer paused a beat and then said, "Good thing you don't offer a money-back guarantee."

"Isn't it nice to have friends you feel so comfortable with you can insult them and know they'll still pick up the check?"

Sawyer ignored the remark. "So you've still got 'yellow fever.'"

"I just like the look of Asian women. Some guys like blondes, some brunettes. Me, I love Asians."

Sawyer looked at himself more as an equal opportunity sex partner. Before he got married, of course. "If I can make it, I will."

Chapter Six

The Palos Verdes Police Station was not that impressive. It looked more like a ranger's station in a national park than a cop shop.

Eric Gregg rose from behind his desk, greeted his former partner and mentor, waved Sawyer to a seat in front of his desk and resumed his seat. "Let me guess," he said. "Justin Wright."

"Just checking in."

"I don't know much. Probably less than you."

"Maybe, maybe not."

"I got a call—after *you* did—from Lomita," said Gregg. "The Homicide Team was already on scene. This is all way too high profile for this office."

"And you ought to be grateful as hell it is. There's going to be a lot of high-priced lawyers working on this case and they're going to try to portray everyone except Justin as incompetent or worse. I hope you haven't said anything politically incorrect in the past twenty years."

"I'm not going to be running this case."

"But you'll be in the loop."

"Which is why you're here," said Gregg. It was not an accusation. Sawyer kept in touch on a regular basis. The former partners went to lunch at least once a month and the two couples—Gregg and his wife, Penny, and Sawyer and Rebecca—got together at least four times a year. At least they used to.

"So, what do you hear?"

"The body's being autopsied this afternoon. With this case, everything's fast-track. The department and the DA want to be on the right side of everything that goes down."

"Understandable."

"I'm hearing Wright might get caught in a political crossfire."

"I know. I'm not trying to influence things; I just want to make sure the guy gets a fair shake."

Gregg nodded. He knew exactly the way things were playing out and what could go wrong. The downtown suits weren't on scene to make sure they caught the killer; they were there to make sure they covered their collective and politically-sensitive asses.

But neither Gregg nor Sawyer considered that anything other than business as usual. Several years ago Sawyer had looked back on his days with the LAPD and come to the conclusion that when he was young he had worked hard to change the world. The last few years he was just trying to figure out where to stand when the shit hit the fan.

"I have no problem feeding you information as I get it. Unless, of course, it compromises the investigation. And I'll be the one to make that call."

"Understood. And thanks."

"You're welcome."

"This has got to be the biggest crime on the Hill since you got here."

"It is. Everyone's got a theory."

"What's your gut tell you?"

"I don't know," said Gregg. "It's too early. I know Justin—not as well as you—but I know him. I also know that, contrary to popular belief, everyone's capable of murder under the right—or wrong—circumstances. I know Riley likes him for it."

"He actually said that he liked Wright for the murder?" asked Sawyer.

"Not in so many words, but that's the feeling I got."

"It's natural to like the husband in a situation like this."

"I got the feeling it was more than that. But I'm not sure. I don't think he had any slam-dunk forensics. Not at this point anyhow. Or if he did, he didn't tell me about it."

"You said the autopsy's being done today?"

"Late this afternoon, early evening."

"Think you could make a call?"

"No problem."

Sawyer knew that what he got from Gregg was merely a quick version of what the defense team would find out a little later. There was no ultimate advantage in knowing the information except that if they knew it sooner, Wright and St. James could react to it quicker and not be blind-sided at a press conference by some reporter with an inside track.

Which reminded Sawyer that he should call Veronica. She had lots of ways to get inside.

"Okay, then. You know my cell number. I appreciate anything you can pass along when you get it. I won't push."

"I know. Happy to do it." Gregg was indebted to Sawyer, though neither man would ever put it that way. Gregg went from a decent cop to a really good one working with Sawyer, who had covered for his partner's early mistakes and helped him grow so that those mistakes were not repeated. And when Sawyer had moved on he brought his partner along with him.

Sawyer walked out of the boutique cop shop thinking about one thing. What made Riley Gaines think Justin Wright had murdered his wife?

Chapter Seven

When Sawyer returned home his answering machine had ten messages, which were about nine more than usual. Nothing like being involved, even peripherally, in a high-profile murder investigation to increase one's popularity.

Four of the messages were from Veronica. The one message he was looking for was not there. Although someone had called and not left a message. Sawyer thought it might have been Rebecca. He didn't know for sure, but that's what he *wanted* to believe. He checked the list of "missed calls" using the Caller ID function on his phone and the caller who had not left a message was listed as an "unknown number."

Their separation wasn't a "legal" separation. But it was real.

Sawyer and Rebecca first met in 1994. She was a real estate agent living in Palos Verdes, and he was a cop working out of downtown, living in Silverlake. One Saturday night she attended a gallery opening in Little Tokyo, not far from Parker Center where he worked. Afterward she and a couple of her friends stopped into a nearby coffeehouse where Sawyer just happened to be playing a song during an "open microphone" hour. They caught each other's eye. Sawyer introduced himself and they went to dinner the following Saturday. And they had been together ever since.

Rebecca divorced her first husband in 1981 when she was twenty-five. There were no children and she didn't remarry again until she and Sawyer tied the knot ten years ago. They were eyes-open, street-wise adults at the time and things hummed along—lots of sex, lots of travel, lots of restaurants…and lots more sex—for the next few years.

In 1999 they moved up the Hill to a new development in Rancho Palos Verdes. Rebecca's real estate business took off in 2001. Between her business and his high-profile as a bestselling novelist, they got invited to a lot of parties and met a lot of people. Life was good.

But a year ago things seemed to change. Sawyer wasn't certain why. Being cynical and a cop, his first thought was that she was having an affair.

Palos Verdes was a small town and Sawyer figured that if Rebecca were seeing someone else he would know. But then, he also knew that friends were conflicted about telling a spouse what the "cheating spouse" was doing. Sawyer knew that sometimes it took photographs depicting wild sex for some in-the-dark spouses to be convinced. Sawyer had known about friends' infidelities and remained silent. It was a tough call.

One of the difficult things about going through rough patches like this was filling in the blanks. Until Sawyer knew the truth he would always fill in the blanks with the answers that made him feel the worst.

He still didn't know the answers.

Rebecca had taken a couple of suitcases to a girlfriend's house last week. She had refrained from saying, "I need some space," but it was essentially the same thing. They had agreed they would not communicate for a while, unless it was important. They agreed that they wouldn't read anything into it when calls didn't come. These were mainly Rebecca's rules.

Each was supposed to be working on things so "we can handle this in a mature manner," she had said over dinner the night before she left. Sawyer noted that she had not said "so we can work this out."

When he watched her drive away that next morning he had the sick feeling that she was never coming back.

Sawyer took the half-finished bottle of champagne he had opened the night before out of the refrigerator, poured the remainder into a half-glass and lay down in bed. He was about five hours shy of a good night's sleep and a full-night's sleep wasn't likely anytime soon.

He unplugged the phone in his bedroom, closed the door and let the answering machine do its job. In less than two minutes he was asleep.

Chapter Eight

Veronica Mays was a player. She was an Indiana girl who had come to LA twenty years ago and leveraged her physical assets, which were considerable, for everything they were worth. In her early twenties those assets were worth a lot and they had not depreciated measurably since then. Now forty-five, she looked more like she was in her early-thirties.

She did a stint at one of the local channels as a co-anchor which earned her a weekend, early-morning anchor shot in New York for one of the big three networks. It all had been going according to the plan until a certain man's wife found out about her husband's affair. And suddenly Veronica found herself with a one-way ticket back to Los Angeles.

However, Veronica was never one to take no for an answer and soon after her fall she caught on with a national cable channel. Her beat was Los Angeles. She was "a contender" again, but time was not on her side. What she needed was a seriously high-profile national story to get her back in the "high life."

Sawyer and Veronica had been an item a year or so before he married Rebecca. And for a moment each had considered the possibility of it being something more. But that conversation usually took place in the middle of the night after too much champagne. Still, they had remained, if not good friends, at least good acquaintances.

Asaka was a Japanese place in Golden Cove, where Hawthorne dove into the Pacific. The prices were reasonable and the food was good. It was Veronica's first time there.

She and Sawyer made small talk while sipping premium sake. Finally they decided to split the Family Boat, which consisted of salmon and tuna sushi, California rolls, assorted

30   Stephen Smoke

tempura, and chicken teriyaki. It came with miso soup, salad and rice.

After finishing off the last piece of tuna Sawyer said, "You know anything I don't know?"

"Isn't that my line?"

"You keep forgetting I'm not a cop anymore."

"You keep forgetting I'm not stupid. The wife of a friend of yours is murdered. You show up about the same time as the LAPD. Add to that your protégé, Eric Gregg, is officially in the loop and I figure you've got the whole thing wired."

"Funny. I thought I was going to have dinner with you and pick *your* brain," said Sawyer. "Look, we can work together on this thing, or apart."

"Is this where you offer me an exclusive if I just hold off on saying anything bad about your client and tell you everything I know? I've seen that movie before," she said without waiting for an answer.

"He's not my client. Besides, I think you're giving me too much credit. I'm not as tapped in as I used to be, but you're right: I spoke with Eric. But he would never tell me anything I'm not supposed to know."

"If you say so. He just knows you wouldn't be stupid enough to tell me something that could come back on him. Still, he's a good source."

"You mean I'm a good source."

"Of course, darling," she said with a smile he hadn't seen in a while and, strangely, realized that he'd missed.

"I can't give you 'an exclusive' because I'm not the inside guy here—that would probably be Riley Gaines. But I'm sure you've already got a lunch lined up with him."

"As a matter of fact... Well, it's not a lunch. But I think we're going to get together sometime tomorrow."

"Good for you." That was also good for Sawyer. Veronica was motivated by something entirely different than he was. To her the Wright tragedy was all about a ticket back to the big time. She didn't give a fuck about Justin Wright. Sawyer could use her ambition, feeding her as little as possible while getting information from her in order to try to stay, if not one step ahead, at least even with the media.

"So, what do you have for me?" she said, holding her drink in both hands, just below her chin, peering over the rim of the glass in a flirty way that looked practiced, but still worked.

"I hear the autopsy will be done by tonight. Maybe even by now."

"You expect any surprises?"

"You never know."

"Also, I know Wright was playing poker with friends that night. At his house."

"I heard that too." St. James had told Sawyer that a *South Bay Gazette* reporter was ready to run with the information about the poker game in the paper's morning edition. The *Gazette* wasn't the *Times* but reporters on home turf sometimes had a competitive edge.

"You know how many poker buddies there were?"

"I'm not sure," he lied. "I think three or four. So, what do you have for *me*?"

"Not a whole helluva lot."

"Come on..."

"I live in Santa Monica. To me Palos Verdes is off the radar."

"Which is one reason we like it here."

"That's fine, but it's going to take me a couple of days to spread some money and the promise of on-camera fame around." She paused and looked Sawyer unwaveringly in the eye. "I always figure out a way to get people to talk."

"I remember," he said, suddenly feeling a little flush. "Okay, so we both know how to reach each other—you've got my cell; I've got yours. If it's important, I'm 24/7. I'm assuming the same on your end."

"24/7," she repeated, still looking him in the eye.

Sawyer paid the check and walked Veronica to her car. He aimed a kiss toward her cheek, but she turned and caught it on her lips. It wasn't a long and lingering kiss, but he felt a sensation he hadn't felt in a while. She smiled, then got in her car and drove away, waving to him as she pulled out of the parking lot.

Sawyer told himself that he had accomplished what he set out to do.

So had Veronica.

Chapter Nine

It was a little after nine when Sawyer walked into The Admiral Risty. Michael was midway through a passionate version of the Eagles' "Desperado." Sawyer stood until he was done. Michael accepted the scattered applause from the small cocktail lounge crowd, stood and welcomed his friend. Sawyer and Michael sat down at a small table next to a window that looked out on the ocean. Michael's date, Carrie Tanner, was working on an apple martini and she seemed pleased to meet Sawyer. She said she was Japanese and recently had divorced her husband of she-purposely-didn't-say-how-many years and received what lawyers called a "handsome" settlement.

Sawyer knew she was at least thirty, but beyond that it was hard to tell how old she was. She had fantastic legs and a slim waist. She was attractive, and she knew it.

After the introductions and small talk, Carrie spoke first. "I've read about you in *Palos Verdes Style*. You're famous."

Sawyer smiled. He knew that not only was fame more fleeting than most people imagined, there was never a checkbox for it on any mortgage application. "Not really," he said. But he knew this was the reason he was here. Michael was trotting him out to impress his new girlfriend. As he looked at her the one thing Sawyer couldn't get out of his mind was what Michael had told him about Carrie plucking her pubic hair.

"Michael said you're involved with the Wright murder."

"Did he?" said Sawyer.

"Yes. He said you're friends with Justin and that you were there last night before the police."

Sawyer shot his friend a smile-covered rebuke and said, "I wasn't there before the police." He also noted that she had referred to Justin Wright by his first name.

"So, you know Justin?" he said.

"We've been on a few committees together."

Sawyer learned early on that in Palos Verdes people knew each other either from the schools their kids went to, the Palos Verdes Art Center, the Norris Theater, or some committee or other.

"We were on the Palos Verdes 75th Anniversary committee together. He seemed very nice."

"He's a good guy," said Sawyer. He was listening, not giving anything away. Especially to his friend's girlfriend. Or would-be girlfriend. The more he watched Carrie talk, the more Sawyer became convinced that this was the most sophisticated woman he had ever seen Michael with. The Tantric class and his other endeavors pulled in women with whom he had sex. But Carrie seemed more than a cut above a groupie. In fact, the more she spoke, the more Sawyer became convinced that his good friend might, in fact, be a little out of his depth.

"So, Carrie, you seem to have me at a disadvantage. You know all about me, but I don't know much about you."

"I'm a rich divorcee," she said simply, guilelessly. If anyone bought that as the whole package, thought Sawyer, they had no clue what this woman was about.

"That's it?"

"I paint a little. I do a little calligraphy."

"She's very talented," said Michael, getting himself back into the conversation.

"I do it for myself. It's like therapy. Michael says you write songs, too."

"I used to. My wife doesn't think it's 'appropriate' for a man my age to play guitar and sing."

"Are you going to play tonight?"

"No, not tonight."

"Oh, come on. Michael says you're good."

"Michael also says the Cubs are going to win the World Series."

The waitress came over and took another order for a round of drinks—another apple martini for Carrie, an Amstel Light for Michael and Sawyer ordered a J. Lohr merlot.

"I'm on," said Michael when the drinks were delivered. He stood and walked to the makeshift stage and started playing his electric piano.

"Michael speaks highly of you."

"He says some nice things about you," said Sawyer, trying to keep a straight face as his mind drifted back to the plucking.

Sawyer's cell phone rang—it was a silent, vibrating ring. Sawyer looked at his phone and recognized Eric Gregg's private number. He excused himself, stood and took the call outside.

"Sawyer," he said.

"Just thought you'd want a heads-up."

"I'm listening."

"You're not going to like it."

"I'm still listening."

"The autopsy's back. Cause of death is what you'd expect, but there was something else…"

"Yes?"

"Judy had sex the night she died."

"Doesn't mean anything. Maybe she and Justin had sex before she was killed."

"Yeah, maybe. But there's more. She had sex with more than one person."

Sawyer let that sink in. "In what time period?"

"They can't nail it down tight, but I was told they have good reason to believe it was in the last twenty-four hours before she was murdered."

"Maybe she had a lover."

"Let me be more specific, Sawyer. When I said more than one person, what I really meant was more than two."

"What?"

"Judy had sex with multiple partners within twenty-four hours of her murder."

"Oh, man…" This was bad and Sawyer knew there was only so much stink you could take off shit. Even if Judy's sexual activity had nothing to do with her murder, the fact that she was having sex with men other than her husband, so close to her murder, would not help her—or Justin—in the court of public opinion.

He thanked Gregg, went to the restroom to compose himself and returned to the table as Michael was finishing a medley of acoustic Rolling Stones songs.

"Anything important?" said Carrie as Sawyer sat down.

"Not really." He noticed that she had finished her drink and was tapping her glass for the waitress to bring her another.

Michael joined Sawyer and Carrie. "So..." he said, in search of praise.

"Good, man. Really good," said Sawyer somewhat absently.

"Thanks. I really like 'You Can't Always Get What You Want.' Carrie said it was her favorite Stones song."

Sawyer was suddenly distracted. He was thinking about how his friend's tragedy was just about to explode onto the national scene as a 24/7 cable TV real-life crime drama.

"Look, I'm sorry, but I gotta go," said Sawyer.

"Oh, come on. I've got another set. I thought we might all do something together after."

"That phone call was something I need to deal with right now. Sorry... I'll take a rain check."

Chapter Ten

Five minutes later Sawyer walked into his house, punched the alarm code, looked for—and found—a bottle of champagne he'd been saving in the back of his wine refrigerator. What the hell. He had hoped to share it with Rebecca on New Year's Eve, but that didn't seem like it was going to happen.

Sawyer was not a teenager. He knew his pain was genuine, but he also knew it would pass. In time. Some pain took longer than others to heal. And if it never fully healed he knew he would adjust to it. He had done so in the past and he would do so again if he had to.

He opened his "man purse" and took out Noah St. James' card. The man purse had been Rebecca's idea. Even though he'd undergone a good deal of razzing from his buddies, it served a real purpose. Everything from keys to credit cards, to odd notes and business cards, was in one place. He hadn't lost anything since he started carrying it.

On the back of St. James' card was his private cell number. The lawyer had several cell phone numbers, but the number he wrote the night before on the back of the card, Sawyer knew, would connect him directly day or night.

"St. James," said a voice.

"It's Sawyer."

"This better be good."

"It's not good." Sawyer told the lawyer what Gregg had told him.

St. James said nothing when Sawyer finished. Sawyer realized that a lawyer with St. James' experience was used to hearing bad news—his clients were generally guilty. Such a person was used to being ambushed by a reporter and to show any inkling of surprise would not benefit his client. After a moment, he said, "Who knows about this?"

"It's all in-house. But that'll change soon. There's no doubt the press will go with this as soon as they can. We might gain some advantage by leaking it ourselves." Sawyer knew that any good reporter would have tentacles into the cop shop downtown and the M.E.'s office as well. And when one media outlet had the information, they all swarmed around it like sharks sensing blood. If he could *control* the leak, then he might be able to at least get something in return.

"I like the way you think, Sawyer."

"You know this isn't good. No matter how we spin it."

"I know," said the lawyer. "You free tomorrow morning?"

"I can be."

"You know where I live?"

"Yes I do."

"Can you come by around ten?"

"I'll be there."

"Good," said the lawyer and hung up.

Sawyer put down the phone, picked up his glass of champagne and went into the bedroom. He undressed, got into bed and turned on the TV.

"It's a Wonderful Life" was just finishing up. Jimmy Stewart was crying tears of joy and talking to angels. Surrounded by his wife and kids and a house full of friends.

Sawyer turned off the TV, poured himself another glass of champagne and lay there in the dark till sleep finally came.

Chapter Eleven

Sawyer awoke at seven. He walked to his office and checked his answering machine—he had unplugged the phone in his bedroom so he could get some sleep. There were two message from Veronica, nothing important. And no messages from Rebecca.

He brewed a pot of custom-blend coffee he had special-ordered through a friend of his who owned a tea and coffee importing business and was *really* into coffee. Sawyer had found a particular coffee he'd liked, discovered where it was grown and then tasted five different blends prepared by his friend. There actually was one that was noticeably different from the rest. He ordered it regularly through his friend—who enjoyed telling *his* friends that he had created a special brand of coffee for a famous ex-cop/writer.

He poured a cup of coffee into an LAPD mug, and then sat down to work the *LA Times* Sudoku.

At 8:01 the phone rang. Sawyer checked the Caller-ID and picked up the phone. "Hi."

"Good morning," said Veronica.

"You must've been pretty aroused calling me that late last night."

"You don't know what you're missing."

He thought about saying that he did, but instead he said, "I might have something for you."

"Where and when?"

"I've got a meeting at ten. Can you meet me at Pavilions for lunch, say around noon?"

"The grocery store?"

"In the Peninsula Center. They've got a great deli and a soup bar."

"Okay. See you then."

"I've got something for *you*," Sawyer repeated with purpose. "Don't come empty-handed."

"I've always got something for you, Sawyer. You oughta' know that by now," she said with a laugh and hung up.

Noah St. James' house was a real mansion: Three stories, a marble staircase, an unobstructed view of the ocean, a half-circle and gated driveway. Sawyer didn't live in a mansion, but they shared the same zip code and, to people who didn't live on the Hill, they were lumped into the same category: Rich bastards.

"Thanks for coming," said St. James and he led Sawyer to a breakfast room overlooking a large pool and backyard. A mid-forties, slightly plump Romanian woman served them eggs, toast and coffee.

"I like your idea about feeding this information to the press."

"I thought you would. I'm having lunch with a woman I know—"

"Veronica Mays."

"You do your homework."

"Actually, I pay people to do it for me. Habit I picked up in college. The important thing is that I know what I need to know in time to do something about it. Can you trust her?"

"More than any other media person I know."

"Okay. Then it's done. She'll have this thing on the afternoon news and the cable news stations will run with it in prime time. Pros and cons?"

"Whatever people thought of Justin Wright before, they'll think less of him when they hear this."

"But will they think he's more likely guilty than they did before?"

"Definitely."

"What we gain from this is that we can start planning our rebuttal now—actually, I've already got someone working on a press release. Also, we gain the confidence of the person we feed this to. It must be someone who can reciprocate."

"Veronica's tapped in. She can feed us things."

The maid brought in a fresh pot of coffee and refreshed each man's cup. When she left St. James said, "Sawyer, I'd like to get things straight between us."

Sawyer waited. He knew what was coming.

"I know you and I don't see eye to eye on a lot of things. And we've often been on opposite sides of the fence. I've always respected you. I'm sure you understood what I was doing, even if you didn't respect it. Right now most people think Justin's guilty simply because he has too much money. By tonight, most juries wouldn't acquit him of kidnapping the Lindbergh baby. And the absolute truth of the matter is that you and I really don't know for sure if he did it or not. I'm sure it won't surprise you when I say I really don't care one way or the other. He didn't hire me for spiritual counseling; he hired me to keep him out of jail. I'm good at that. And I intend to achieve that result for Justin...one way or the other.

"I know you and he are friends and that you and I are not—although, as I said, I do respect you. I've got private investigators, but no one as tapped into Palos Verdes as you are. I also want you to know that I might know things I can't, or won't, tell you. I hope you understand."

"I understand."

The two men made small talk for another five or ten minutes, then Sawyer stood and St. James walked him to the door.

"By the way," said Sawyer. "I actually *do* care whether or not Justin murdered Judy."

"I know." He smiled as though Sawyer had said something naïve, but charming. "Keep me posted on your meeting with Veronica Mays. I'm curious to see how aggressively she takes the bait."

Chapter Twelve

Sometimes it was best not to know how good...bad things feel.

Sawyer knew that it was impossible to un-ring a bell. And like Pavlov's dog, once you linked the stimulus with the reward, with the pleasure, most people performed right on cue. The problem, he reasoned, was that once you started depending on something or someone for pleasure, it was tough to ever find your way out of the maze. Such dependency made you insecure because there was always the fear you could lose that something—or someone—you now needed desperately to make your world keep spinning.

Still, Sawyer knew the truth was that we all lose everything and everyone in the end.

Sawyer wasn't sure what Justin Wright was afraid of losing, but he figured that whatever it was, he had either lost it or was about to.

It was only about eight minutes from St. James' mansion to Wright's mansion. The day was clear and Sawyer could see Catalina on his right as he drove south on Palos Verdes Drive.

He was thinking about secrets. Secrets known could be embarrassing, humiliating and sometimes devastating. But undiscovered secrets were often much worse.

He knew that certain deeds that remained hidden haunted you and that such apparitions were dealt with in different ways. People without a conscience slept better. A person with an intact conscience had two choices: Get rid of the guilt or get rid of the conscience. Those who chose to exorcise their guilt did so in several ways. The simplest and most straightforward was to come forward and admit indiscretions, bad behavior or lapses in judgment. That was the road less traveled.

The other choice, Sawyer knew, was often a subconscious one in which a person orchestrated his own demise or punishment. The ensuing drama was part "acting out," part self-abuse. The latter showed, if not remorse, at least a self-knowledge that one had done wrong.

Sawyer wasn't sure how Wright was going to handle the public revelations of his secrets. He knew the man, now in his early seventies, was strong. But Sawyer had observed that scandal affected young and old differently. The young were often resilient and capable of bouncing back. Sometimes they seemed incapable of feeling shame about anything and often used the notoriety to their benefit.

As a rule, Sawyer had observed that older people didn't handle scandal as well. They often felt a sense of shame that, in the twenty-first century, was about as common as a human tail. And older people did not have the time, or sometimes the energy, to rehabilitate their reputations.

Sawyer felt bad for Justin. He knew that the vast majority of people simply viewed Judy's murder much in the same way they viewed a TV reality show. Reactions to tragedies usually had more to do with how close to you they occurred. Hurricanes didn't bother people in L.A. No one in Miami lost sleep worrying about earthquakes. It was a sad commentary, but generally the further you were away from disaster, the more of it you wanted to see on TV.

Which partially explained why people loved scandal. *Other* people's scandal.

And why people around the country were tuning in cable news to get the latest on Justin Wright.

Chapter Thirteen

Wright poured half-glasses of Bookers for himself and Sawyer, and then they took seats in the library—Wright in his customary chair, Sawyer on the couch.

"You know...about..." It was hard for Wright to say.

"I'm not here to judge you, Justin. But when you're the kind of rich you are, there's a ravenous tabloid world out there that looks at you as though you're raw meat. They're going to turn over every rock and when they can't find something they'll make it up. When they can't find someone who will tell them the truth, they'll find someone who will tell them a lie millions of people want to hear—and dare you to sue them. For the media, destruction of the rich and powerful is a sport."

Wright just rolled his glass between his hands, sighed deeply and nodded.

"This'll get worse before it gets better," said Sawyer.

"That your idea of a pep talk?"

"It's my idea of a straight dose of reality."

"My wife's been murdered, Sawyer. I was the one who found her body on the floor. That's about as real as it gets."

Sawyer didn't argue. His friend had been through as bad an experience as anyone could imagine, and it kept getting worse by the hour. He had not had time to grieve and people who might otherwise be sympathetic and supportive stayed away. People didn't want to see themselves on the evening news. One of Wright's associates confided to Sawyer that he didn't even call because he feared his phone number would be flagged if police were monitoring incoming calls.

People were afraid. And they had reason to be.

Wright was probably the most afraid. He had the most reason to be.

"How are you *really* doing?" said Sawyer after a while.

"I honestly don't know, Sawyer. It's bad, really bad. It's all kind of a blur. Sometimes I think it's going to be okay when the truth comes out… I want my old life back."

"It may be okay one day—but not soon. And your old life's never coming back."

"I'm starting to get that feeling."

Both men sat in silence for a moment. The phone would ring periodically in another room; Sawyer could see that the phone in this room was unplugged. If St. James needed to reach him, Wright had his private cell in his pocket. Sawyer let the silence run. He knew that Wright knew he was there to talk and he knew what they were going to talk about. It wasn't easy for either man.

"I really appreciate you being here for me, Sawyer. After spending so many years with so many people's noses up my ass, it suddenly seems kind of lonely. There's really just you and Noah and Nathan. And I know Noah wouldn't be so supportive if I weren't paying him double his usual fee and he wasn't guaranteed so much TV time."

"How is Nathan doing with all this?" Nathan was Wright's son from his previous wife, Natasha.

"He's okay. He's a strong kid. A good kid." Wright sipped his Bookers and thought about what to say next. How to broach the subject. "Noah told me what you found out from the autopsy…and what you plan to say to the reporter. Thanks."

"Anytime the media wants dirt on you, I'm willing to oblige."

"No, seriously. This is… I don't know this world."

"I know it. St. James knows it. It can chew you up and spit you out no matter how much money you've got."

"About the…uh…"

"Look, Justin, I would never ask you these kinds of questions if I didn't have to. If I go to my contacts and tell them something that isn't true and it makes them look bad later, I burn a bridge. I can work with the truth; I can sculpt it into to something that can't be used as a weapon against you. But if you tell me a lie and I go with it, it can come back to hurt you. Badly."

"I understand. But this is really tough." He paused and sipped his bourbon. "Judy and I love...*loved* each other very much. She understood me. When we first got together we had both been around the track a few times. It wasn't like she was a twenty-year-old supermodel taking 'the rich old guy' for a ride. We both knew what we were getting." He paused again. "I always thought she was beautiful," he said. He smiled. Suddenly he was somewhere else.

"She was a beautiful woman," said Sawyer, partly because he knew Wright wanted to hear him say it, and partly to bring the old man back from somewhere far more pleasant than where he really was. He needed to focus.

"We enjoyed life. Money was never a barrier to anything we wished to do. We traveled when my schedule allowed. She decorated all our houses. She was on all the best committees and we were generous." He looked at Sawyer and said, "She genuinely liked to help people. I know this is not important and it's going to get lost in all the other bullshit, but she did—she really helped a lot of people. She was a good person, Sawyer."

Sawyer knew Judy. After all her good work the only thing people would remember about her was that she was a tramp. Millions would be totally focused on the details of her sex life. No one would be interested in the many people helped by her kindness and generosity. He had read somewhere that Madonna was much more well known than Mother Theresa. Sawyer had long ago concluded that life wasn't fair. But sometimes it was downright stupid.

"Judy and I had a 'mature' relationship. We loved each other, but we never judged each other."

Sawyer wasn't a psychologist or a priest, but he realized that Wright was giving him a kind of confession. Not of murder. Wright was trying to explain the context for what happened the night of the murder. Or maybe it was just Wright being honest about his life for the first time.

"Judy was extraordinary. She really was beautiful, wasn't she, Sawyer?" said Wright, finding it difficult to get beyond that point.

"Yes, she was." There was no doubt about that. The first time Sawyer met Judy Wright was just after he moved to Palos

Verdes. She was not the youngest person in the room, but she was the most attractive. Sure, she'd had a nip here and a tuck there, but it was only restoration—not creating something from scratch. She had been runner-up in the Miss California Pageant—the year was not disclosed, but there were a couple of photographs of her wearing her sash and smiling for the cameras. She was a beauty. But it didn't stop there. She was book-smart, street-smart *and* beautiful.

Sawyer thought he knew Judy. Now he wasn't so sure. He knew she was comfortable in her own skin. She knew what people thought of her and she was aware of her place in the world. She never flaunted her wealth and she was kind and patient with people with whom she did not have to be kind and patient. Sawyer had seen people on the Hill, especially insecure women who hadn't made the money themselves, treat other people badly simply because they could. Judy was not that way.

"Something happened about a year ago." Wright sighed deeply and took another sip of Bookers. "Some friends invited us to a swing club. We'd been faithful to each since we were married and I just thought it would be fun to spice up our sex life.

"Anyhow, we went to this club and during the evening some guy started talking with Judy and asked her if he could take her into a room and have sex with her. You've got to understand, this was completely unique for both of us. Judy took me aside and told me what the man said. She said she would do whatever I wanted her to do. If I said no, she would tell the man no. If I said yes, she would...go into the room.

"I'm telling you, Sawyer, it's hard to explain but I was suddenly very turned on by the idea of Judy having sex with another man. I guess it goes back to the idea that I've always wanted people to envy what I have. So I said yes. But with one condition: I wanted to be in the room at the time."

"That's pretty out there, Justin. You know that, don't you?"

"Yes. And I wouldn't be telling you any of this if I didn't feel that you need to know. So, we all went into a room and...they had sex. Later, Judy said she felt very inhibited because she wasn't sure how I felt. So even though the man got off, she did not."

"How *did* you feel?"

"It was strange. I felt kind of numb. But the sense of eroticism was overwhelming. It was exciting for us both whenever we discussed it for several months afterward. We climaxed together to that sexual memory over and over again. And we started fantasizing about how to expand on it.

"I told you there was a poker game the night Judy was murdered. That was only partially true. The poker game was the cover story the four men told their wives. Each of those men was here to have sex with Judy. For almost a year we've been inviting...men over. Four men. Men with whom Judy thought it would be fun to have sex. It was always her choice but I have to say that I enjoyed it just as much as she did."

"These men... You're talking about Rosenberg, Arquette, Sanchez, and Woodbridge?" said Sawyer, referring to the men Wright had identified as his poker buddies.

"Yes. You know them. They're not 'young studs.' All are extremely successful. They were friends. I know it sounds weird."

Sawyer thought that was a bit of an understatement.

Robert Sanchez was a big-time shipping magnate who spent most of his time these days fishing off Catalina on his 74-foot yacht. Jake Woodbridge was a former city councilman who still had serious clout. Danny Rosenberg ran a well-known accounting firm on the Hill, and Tony Arquette used to be the chief of police in Dallas before moving to Palos Verdes about ten years ago.

"Judy and I had a lot to lose. We were vulnerable to blackmail. The wrong person could use our 'indiscretions' against us. The people we invited were pretty much the same as us. They were successful professionals, married and had no history of cheating on their wives. Each still had an interest in sex, but they wanted something safe, just like *we* wanted something safe. It seemed to work. Until now.

"Being successful and married gave them all something to lose. Kind of like a mutually-assured-destruction pact. It also kept one man from becoming too attached to Judy. That's what's going to be the hardest thing to explain about this whole arrangement: Judy and I were very happy with it and we were both very much in love with each other. We no longer had sex in order to procreate; we did it for fun and to be intimate. Judy never told any of these men she loved him and she would never see any of them behind my back. What we did, we did together. And God help me, I truly enjoyed other men admiring Judy's sexuality."

"You've got to prepare yourself, Justin. When the press breaks this story tonight, all your 'friends' are going to cover themselves first and they're going to cut you loose. This revelation is a potential tsunami that can rip their lives apart. They're not going to be there for you."

"No one knows who they are."

"Not yet and it won't come from me. But there's a very good chance that the names will eventually come out. And you've got to assume that whatever they know about you and Judy, the police, and maybe even the press, are going to know soon. Your friends are going to be scared and they're going to get the screws put to them pretty hard. They're going to want to look cooperative, like they've got nothing to hide. Which, of course, they do."

"I would think they'd know enough to keep their mouths shut."

"People aren't used to being murder suspects. It isn't like on TV. Most people don't have a criminal defense attorney on speed dial."

Wright winced a little, almost imperceptibly. Sawyer figured it was a memory of something personal and hurtful he knew would now be divulged to the world. What had started out so private was now about to become one of the most public sex scandals in years.

"So this has been going on for about a year?"

"Since last December."

"And no one wore condoms?" asked Sawyer, thinking about what Gregg had told him about multiple DNA samples indicating Judy had had sex with multiple partners.

"Sometimes, but not always. No one was worried about AIDS or STDs. The men were married and didn't fool around, except with Judy. It was a pretty closed circle."

"That sounds odd. I mean, who wouldn't wear a condom if you're going to fool around?"

"I know it sounds strange. But you have to understand the context. I know these men and so did Judy. We believed them when they said they didn't fool around. It seemed like the perfect situation for everyone. Before being admitted to the group each man had to provide a clean bill of health from a physician. And let's be honest. It really feels...different wearing a condom."

"I'm not a big condom fan either, but it sounds, well...messy."

"Not everyone actually 'came' *inside* Judy. Some did, some came...elsewhere."

Sawyer sighed deeply and said nothing. Now he had a better understanding about the DNA found in—or on—Judy. If she had DNA from semen *on* her, and she showered at least once a day, then it would be logical to assume that the DNA was probably less than twenty-four hours old.

Even though he understood it better didn't mean it was going to play any better. It still added up to the same thing. "If you didn't kill Judy—"

"I didn't, Sawyer. I swear!"

"I know, I know," he said, holding up his hand. "Then it was most likely one of the four poker players. Do you think anyone is more capable of murder than any other?"

Wright shook his head. "Of course not."

"You've got to start looking at this thing realistically, Justin. If one of *them* didn't do it, then you move to the top of the list."

"There must be another possibility."

"Maybe. But until someone comes up with a plausible alternative, there are only two likely explanations: Either you did it, or one of your four buddies did. Think about it. Has any one of these guys seemed more focused on Judy or obsessed with her?"

"No. I would have noticed. She would have noticed too."

"And she would have told you?"

"Definitely."

"Any of these guys have any history of violence? Any of them like to play rough with Judy?"

"No and no. Our sex was pretty ordinary."

"That's probably not something you want to say again out loud."

Wright coughed a tiny, but sad laugh and sipped his Bookers.

"I'm going to look at these guys hard," said Sawyer. "If there's anything you can tell me that'll give me a head start, let me know."

"I can't think of anything. But I know it's important. I'll think about it."

"Good." Sawyer tossed down the remaining bourbon and showed himself out.

Chapter Fourteen

There wasn't much of a lunch crowd at Pavilions grocery store. Sawyer ladled himself a bowl of tomato bisque and Veronica ordered a Greek salad with extra dressing. They took their food to an area of empty tables.

"So, whatcha' got for me?" said Veronica after she finished her first bite.

Sawyer made a face and looked as though he was about to say something that was difficult to say. Being a good cop qualified him for a number of professions in which he needed to stretch the truth with a straight face. He had appeared in cameo roles for several television shows and movies based on his books. It wasn't that hard. In one he played a guitar-playing homeless guy set up outside the Greyhound Bus Station in downtown L.A. On the set of another TV movie based on one of his books, he met Dennis Farina, an ex-Chicago cop. Sawyer always believed Farina was the most believable cop on the screen. He knew how to be a cop in ways they didn't teach in an acting class.

Sawyer leaned closer to Veronica and spoke in a conspiratorial manner. "Judy had sex with multiple partners the night she was murdered."

Veronica's fork stopped halfway to her mouth. "You're kidding me!"

"No."

"Are you serious?"

Sawyer knew what she was really thinking. She couldn't believe her good luck. "Apparently it was a swing club kind of thing where Justin and Judy had a group of guys over every week."

She chewed and pondered not so much *what* he'd said, but *why* he'd said it. "This can't be good for Justin. Why are you telling me?"

"I don't see how this hurts Justin." Even though he knew exactly how it did.

"You don't?" she said incredulously.

"No. Frankly I think this pretty much takes Justin off the hook." Sawyer thought of how Farina would have played it. Straight face and all.

"How can you possibly say that?"

"If she had three or four other partners the night she was murdered, to me—an ex-homicide cop—that means not only three or four other suspects, but several additional female suspects who might be very angry with the woman having sex with their husbands."

Sawyer maintained eye contact with Veronica, trying his best to sell it. If she knew she was simply being used, what he would get from her down the line would be limited.

"So the cops really think one of these other guys killed her?"

"That's what I'm hearing."

"That's incredible. People are going to be bidding for movie rights by the end of the week."

"I feel sorry for Justin."

"Most people don't."

"Most people don't know how devastating this has been for him. And now *this*. No husband wants this kind of thing spread around the world on TV and in the tabloids."

"So explain to me again why you're telling me this?"

"I trust you."

"I hope you're not trusting me to *not* go with the story."

"No. I'm trusting you to handle it in a classy manner." Again, with the little white lies.

"Thanks. I'll do my best."

"I know you will. That's all I can ask."

"Does anyone else have this?"

"I'm sure if anyone did it'd be everywhere by now. It's yours 'exclusively,'" he said, making his point.

"I appreciate it."

"It won't be the last thing I can toss your way."

She smiled as she chewed on an olive. "Okay. What do you want from me?"

"You're hard-wired in to a number of good sources of information. I give you a heads-up, you do the same for me. Everybody's happy. The more I get from you, the more I give you. This is my show of good faith." He didn't say that now it was her turn. He didn't have to.

"So this is solid? I'm not going to get sued if I say that a dead woman had sex with multiple partners on the night she was murdered?"

"No."

"Where can I go for confirmation?"

"Call any of your connections in the M.E.'s office and at least get someone to 'not deny' what I told you. Trust me, it's rock solid."

"I believe you. You've never lied to me." Then she smiled coquettishly. "Except that time you told me you'd never leave me."

Sawyer laughed. "I never said that. If I had, you would have bolted."

"I know. But it sounds nice to think of it like that."

"Yeah... Survivors get to rewrite history."

When Sawyer was in his car he called St. James' private cell. "She went for it?"

"Yeah. So brace yourself. It's going to be a long night."

"Wright's 'spokesperson' is going to earn her keep tonight."

Sawyer hung up and sat in his car for a moment, marveling at how artificial the real world had become.

Chapter Fifteen

Sawyer knocked on Eric Gregg's open office door and his old partner looked up.

"Got a minute?"

"Sure."

Sawyer went inside and closed the door behind him. The office was nothing fancy, but it was more than functional. On the desk was a framed picture of his wife Penny standing in front of a glacier. Next to that was a photo of Gregg's son, Donny, in his little league uniform holding a bat. On the wall behind the desk were photos of Sawyer and Gregg at Sawyer's retirement party.

Sawyer sat down and told Gregg about his conversation with Wright, including the names of the guys involved.

"I know these guys. Not well, of course. But I see them at fundraisers and I get invited to their parties now and then. They like to have a badge in the party photos."

"I know these guys, too," said Sawyer.

"You should. You're one of them. Are you going to talk to them?"

"I'm going to try. I know Sanchez and Rosenberg better than the other two," said Sawyer. "I met Sanchez at a fundraiser at the Art Center. He introduced himself, told me he'd read my books and asked me out on his boat. I met Rosenberg at a fundraiser, too. I think it was for some beautification project. Anyhow, he also had read a couple of my books and I asked him a couple of tax questions. He seemed like a nice guy."

"For a rich guy living in Palos Verdes."

Sawyer smiled. He knew what Gregg meant. Some people who lived on the Hill not only thought they *walked* on water, they also took credit for importing it from some fancy place in Europe.

"Woodbridge solicited my endorsement for his last election," said Gregg. "He trotted me out at fundraisers when he wanted people to think he was a law-and-order type. Not a real burning issue here in PV."

"Until now," said Sawyer. "I know Arquette fairly well. Most of the time I've spent with these guys has been at Justin's soirées or on his boat."

"You got a read on this thing?"

"I really don't. Either Wright murdered his wife or one of the four 'Club' members did. Wright thinks there's another possibility."

"Like what?"

"Hell if I know and he doesn't either. The 'intruder theory' doesn't have a great track record with juries."

"If you had to make a guess…"

"It would be hard to bet *against* Wright or the other four guys. They never seem to lose."

Sawyer stood and shook his ex-partner's hand. "When I've got something, I'll give you a shout."

"Same here."

Chapter Sixteen

Sawyer called Sanchez as soon as he got home. The news wouldn't hit the media echo chamber for another couple of hours. He would try to see Sanchez and Rosenberg immediately, before the prime time news cycle kicked in and they started to panic. Their names weren't out there. Not yet. But they had to believe that it was only a matter of time before their lives and reputations were going to be destroyed one revelation at a time.

Sanchez sounded a little shaken when he took Sawyer's call. He asked Sawyer to meet him on his boat in Redondo Beach.

Thirty minutes later the two men sat on Sanchez' yacht, the *Angel's Breath*, looking out over what would, under ordinary circumstances, be a beautiful Pacific view. For Sanchez it was not a beautiful day and the only reason he wanted to meet on the boat was to get away from the rush of trouble he knew was headed his way.

Sanchez poured them both a glass of Jordan Cabernet Sauvignon—without asking Sawyer what he wanted.

Sawyer recalled that Sanchez considered himself a connoisseur of wines, tequila, and Italian food. Sawyer always thought it better to find a great moderately priced wine than to pay fifty dollars to try to impress your friends with your "expertise." Sawyer figured that anyone could find a great fifty-dollar bottle of wine. But maybe that kind of thinking just came from spending most of his life cashing a cop's check.

"I didn't kill Judy." Sanchez was not one to beat around the bush.

"Somebody did. And either it was one of the four members of the Club…or it was Justin."

Sanchez nodded. "So, you know."

"Everyone's going to know, Robert. Sooner or later. What happened after Justin went to bed?"

"What do you mean?"

"Seems like a straightforward question."

"We…you know…"

"You had sex with Judy."

"Yes."

"All at once or separately?"

"Separately, of course," said Sanchez as though Sawyer had asked a ridiculous question.

"Who was the last to leave?"

"I'm not sure."

Sawyer cleared his throat purposefully, then said, "You don't have to answer me, Robert, but my friendly advice is that you're going to need to come up with better answers than that."

"I really don't know who left when. All I know is that I left first."

"Okay. That means Rosenberg, Arquette and Woodbridge were still there."

"That's right."

"So if I asked them they would corroborate your story…that you were the first to leave?"

"All right, all right… It could have happened a little differently than that. I'm not sure."

"It's a good thing I'm the one you're taking for a test drive with that story. You're making yourself look good for Judy's murder."

Sanchez shook his head and stared out over the Pacific. A couple of small boats were returning to port. "We all left at the same time."

"If you all left at the same time, then how do you account for Judy's murder?"

"I can't."

"Your story leaves Justin holding the bag. Do you really think he killed Judy?"

"No." He paused. "I don't know. All I know is that I didn't."

"You say you all left together."

"That's right."

"Did you actually see each man get in his car and drive away?"

"I don't know. I wasn't thinking about it. All I know is that we all walked out the front door at the same time and I got in my car and drove home."

"So it's possible that one of you either did not drive away or immediately returned, unbeknownst to the other three."

"It's possible. I can't say one way or the other."

"How did you feel about Judy?"

"What do you mean?"

"Did you like her? Did you love her?"

"She was great. I liked her a lot. We all did. I wasn't in love with her, if that's what you mean."

Sanchez sipped his wine and stared out at the Pacific again.

I really loved Judy. And I know she really loved me, too. At least in the beginning. I know it all sounds stupid now.

She first approached me in late December last year when Justin was in Japan on business. I remember that first night. God, she was beautiful.

She asked me to meet her for a drink at the Hilton. She got there before I did. She was in a dark corner booth in the bar and she had sunglasses on. Indoors. It seemed so pretentious, but she had the style to pull it off.

We were just talking. Small talk mostly. We knew each other from social gatherings. After a few drinks we both were feeling...comfortable. We talked about how wonderful it was to live in Palos Verdes. We talked about my work—she compared me to Aristotle Onassis. My shipping business is big, but nothing like that. Still, I was flattered.

We talked about places we liked to vacation, that kind of thing. I could tell there was a spark between us. We both felt it.

We were having such a good time we decided to have dinner. She said Justin was going to be gone for a few days and asked if it was okay to call me.

I said yes.

The next couple of nights were unbelievable. She was my perfect woman.

But of course she wasn't mine. She was Justin's wife.

The third night in a row we saw each other, we'd been drinking a bit and I felt her leg touch mine under the table. At first I thought it was an accident, but then after a while I knew that she was giving me a signal. I was on fire. I had never been so aroused in my life.

I told her I could get a room at a nearby hotel and she said she would like that. But...

She said she couldn't "disrespect" Justin—she would feel too guilty. Also, she said it would be a risk for both of us to be seen going into a hotel room. I suggested we go back to her house— after all, Justin was away. She said she wouldn't feel right having sex in Justin's house while he was away.

Then she made the most incredible suggestion. She begged me not to judge her. To hear her out.

She said that recently Justin had become obsessed with the idea of a "private swing club." She made some specific complaints about her marriage, about Justin, that I was embarrassed to hear and don't feel I should repeat. The bottom line was that he enjoyed watching her have sex with other men. Sometimes he participated, sometimes he did not.

She said that Justin had suggested several men from the Hill join their own private club. She said the men had been Justin's choices, but that she wanted to make sure there was at least one person she really wanted to make love with. And she chose me.

I was shocked. I would never have thought such a thing of Justin or Judy. Hell, I would never have believed anything like that could ever go on up on the Hill. But I was hooked on the woman. Everything about her...everything about her sexuality intrigued me.

She said she would try to manipulate Justin into asking me to join their club. She explained that she felt obligated to Justin— things had not always been bad between them and he had given her a great deal. She begged me to consider it.

My marriage had not been good for some time. She didn't have to sell me that hard. I was falling in love with her and if that was the only way we could be together, then so be it.

The following week, Justin, Judy and I went out to dinner. Justin invited me to join their group. Apparently Judy had convinced him. I actually think he believed it was his own idea.

Each week, when I had an orgasm, she would always whisper in my ear—so the others couldn't hear—that she loved me. She was the great love of my life.

Finally Sanchez turned back to Sawyer and said, "The sex was good. That's really about all there was to it. I mean, who passes up a good free piece of ass, right?"

"If it's really *that* good, then it's usually not free. One way or another," said Sawyer. But he realized he was preaching to the choir. "Was anyone in love with Judy—besides Justin?"

"I don't think so. Everyone knew Rule Number One: No sex or any romantic relationship with Judy outside the Club. Plus, we were all married. It seemed like a perfect arrangement for everyone."

"And your wife thought you were playing poker."

"Yes. A once-a-week poker game. Like I said, it all seemed perfect. She knew where I was and she could even call me there. She knew the other guys in the game and she knew Justin and Judy."

"She just didn't know you and your buddies were fucking Judy."

"My daughters are going to hear about this," said Sanchez, as though saying it out loud might shame someone into silence. "What am I going to tell them?"

"Was anyone ever violent with Judy?"

"No. Definitely not. The sex was pretty..." Sanchez stopped himself. "Okay, it wasn't ordinary, but there was no rough sex, if that's what you mean."

"Did you ever sense that one of the four of you felt possessive of Judy, or jealous, or wanted more?"

"No. Not really."

"What does that mean?"

"When Danny separated from Linda, he saw Judy a couple of times for lunch. I think he was feeling her out to see if she might be interested in...something more."

"How do you know this?" Sawyer was thinking that Justin either didn't know this, or had decided not to tell him.

"Danny told me. I told him to back off. I knew Justin wouldn't have liked it."

"He didn't mind his wife having sex with another man, but would object to her having lunch with him?"

"I know it's hard for someone like..." Sanchez stopped himself. "I know it's hard to understand if you're not in the middle of it, but what Judy did with us was not being disloyal to Justin. It was more like something they enjoyed doing together. I know Justin liked the fact that we were all sexually attracted to his wife and couldn't have her. At least not the way he had her. Danny told me that Judy said a one-on-one relationship between the two of them wasn't possible. End of story."

"How did Danny take it?"

"He felt rejected. But as far as I know, that was the end of it."

"You sure?"

"Yes. I even spoke with Judy about it. She confirmed that Danny had approached her, but that he had later apologized and things got back to normal."

"Any other situations like that with Arquette or Woodbridge?"

"No. And I think I would have known."

Sawyer's phone began to vibrate. He looked down at the Caller-ID number on the tiny screen and recognized Danny Rosenberg's number. "Here's my cell number," said Sawyer, taking out a card and writing down his number. "Call me anytime. If you want it off the record, we can do it that way. I'm trying to help Justin because he's my friend and I believe he's not guilty. As long as you didn't kill Judy, then we're on the same team and maybe I can help you, too."

"Okay," said Sanchez, pocketing the card.

Sawyer felt a twinge of guilt. He was, after all, the person who gave the information about the Club to Veronica Mays.

Chapter Seventeen

By the time he reached his car Sawyer had set a meeting with Rosenberg in fifteen minutes at the Red Onion on Silver Spur. The Red Onion was the original restaurant in the famous chain and a Palos Verdes landmark. The owner proudly displayed photographs of Ronald Reagan and other political luminaries on the wall, as well as a considerable amount of sports paraphernalia, most notably from the University of Southern California.

Danny Rosenberg was five minutes late and he looked upset when he sat down in a corner booth in the bar. He ordered a Patron Margarita on the rocks, no salt and Sawyer ordered a straight shot of Patron over ice.

After the drinks were served, Rosenberg said, "My mother is going to hear about this," as though it made a difference.

"How do you think your wife's going to handle it?" said Sawyer.

"Ah hell, she'll just use it against me in the custody case. Perfect timing."

"I didn't know you were getting divorced."

"Yes. My marriage has been over for a long time."

Sawyer had heard men and women say that. What they often meant was that the *sex* had been over for a long time. He also knew people with good marriages in which the sex had been over for decades. Different people had different expectations of marriage.

"I hear that when things started to go bad with Linda you approached Judy."

"About what?" asked Rosenberg, looking like a deer in the headlights.

"About taking the 'relationship' to another level."

"Who told you that?"

"Justin," said Sawyer, even though that wasn't true.

"Justin said that? I had no idea he knew."

"So it's true."

"Should I be talking to you?"

"Why not?" Cops usually answered questions with questions. "I agreed to see you because I thought we've always been, if not good friends, at least friendly. I thought you called to…I don't know. Can what I say to you be used against me?"

"I'm not a cop anymore. But I *am* Justin's friend," said Sawyer, not answering the question. "I'm not here to hurt you. I'm just trying to figure out who killed Judy, and the five of you are the only logical suspects."

"You really think one of us did it?"

"Like I say, it's logical. So, about you and Judy… How did you feel about her?"

"I talked with her when Linda and I separated. But she made it quite clear that she wouldn't see me…sexually outside our weekly encounters."

"How'd you take it?"

"Honestly? I felt rejected. But what the hell, I still got to have sex with her every week if I stuck to the rules."

"And did you stick to the rules?"

"Definitely."

"Were you in love with her?"

Rosenberg coughed uncomfortably. "Are you kidding me?" He sipped his margarita and toyed with the rim of the glass, suddenly far away.

I loved Judy.

She first approached me in April of this year when Justin was in Scotland on a golfing vacation. God, she was beautiful.

She asked me to meet her for a drink at the Franciscan—a little restaurant over on Sepulveda. She got there before I did. She was in a dark corner booth and she had sunglasses on.

The conversation started innocently enough. Of course we knew each other from social gatherings. We had a few drinks and we both loosened up a little. We talked about life in Palos Verdes, what a wonderful place it was to live. We talked about my work—she was the first person I'd met in a long time that didn't think accountants were necessary-but-boring paper pushers. There was a spark there from the beginning. We both could feel it.

We were having such a good time we decided to have dinner and stretch out our time together. She said Justin was going to be gone for a few days and asked if it was okay to call me.

Of course I said yes.

The next couple of nights were like none that I'd ever known. She was the woman I'd always wanted.

But of course she wasn't mine. She belonged to Justin.

The third night in a row we saw each other, we'd been drinking a bit and I felt her touch my leg under the table. At first I thought it was an accident, but when she did it again, well... I'd never been so aroused in my life.

I suggested that I could get a room at the nearby Marriott and she said she would like that. But...

She said she couldn't do that to Justin—she would feel too guilty. Also, she said it would be too risky.

Then she suggested something incredible. She begged me not to judge her. She said that Justin was obsessed with watching her have sex with other men. She also said that Justin wanted to form his own "private swing club" made up of powerful men who lived on the Hill. She said she wasn't interested in the men Justin had selected, but that she would go along because Justin had been so good to her for so many years.

While I admired the fact that Judy would go to such lengths to satisfy Justin in what was obviously an unhappy marriage, I was nonetheless shocked.

She said that if I could join their club, at least she would be "making love" to one man. She said that she would try to manipulate Justin into asking me to join the club. She begged me to consider it.

Although I was married, my marriage had not been good for some time. The following week, Justin, Judy and I went out to dinner. Justin invited me to join their group. Obviously, Judy had convinced him to the point that he actually believed it was his own idea.

The first time I made love with Judy it was like discovering sex for the first time. At the end of each weekly session she

*would whisper in my ear—so the others couldn't hear—that
she loved me.*
She was the great love of my life.

"So you didn't love her…" said Sawyer.

"Of course not," said Rosenberg. "In the final analysis I don't
think I ever had any real feelings for her at all. The sex was
good and my marriage was on the rocks. That's about all there
was to it."

"So what do you think happened to her?"

"I have no idea, Sawyer. I swear. The four of us left about
midnight and I never saw her again."

"So you think Justin did it?"

"I didn't say that. I just know that I didn't."

"What motivation would Justin have?"

"I don't know. Jealousy?"

"Jealousy? You've all been doing his wife for about a year
and suddenly he gets jealous? What changed?"

"I don't know."

"That doesn't ring true to me."

"I know. It doesn't make any sense."

"Can you think of anyone who would have had a motive to
kill Judy?"

"No. No one."

"Was there anything…*anything* at all that you observed or
she told you that seemed out of character or, looking back,
might have been some kind of red flag?"

Rosenberg pondered the question, looking away from Sawyer
for a moment. Then he turned back and said, "No. Besides a
couple of lunches and bumping into each other at social
gatherings, the only time we saw each other was when we got
together at Justin's one night a week."

"Okay," said Sawyer. He stood and tossed a twenty dollar
bill on the table. "You know my number if you think of
anything. Unless you did it—and I don't think you did—I can
do a few things the cops can't." That was true, but Sawyer
wasn't looking to do Rosenberg any favors.

"Okay, thanks."

"Your lawyer's going to tell you different. He's going to tell you not to talk to me."

"Do I need a lawyer?"

"Everybody needs a lawyer. Difference between you and everybody else is that you can buy one who dresses better."

Rosenberg started to laugh, but wasn't sure what part of what Sawyer said was supposed to be funny.

Chapter Eighteen

When Sawyer got home there were fifteen messages on his machine. He knew what that meant—Veronica Mays' report had aired on the East Coast. Cable news networks generally didn't stagger programs, especially news programs. A six in the evening news show started at three on the West Coast. Sawyer looked at his watch. It was 5:30, which made it 8:30 in New York. Even though Veronica was working out of a studio in Los Angeles, she was "breaking news" during prime time in New York.

Most of the messages were of the did-you-hear variety and he didn't bother to write down the names. There were two calls from St. James, but there was no urgency in his voice. There was a call from Wright and he didn't sound good. There was a call from Michael asking to get together for a drink later. There was a call from Veronica. She sounded excited. She thanked him and said she had something to tell him and to call her on her cell. Eric Gregg called and asked Sawyer to call him back.

Still no call from Rebecca.

Sawyer poured himself a cup of coffee, hit the 50-inch TV's on-button and sat down in the black leather recliner. The first thing he saw was Veronica's face. She looked good onscreen. Even in high-def. He knew what she was saying and felt an odd feeling of pride at being the one pulling the strings behind such a big story. Of course, he had done it before when he carried a badge. But this was different.

When she was finished, Sawyer called St. James, who told him that there was nothing new and that the spokesperson was preparing a statement that, while it accused no one, tried to throw the scent onto Wright's four friends, who remained unnamed. The whole thing was nasty and Sawyer knew it was just beginning. The public didn't realize how vicious the media really were. Even if they did, thought Sawyer, they probably wouldn't have cared. The way he looked at it, other people's pain fueled 24/7 cable and it made a lot of small people feel better about their even smaller lives.

Sawyer caught Eric Gregg on his cell. "You called?"

"Riley Gaines called about an hour ago and asked me about you. He wanted to know how you were involved."

"What did you say?"

"I told him the truth. Or at least a defendable version of it. Obviously, he knows about our relationship. I assured him that I wouldn't be telling you things I shouldn't, but that you had stopped by and we talked a little about the investigation. I told him I mainly listened."

"Which is the truth. You know I don't expect anything from you that's going to jam you up. We're one hundred percent clear on that, right?"

"Yes."

"Bottom line is that Justin's a friend, but you were my partner. I'll help Justin, but not at your expense."

"I know. Don't worry about it. I know the rules. I'll do what I can, nothing more."

"Understood."

When Sawyer hung up he realized that Gregg had not asked him if he had spoken with any of the men from the swing club, even though Sawyer had told Gregg that was what he planned to do. Sawyer knew it was not because his old partner had forgotten.

Sawyer called Michael and told him he'd stop by Admiral Risty around nine.

Then he called Riley Gaines. "Hey Riley, long time, no talk."

"I wondered when you were going to call."

"How about I take you to breakfast tomorrow morning?"

"I'm not going to give you anything. In fact, I was going to call you and see where you fit in this thing."

"I'm not involved. Not really."

"Yeah, I remember you always had a sense of humor."

And Sawyer knew that Gaines had none. "So, tomorrow morning?"

"I'll be down in Palos Verdes about ten."

"Marmalade. It's in the Avenues shopping center."

"Yeah, I know it. See you at ten," he said and hung up.

Sawyer turned off the television, went into the bedroom, stripped off his clothes, set the alarm for 8:15 and unplugged the phone again.

Chapter Nineteen

Michael Hall was in good voice. The crowd was small but appreciative. Sawyer sat down at a corner table and ordered a Grey Goose martini, neat.

After his set Michael joined Sawyer and ordered a Boodles martini with a twist. When Hall's drink was delivered, Sawyer said, "So, where's Carrie?"

"She's going to New York for the holidays. Called me this afternoon and told me she was going."

"I take it she didn't ask you to tag along."

"No."

"Oh well…"

"That's life," said Hall with a sigh. "Good thing I'm a Tantric master."

"Which is why I'm here: I'd like to ask your 'professional' opinion about something."

"Shoot."

"Are things really so wild sexually on the Hill? I thought this was just a sleepy little town where money came to die."

"To be honest, it's not as wild as what Wright and his friends were doing, but people are…let's just say they stay active. Women on the Hill aren't kids anymore, but they take care of themselves. As a group they're very health conscious. And what nature didn't provide—or stopped providing—they replace or enhance. There are a lot of good-looking women up here who are divorced, widowed, or simply bored with their husbands."

"Sounds like 'Desperate Housewives.'"

"Trust me. I know a lot of these women. They're not desperate and they sure as hell aren't housewives. Besides, I like being with a woman who remembers Paul McCartney when he was with his 'old' band."

"Do you know any of the men Judy was sleeping with?"

"Have their names been released?"

"No, I just thought you might have heard something through the grapevine."

"No. But Judy used to come to my class now and then."

"Really?"

"You sound surprised."

"Did you ever sleep with her?"

"Never had the pleasure. But I could see what other men saw in her. She was something."

"Did she come to class alone?"

"As a matter of fact, no. She always came with a friend."

"Got a name?"

"ShyAnn Sands. She's late-forties, divorced, drives a two-year-old Benz convertible."

"You seem to know a lot about her. Did you date her?"

"We had coffee a couple of times. And no, we never had sex. But we flirted a little. I have a rule that I never date women whose names are purposely misspelled. In the back of my mind there's always the thought that the name was *not* purposely misspelled. Therefore, if I dated such a woman, I'd always have to wear 'long pants' before wading into that gene pool—if you know what I mean..."

"You got her number?"

Hall took out his PDA, pressed a few tiny keys, and read off a local number, which Sawyer wrote down.

"You think she would know about Judy's private club?"

"I don't know. I wouldn't be surprised. They seemed pretty tight."

"Did she ever talk about Judy when you two got together?"

"Not that I remember. At least nothing comes to mind. We just mainly talked about the class—you know, channeling our spiritual and sexual energy, that kind of thing."

"You live an interesting life, Michael."

"I got no complaints."

Chapter Twenty

Sawyer called Wright on his way home from Admiral Risty and asked him about ShyAnn Sands. He told Sawyer he'd heard Judy mention the name, but that he had never met her. When he hung up Sawyer called Sands' number, got an answering machine, but didn't leave a message.

It was about ten when Sawyer parked in the driveway and let himself in. He made himself some hot chocolate from scratch, lit the fireplace and sat down in the living room across from the flames.

Fifty years into his life Sawyer really couldn't define the word love, even though he'd thought a lot about it lately. The Hallmark definitions usually had to do with respect, admiration and an appreciation of someone developed over periods of ups and downs, multiple hairstyles, career triumphs and defeats, mistakes and reconciliations. But he couldn't help thinking that there was more to it than that. Something more raw, more visceral.

Great love stories were almost always unrequited affairs, thought Sawyer. What if Romeo and Juliet had married and stayed together for fifty years? They might have been happy, but they wouldn't have been famous. No love songs would have been written about them.

Living together—and loving together—when passion faded was really the measure of love, he thought. Certainly not all feelings died, but the intense infatuation of a new relationship could not be sustained forever. Infatuation was like a sprint—almost everyone could run around the block. A marriage was like a marathon—it took work; more work than most people were willing to put in.

Sawyer recalled seeing a TV show where several scientists said they believed that "love," or the feeling of "being in love," lasted only a few months. So where did a loving couple go from there? Did people really learn to live lives of quiet desperation? Did they give up parts of themselves in order to conform to a path of least resistance? Did they compromise in the name of harmony to the extent that little of themselves remained? And did those changes—the smoothing of rough edges—really create a better fit? A better marriage? A better person? Or did it just make people feel more comfortable being the person someone else wanted them to be?

Sawyer pondered these things as the flames danced, flickered and began to fade. Out of the corner of his eye he saw the phone.

And waited for it to ring.

Chapter Twenty-one

Riley Gaines was no one's fool. He had worked his way up the ranks and into Homicide by being smarter than everyone else and working harder than most. He played it straight down the line. He didn't do any favors—unless it was absolutely necessary. He never railroaded anybody—not knowingly anyhow. He had no ambitions to be Chief. He was happy doing what he did—putting the bad guys in jail, letting the chips fall where they may.

He and Sawyer knew each other. They respected each other but weren't in each other's fan club. They had only worked together on one case and it had ended with the murderer getting life without parole.

Marmalade was about half full by the time Sawyer arrived, ten minutes early. Riley Gaines was right on time. Sawyer stood and waved Gaines to a booth. Coffee was offered and poured and each ordered eggs rancheros.

"You said yesterday that you were planning to call me..." said Sawyer.

"I hear you're at the center of this thing."

Sawyer laughed modestly. "Hardly. I'm just a friend of the victim's husband."

"Really? I hear you're advising St. James and Wright."

"I wouldn't use the word 'advising.'"

"Don't play games with me, Sawyer. You're not in my crosshairs but things can change. Fast."

"I don't react well to threats, Riley."

"I'm not threatening you, Sawyer. I'm just telling you not to muddy the waters. You're not a cop anymore. I am and I'm in charge. Look, I'm not trying to come across as a hard-ass, but if that's the way it feels to you, that's okay too. If you were in my shoes you'd to the same thing."

Sawyer thought about arguing but he knew Gaines was right. Gaines was not a political hack and he wasn't out to lock up the wrong guy—especially the wrong "rich guy." At the same time he wasn't impressed by bling, even old-money bling, and he wouldn't tolerate Sawyer, or anyone else, getting in the way. As long as Sawyer stayed on the periphery and played by the rules, he would have no trouble with Gaines. If not, Gaines had no problem kicking his ass.

"I thought this was going to be a friendly breakfast."

"Really? You just said breakfast." That was as close as Riley Gaines got to a joke. "I know it was you who orchestrated the release of Veronica Mays' swing club story."

"What makes you think that?"

"Come on, Sawyer. You and Mays used to have a thing—everybody knows that. You found out the M.E. discovered multiple DNA on the victim… Hey, it was the smart thing to do. Give the vultures some meat they're going to get anyhow; it makes them think you're feeding them information, when the exact opposite is true: you're setting them up to give *you* information."

"You still have more information than I do."

"I should. I'm in charge of the fucking investigation."

"So why did you agree to meet with me?"

"I just wanted to let you know that I know what you're doing. Like I said, as long as you stay on your side of the fence, you got no problem with me. But you cross that line—and you more than most people know exactly where that line is—you've got a serious problem with me. Ex-cop or no ex-cop."

"Okay. I got it."

"Good."

The two men small-talked over breakfast and, as the dishes were being cleared away and a last cup of coffee was poured for each, Sawyer said, "What do you think about this, Riley? Seriously."

"I'm not sure, but Wright's at the top of the list. By the way, I'm not ready to buy into the swing club members as suspects. Not yet anyhow."

"So you really think Wright did it?"

"Look Sawyer, you and I both know these things usually aren't that complicated. Look at O.J. It wasn't complicated. It didn't really make any difference that Mark Fuhrman said a 'bad word' ten years before the murders. You know me. I'm not approaching this with tunnel vision; I'm open to other reasonable explanations, but I'm not buying some scenario dreamed up by a screenwriter."

For a moment Sawyer wondered why Gaines had bothered to meet with him at all and why he was telling him his feelings about Wright being the target of his investigation. But it only took a second to figure out. He wanted to deliver the message that he was willing to work with Wright and St. James on some kind of plea deal. Sawyer was the go-between.

"I still don't think he did it."

"Yeah, well, Wright can't use 19th Century slavery as a defense and Johnny Cochran's dead. I know that Noah St. James is famous for smacking a jury with a stupid stick, but I just want you to know that I won't let that happen. Police incompetence will not be an issue in this trial. If Wright did it, he's going to jail. The only question is for how long."

Sawyer believed the man. He grabbed the check, shook Gaines' hand outside the restaurant and walked to his car. He didn't know what to tell Wright. Except that if he was guilty he should be worried.

And maybe even if he wasn't.

Chapter Twenty-two

ShyAnn Sands answered her phone and, after Sawyer shared with her his list of mutual friends, she agreed to meet him at the Starbucks at the corner of Hawthorne and Palos Verdes Drive.

She ordered a macchiato, Sawyer just got a standard cup of joe—for about three times what he used to pay for it at a diner on Broadway when he was working downtown.

They sat outside under an outdoor propane heater. It was warm for December, but there was still a chill in the air off the Pacific, just a few hundred yards away.

"I still can't believe Judy's dead," said ShyAnn. Sands was blonde, slim, and just barely brushed up against five feet. She had about as perfect a body as money could buy, but she'd obviously had a pretty good foundation on which to build. Her nose was cute and just ever-so-slightly upturned. Her teeth were bleached and lined up perfectly. He figured she had a lot of practice flashing her smile, but couldn't bring herself to use it this morning. "Should I be talking to you?"

"Don't know why not," said Sawyer. "You didn't have anything to do with Judy's murder, did you?"

"Of course not."

"I'm simply doing what I can to help Justin."

"I understand. I know who you are—I've read about you in the local papers—and I think Judy mentioned your name once. I just don't want anything I tell you winding up in some tabloid or coming back to hurt somebody."

"Who could it hurt?"

"Judy, for one. Look at what the media's doing to her reputation."

"I know. It's not right. So you knew about Justin and Judy's private club," said Sawyer.

ShyAnn started to say no, but bit her lip and sipped her macchiato. "Not really."

"Which means what exactly?"

"She told me about it. I was shocked. And I'm not easily shocked."

"What did she tell you about it?"

"What she was doing."

"Did she tell you with whom she was doing it?"

"Yes."

"She must have really trusted you."

"I think I was her best friend."

"That's odd."

"What?"

"Justin said he'd heard Judy mention your name, but he'd never met you."

"That's true."

"How can you be Judy's best friend and never meet her husband?"

"It happens. We met a few years ago at a local health club—Palos Verdes Fitness. We really hit it off. I'd just gotten my divorce and I was starting to 'get out there' again. She encouraged me and we just started hanging out together. We'd meet for drinks at various restaurants and bars in the area and talk."

"About what?"

"Men. What else?"

"Did she ever tell you about anyone other than the four men she saw weekly?"

"Not in so many words, but I think she was 'seeing someone.' I don't know if it was one of the four guys or someone else. She wouldn't tell me."

"Seems she told you everything else. She felt comfortable telling you about having sex with four guys, but wouldn't tell you about an affair?"

"I know, I know... It doesn't make sense. It was kind of like she was 'protecting' the relationship."

"Do you have any idea whom she might have been seeing? Even an educated guess?"

"No. But I do know she thought things were coming to a head."

"How so?"

"I don't know exactly. She said things were getting out of control."

"She said that?"

"Yes."

"And *did* things get out of control?"

"I don't know. Maybe that has something to do with what happened to her."

"You mean you think maybe her lover murdered her out of jealousy?"

"Wouldn't it seem more likely that *Justin* murdered her out of jealousy?"

"That's not the way I see it," said Sawyer, but he knew a lot of people would.

Both were silent for a moment, taking in the panoramic ocean view.

"Judy was a good person," said ShyAnn finally. "I hate what the newspapers and TV shows are making her out to be. She wasn't like that."

"I know," said Sawyer. But what he was really thinking was that he didn't know Judy Wright at all.

Chapter Twenty-three

Sawyer checked his cell on the way back home. St. James had called. Nothing urgent, but it was "important." And Rebecca had called.

Sawyer called St. James back and spoke with him as he pulled into his driveway and turned off the car. He told him about his conversation with ShyAnn Sands and about her speculation.

"I like the 'jilted lover' angle," said the lawyer. "I can work with that."

"That's not exactly what she said."

"I'm just thinking out loud. This can take us more than halfway to reasonable doubt. If we can find the lover."

"Maybe. I'd like to talk with Justin again."

"Fine. He trusts you. And so do I…in case that means anything to you."

"Thanks." It really didn't mean that much to Sawyer to mean that much to St. James. But then, one of the definitions of being a friend, in Sawyer's book, was being able to be counted on in times of trouble. St. James never backed down from a fight. He could do worse than to have Noah St. James as a friend.

Sawyer walked inside, poured himself a Splenda-sweetened Diet Coke, and then called Rebecca back.

"Hi, Rebecca."

"Sawyer?"

"Yes."

"Thanks for calling back," she said politely. "I'd like to meet with you."

"Okay. When?"

"Sooner the better."

"Okay. How about this evening?"

"That's fine. Where?"

"Why don't you come home?"

"Why don't we meet at Chez Melange?"

"How about seven?"

"That's good. See you then," she said and hung up.

He called Wright and set an appointment for two p.m. Then he unplugged the bedroom phone, set the alarm for one-thirty and went to bed.

But he couldn't stop thinking about the fact that Rebecca didn't want to meet with him in their home.

Chapter Twenty-four

Sawyer ran the media gauntlet outside Wright's mansion. Wright buzzed Sawyer in the gate. He parked in the underground garage and took the elevator up to the first-floor foyer where Justin greeted him and ushered him into the library.

"You remember Nathan?"

Sawyer shook hands with a tall, good-looking young man he vaguely recalled meeting at one of Wright's summer theme parties—something to do with Italian wines. Sawyer remembered that Judy had been dressed in a very low-cut serving wench's outfit. It was an image that stuck with Sawyer for some time.

"Nice to see you again," said Sawyer, extending his hand. As the two men shook hands Sawyer was struck by Nathan's deep and penetrating blue eyes, which were accented by his dark features.

"Thanks for helping my dad, Mr. Black."

"Please call me Sawyer."

Nathan nodded.

"Friends do for friends," said the former detective. "And I'm not sure how much I'm helping."

"Nonsense," interjected Wright. "Sawyer is my rock. Noah may think he's running the show, but I feel more comfortable with you, Sawyer."

Sawyer declined a glass of bourbon and then the three men seated themselves in the library.

Sawyer pegged Nathan Wright for somewhere between twenty-two and twenty-five. He was still at the age where it was hard to tell whether his fitness came from regular exercise or good genes.

"Nathan's a good kid," said Wright. "No silver spoon in his mouth. I told him when he graduated from college to take a year off, find himself—or whatever the hell they call it these days—then come back and tell me what he wanted to do. I told him I'd pay for everything. But I also said, 'After you get on your feet, you're on your own.'"

Nathan flashed a heard-it-all-before grin and sipped his father's high-end booze. "That plan sounded better when I was seventeen," said Nathan good-naturedly.

"A Harvard grad… You'd think he could land a decent job," said Wright with a laugh, but Sawyer could tell that he was proud. Especially of the Harvard part. Every Harvard graduate Sawyer knew would always find a way to work Harvard into the conversation whenever they met someone new.

"So, what do you do, Nathan?" asked Sawyer, not because he was particularly interested, but because he knew that was his line. Besides, it felt good to pretend the world wasn't coming to an end.

"I own a kayak shop down on the Redondo Pier."

"And guess what?" said Wright. "Been in business less than a year and some national outfit has already approached him about franchising."

Sawyer was thinking that the rich get richer even when they open a God damned kayak shop. But what he said was, "That's great."

"The kid's a genius," said Wright and he poured himself another drink.

Sawyer could tell by the way Wright spoke that this wasn't his first, second or even third drink. It wouldn't have surprised Sawyer to find out Wright had been drinking ever since he discovered Judy's body.

One of the cell phones on Wright's desk started playing a riff from an Andrea Bocelli song Sawyer had heard a hundred times but still didn't know the name of. Wright stood and said, "I gotta take this." He walked over to his desk, picked up the phone, took it into a room off the library and closed the door.

"I'm sorry about your stepmother," said Sawyer.

"Thanks. She was a good person."

"You two got along?" Sawyer recalled the acrimony that surrounded Wright's divorce from his first wife, Natasha. It lingered, according to Rebecca, in the form of Natasha taking every opportunity to tear Judy down.

"My mom didn't like her. I guess everyone knew that. But Judy and I got along fine. In the beginning it was a little awkward because I was living with my mom. After I went away to school and started coming back for vacations, Judy and I got along better. She told me I had one mother and that she wanted to be my friend. I respected that."

"So, how is your mother?"

"Fine. She's busy all the time."

He knew that Natasha had been through lots of men. It was more appropriate to say that lots of men had been through her money and no one had stuck around. Still, Justin paid her enough money so that the gravy train never ground to a halt.

"How does your mother feel about…"

"Judy's murder? I know this doesn't sound very nice, but she kind of feels like my father's finally getting what he deserves."

"That's probably what a lot of people think. All they know about your dad is that he's richer than they are, has a lot more sex than they do, and with a more attractive partner. People are jealous."

"You think my mom's jealous?"

"What do you think?"

Nathan didn't answer immediately. "Even if she is, she doesn't kill people. She wants them to feel more pain—she sues them."

"Sorry about that," said Wright as he came back into the room and set the cell phone on the desk.

"Hey, I've really got to go," said Nathan. He stood, hugged his father, shook Sawyer's hand, and left.

"Great kid," said Wright when his son had gone.

"Yeah, seems like it. He said things are still pretty chilly between you and Natasha."

"Never worse. And this…this will just make her more self-righteous than ever."

"How do you think Nathan's taking Judy's death?"

"Seems to be handling it okay."

"Were they close?"

"What's that supposed to mean?"

"I mean she was his stepmother for about fourteen years of his life and she was just brutally murdered. I know he was closer to his own mother, but you all lived within a few miles of each other. I guess what I'm saying is, were they like mother and son, or more like friends?"

"Friends," said Wright. "Sorry, I'm a little tense, as you can imagine. Nathan never called Judy 'Mom' and he was always 'loyal'—that's how Natasha puts it—to my first wife. But Natasha's hatred didn't rub off on Nathan. He and Judy seemed to get along fine."

"I'm trying to get a picture of Judy that even you might not have, Justin. Because if you didn't kill her—and I believe that you didn't—then someone looked at her in a way that you're not aware of. Someone hated her so much, loved her so much, or felt so passionately about her that he—or she—was driven to murder. Think about that, Justin. We don't have a serial killer on the loose in Palos Verdes. This is a crime of passion. A passion so intense that someone you and I would call a 'normal person' became so obsessed that he actually murdered someone."

Justin thought about that for a moment. What Sawyer said was true. Judy's murder was not a robbery gone wrong—nothing was taken. It was not one in a series of rapes or murders in Palos Verdes. Obviously, someone intended to kill Judy. Specifically.

"I have to say this, Justin—not to hurt you or make your life more miserable than it already is—but we've got to talk about this."

"I understand," said Wright, although he wasn't exactly sure what Sawyer was going to say.

"It's likely, though not one hundred percent certain, that your wife was murdered by someone who believed, rightly or wrongly, that she was someone special in his life."

"What do you mean?"

"I mean that Judy may have had a lover. Or there might be someone who thought he was her lover, or wanted very badly to be her lover."

"She had a number of lovers."

"I mean 'lover,' not just a sex partner."

"Where are you going with this?"

"Did you know that Danny Rosenberg approached Judy about having a more—how shall I say this—'intimate' relationship?"

"He got to have sex with her every week. What's more intimate than that?"

"I think it wasn't enough for Danny. For one thing, his marriage to Linda was falling apart."

"He knew that seeing Judy outside the Club was strictly against the rules."

"Not everybody plays by the rules."

Justin thought about that as he sipped his bourbon.

"To her credit, from what I hear, Judy followed the rules," said Sawyer, anticipating Wright's next question.

"So she rejected Danny?"

"Yes."

"How'd he take it?"

"To hear him tell it, he was disappointed, but he figured that sleeping with her once a week was better than not at all."

"I see…" said Wright, but he was somewhere else.

"The thing is, Justin, a husband isn't always the best person to ask about who his wife really is or isn't, and what she really feels. There's a good chance there's something extremely important that you don't know about Judy's life that ended up getting her killed. That's the reason I asked about Nathan. Everyone Judy was close to might have a piece of the puzzle—perhaps even pieces you not only don't have but would never guess existed. I need to find those puzzle pieces and fit them into place. For example, ShyAnn Sands knew about your 'private club' and she also believed that Judy was having an affair—separate and apart from the Club. But she didn't know who that person was."

"ShyAnn said that?"

"Judy may have had a secret life. I know you wanted to give her 'space' and privacy, but she's dead and you're going to jail unless the cops can come up with someone other than you to pin it on."

"I understand," said Wright again.

"I want to make sure you do. What I'm asking is for you to dig into places Judy might have tried to hide things. Go through her closets and drawers, everything the police didn't cart away. See what you can find. Did she have a diary?"

"I think so."

"And the cops didn't take it?"

"No."

"Why not?"

"It isn't here in the house. It's in her studio in San Pedro. To be honest, I'm not really sure it's a diary. She said she kept a 'journal' to document her growth as an artist and to record her general thoughts about life. She kept the book in her studio because that's where she painted."

"And the police don't know about the studio?"

"I didn't tell them."

"I didn't know Judy painted."

"She took a few classes at the Art Center. She took some private lessons from a guy at Angel's Gate in San Pedro."

"You remember the guy's name?"

"Not off the top of my head. But I've got a few cancelled checks made out to him. I can get them for you."

"Good. You have a key to Judy's studio?"

"No, but I know the address. I send a rent check for the studio every three months." Wright stood, walked to his desk, opened a drawer, withdrew a large checkbook, looked through several pages, wrote down something on a piece of paper and handed it to Sawyer, who looked at it and saw that it was only a block or two from The Whale and Ale.

"Lots of artists' studios and galleries in this area."

"Yes. First Thursday of every month they've got an 'art walk' where people check out all the studios and see artists' work. Judy found the atmosphere very inspiring."

"Any reason she didn't give you a key?"

"She never offered and I never asked. I just paid the rent. The only reason I know the address is because she told me the owner lives in the building, and he's the guy I send the checks to."

Sawyer stood and said, "You have a piece of paper with your letterhead?"

"Sure." Wright took out a piece of paper from a drawer.

"Write this: 'I authorize Mr. Sawyer Black to be my legal representative to remove my wife's belongings from the studio for which I pay rent. Be aware that failure to comply with this legal instrument may result in serious and immediate legal sanctions.' Sign it and date it."

"Legal sanctions?"

"Don't worry about it. It sounds like 'legalese.' That scares people who don't know better."

Wright signed the document and handed it to Sawyer, who folded it and pocketed it.

"If I need help selling this I'll call you. So be available."

"Thanks, Sawyer," said Wright. He shook his friend's hand and walked him to the door.

When he was in his car Sawyer checked the digital clock. It was three o'clock. He didn't have another appointment until his 7 pm meeting at Chez Melange with Rebecca. He drove down the hill on the ocean side and took the back way into San Pedro.

Chapter Twenty-five

San Pedro was a working class town and one of the major ports through which goods entered the United States. The 110 Freeway was Los Angeles' oldest freeway. At the far northern end was Pasadena. It dead-ended into San Pedro on the south. Pasadena was old money and museums.

San Pedro, on the other hand, was not old money or even new money. For years the city had tried to revitalize its old neighborhoods the way Pasadena had done but it had never quite worked. It wasn't because of the restaurants. They were some of the best in Los Angeles and Sawyer frequented many of them. And there was no doubt that some of the South Bay's most talented artists were in residence in San Pedro.

Even so, the crowds—at least in the numbers city fathers had hoped for—never materialized. San Pedro always seemed to be in a state of becoming. And never fast enough for retailers paying the rent, waiting for the rebirth.

Sawyer drove past Marcello Restaurant, an Italian place he often took friends. He parked in front of an old three-story, white brick building, put a couple of quarters in the meter, walked into the foyer and pressed the manager's buzzer located just to the right of a large locked glass door. Someone inside yelled, "Just a minute." Sawyer heard the man through the door. Apparently the intercom wasn't working.

A husky bald man who looked to be in his mid fifties opened the door. He had the demeanor of a man who had just been awakened from a nap. "Can I help you?"

"I'm here to take a look at Judy Wright's studio."

"Yeah, I heard about that," said the man unresponsively.

"You got a key?"

"Sure. It's my building. But I'm not sure I can let you in."

"I'm her husband's representative and I'm here to collect her things before the media gets wind of this and starts stealing things. You understand, I'm sure."

"Yeah but, I don't know who you are. You might be the media yourself."

"I just came from her husband's office and he gave me this." Sawyer withdrew the letter Wright had written and handed it to the man.

"How do I know this was written by Mr. Wright?"

"Compare it to the signature on his check. He paid the rent, right?"

"Yeah, but I don't have any checks he wrote. I cashed them all."

"You have a phone?"

"Of course. Call the number on the top of the letterhead. Talk to Wright yourself. Ask him anything so you can satisfy yourself that he's actually who he says he is. He needs to retrieve his wife's things immediately and you need to comply. Legally, Mr. Wright is actually the tenant because he's the one who's paid the rent. Your obligation is to him. I'm sure you know who Mr. Wright is."

"Of course."

"He would be grateful if we can do this so as to preserve as much of his wife's dignity as possible. If on the other hand you attempt to use this tragedy for your own purposes—"

"No, no, no. I liked Judy. She was great. Okay, okay, I'll make the call."

The man closed the door and disappeared into his apartment, leaving Sawyer standing in the outside foyer.

A few minutes later he reappeared and waved Sawyer inside.

"Her studio's up the stairs, the last door on the right." He handed Sawyer a key, went back into his apartment and closed the door.

Sawyer walked up the old wood stairs and followed the hallway to the end, put the key in the door and opened it. The room was dark. He hit a switch, a bare bulb hanging from the ceiling came on, and Sawyer closed the door.

There was an easel at the far end of the room, but it was empty. Instead of chairs there was a sofa. The blinds were drawn and without the inside light the studio was black as midnight. There was a half-refrigerator just to the left of the sofa. Sawyer grabbed a paint cloth and used it to open the refrigerator, careful not to leave fingerprints.

Inside was a bottle of Ketel One vodka, a jar of olives, some moldy Swiss cheese, and an onion bagel. There was a bottle of vermouth on a side table next to the refrigerator.

Sawyer closed the refrigerator and scanned the room again. There were a few canvases leaning against each other on the floor next to the easel. He looked through them. Lots of abstracts and a few Palos Verdes landscapes.

Two scented candles—one cinnamon, one rose—were on the side table alongside a box of Kleenex. There were also two books next to the candles—a coffee table art book, *Palos Verdes Peninsula Artists* and *Song of Life*, a book of poetry by Bernadette Shih. Sawyer looked inside both books. Neither was signed.

The side table had a drawer, which Sawyer opened. Inside was a small leather-bound notebook, tied together by a thin leather lace wrapped around the volume. He untied the lace and opened the book. At first glance it seemed like general notes and musings about her art classes. There was an entire section dedicated to *plein air* painting, another to life drawing, and another to "my Fauve period." Scattered throughout the book, in no apparent order, were short poems. He scanned one:

Share communion with your lover
Your glass is full but you must taste it
Don't save your kisses for tomorrow
A lonely life is one that's wasted

There were more verses like that. Out of context it was difficult to know what they meant, if anything. Some people used poetry as an outlet for fantasy, others as a form of therapy. In neither form were the words to be taken literally. Judy could have written the poems about her husband. In fact, he wasn't even sure if it was Judy's notebook. He quickly scanned the book for phone numbers, saw none, then pocketed it and continued to look around.

There was no phone, but that was not unusual in an age where some people had only cell phones and I-pods to connect themselves to the "real world."

Just then he heard a noise from the studio next door. Someone had just come in. Sawyer went outside and knocked on the neighbor's door. A man in his early forties opened the door. He looked a little rough. Sawyer could smell gin on his breath.

"Yes?"

"I'd like to ask you a few questions about your neighbor."

"Which one?"

"The woman next door," said Sawyer, tilting his head in the direction of Judy's studio.

"You mean J-Lo."

"J-Lo?"

"Because of her... You're not her husband, are you?"

"No," said Sawyer with a relaxed, easy laugh. Apparently the guy didn't know what had happened to Judy. Sawyer knew people like this. Unplugged people. No TV, no Internet, no cell phones. They read a lot, drank the best booze they could afford, and stayed to themselves. The world could go to hell.

"I called her J-Lo because of her butt. It was like J-Lo's."

"And you know this how?"

"I've got eyes."

"Mind if I come in?" said Sawyer, making his way toward the door.

"No, I guess not."

Sawyer pushed past the man into the one-room studio.

"You live here?"

"Sometimes," said the man as he closed the door. "And you're...?"

"I'm an old friend of J-Lo's. We go back to our college days," said Sawyer, making it up as he went along. It wasn't that hard. This guy was not a tough audience.

"Really... She never struck me as the college type."

"Yeah, well, USC... Go Trojans."

"Whatever. I'm not into sports. I take it she's not in."

"Right. I was just wondering if you could tell me where I could find her; you know, places she hangs out, people she hangs out with. That kind of thing."

"What's your name?"

"John," said Sawyer. He'd told worse lies. "And yours?"

"Tony."

They didn't bother to shake hands.

"Tony, can I level with you?"

"I'd appreciate that."

"You got something to drink?" Guys like Tony always had something to drink, thought Sawyer. And they didn't need a good excuse to put it to work.

"All I've got's bourbon."

"You're reading my mind."

Tony opened a small paint box, removed a tray and produced a bottle of Jack Daniels. He made a show of washing out two glasses under a dirty faucet in the corner and returned with two one-third-full half glasses. "Cheers," he said, as he handed Sawyer one of the glasses.

"Cheers."

"So, you were gonna start telling me the truth."

"Right. I'm not an old friend of hers."

"No kiddin'," said Tony with a smirk.

"Yeah, well... J-Lo's husband is a friend of mine and he's kind of worried about her. He pays for her studio and she spends a lot of time here—according to him—so I'm just trying to get a picture of what *really* goes on. If you know what I mean..."

"You mean is she fucking other guys?"

"That's one way to put it."

"I don't know. She wasn't fucking me. Not that I would've turned it down, but we hardly ever spoke."

"And why should I believe you?"

"First of all, you're drinking my bourbon. Second, I don't give a flying fuck whether you believe me or not."

"But you were friends."

"I wouldn't say friends. We talked every once in a while when we passed in the hallway. I still have no idea what her real name is, or what her real life is. We have a lot of 'posers' here in San Pedro. People who live a Bohemian lifestyle when it suits them, then go back up the Hill to their *real* life. This is it for me. I paint and drink and that's about it. I'm the real deal. For better or worse."

Looking at the man, Sawyer decided it was probably for worse most of the time. "How often did J-Lo come here?"

"I dunno, maybe four times a week. That's just a guess because I didn't really keep track."

"Was she serious about her art?"

"Not as serious as me. I could tell this was a part-time thing for her. Not that she didn't have some talent, but she wasn't committed enough to develop it."

"Did she have visitors?"

"Not many."

"Men or women?"

"What do you think?"

"So, was it men or one man?"

"I don't know. Like I said, I really wasn't paying attention."

"I imagine you'd pay attention if she was having sex with somebody next door."

"You're right, I would. But I never heard anything like that. Doesn't mean it didn't happen, but I never heard it."

"You have a regular schedule?" Sawyer took a shot.

"Kind of. I got a part-time day-job painting houses for a buddy of mine. That's how I make ends meet. He pays me off the books. Mondays, Wednesdays and Fridays I work from about nine till about four."

"You ever tell your schedule to J-Lo?"

"As a matter of fact, I did. And she would also know that about five every weeknight I go down to Danny's Pub, about two blocks east of here, for Happy Hour. I nurse a beer for a couple hours so I can partake of the free all-you-can-eat calamari. It's not like it's fresh, but it's dinner."

"So you're gone during the day and early evening a lot."

"That's right."

"So she could be having wild parties next door and you'd never know."

"I suppose so."

"Did you ever see any one specific person besides J-Lo at her place?"

Tony leaned back against the wall, tossed his head back, took a deep breath and scanned through what was left of his memory. "There was a guy. I think I saw him more than once, but I can't be sure. High cheek bones, bald, slim, attractive, well-dressed."

"How old?"

Tony shook his head. "Hard to tell these days, what with plastic surgery and all. Being bald makes it even harder. Looked like he could have shaved his head. But I'd guess forties if the guy worked out. Hey, I gotta get goin'," said Tony, looking at his watch.

"Thanks," said Sawyer. He stood, leaving the Jack Daniels behind. He knew it wouldn't go to waste.

Tony locked his door and went downstairs. Sawyer went back to Judy's studio. He looked through her paintings for any sign of anyone who looked like the man Tony described. Nothing. He scoured the room again, looking under the sofa, behind tables and underneath drawers, even in her wastebasket, but the place was clean. Too clean, he thought.

Sawyer locked up and walked out onto Seventh Street. It was five o'clock. He had time for a quick drink at the Whale and Ale before heading home. As he walked toward the restaurant the wind off the Pacific picked up and he lifted his collar to protect against the chill. He wasn't sure if Judy had used the studio to meet men, or a man, but he knew it was possible. An alcoholic with an off-the-books day job and a free Happy Hour dinner within walking distance ran more predictably than Amtrak.

And though he knew Judy had never gone to college, he knew that she was smart enough to get Justin to divorce his first wife, and that took more than a good-looking butt. If she had wanted to create a more dependable rendezvous location, she couldn't have dreamed up a better spot.

Sawyer sat down at the bar and ordered a Pimm's Cup the way only a British pub could make it—in a pewter mug, with a cucumber, lemon and ginger beer.

He sipped his drink and called Jake Woodbridge. When the former city councilman initially declined to meet Sawyer for a drink at the Whale and Ale, Sawyer mentioned Judy's name and suddenly the man had an opening in his schedule.

That gave Sawyer about half an hour to continue reading Judy Wright's diary.

Chapter Twenty-six

Sawyer knew Jake Woodbridge through Justin Wright. They had played golf together, fished and drank on Justin's boat and attended dinner parties and fundraisers, with their wives, at Wright's home.

Jake Woodbridge wasn't the most famous politician Sawyer knew. But he was a powerful man, nonetheless. And he loved politics the way some men loved golf, single-malt Scotch, Cuban cigars...or women.

"Politics is the art of promising something for nothing while trying to get people to believe you really think it's possible," Woodbridge had explained to Sawyer one afternoon on Wright's veranda as the two men looked out over the Pacific, smoking cigars and drinking bourbon. "Most people really don't care how things get done as long as they don't have to pay for it."

This hadn't come as a revelation to Sawyer because the further up the chain of command he had gone with the LAPD the more he understood about politics.

Woodbridge was a thin man, balding in front, but with thick hair on the sides. He was fit. According to him he played tennis at a "semi-pro" level, whatever the hell that meant, thought Sawyer.

"This is unbelievable," said Woodbridge as he sipped a glass of merlot.

"Believe it. And fast."

"I spoke with my lawyer and he said I should be careful what I say to you."

"You should be careful what you say to anyone now," said Sawyer. "I'm not here to hurt you, Jake. We're all friends..."

"Yeah, that's easy to say when we're all playing golf or sitting around in some Catalina bar talking about getting laid. But this is different."

"You're right. This *is* different."

"Look, I'm sorry about what happened to Judy, but I had nothing to do with it. I swear," said Woodbridge, as though convincing Sawyer made a difference.

"I didn't think you did. I'm just trying to understand what happened that night."

Woodbridge touched the rim of his glass with his index finger. "This club... Out of context it all sounds perverted. But it wasn't like that. We were all friends."

"Tell me what happened that night"

"If I tell you..."

"It could be used against you," said Sawyer. He felt that telling Woodbridge the truth would make the politician trust him more.

"All I'm going to tell you is what I'll tell the police. Because it's the truth. I didn't kill Judy and I don't know who did."

"Okay."

"I arrived about eight. That was the time we told our wives Justin's 'poker game' started. So, we were all there by about eight-thirty. Drinks were set up in the library and we all started drinking. Everyone liked to loosen up before things got started."

"Was anyone ever not able to...perform?"

"No. But then who could really tell? Viagra was always available if you wanted it. I tell you, Sawyer, it was another world for me. What happened with Justin and Judy... I'd never been involved in anything like that before. Justin and Judy were very different kinds of people."

"What do you mean?"

"I think Judy was kind of along for the ride. You know Justin. He's a 'presence.' When you're around him, you know he's running things. He built one of the most successful companies in the world. That didn't happen by luck. The man's hands-on. He's not a 'control freak' in the sense that he has to do everything himself. But he's a control freak in the sense that he has to control the outcome."

Sawyer knew that Wright didn't really have to control everyone and everything. He only wanted to control the people and things that meant something to him. Sawyer never fell into that category and he was thankful for that.

"Anyhow, we drank, talked, played a little poker, and then Judy came downstairs. Justin always started things. It was like a polite kind of protocol. She was wearing a T-shirt and high heels. Nothing else. She walked in, over to the card table and stood next to Justin. She spread her legs slightly and Justin started rubbing her...between her legs. She started moaning... Justin stimulated her to orgasm and then Robert..."

"Sanchez?"

"Yes. Robert stood and went around behind her. He took her into a small room off the library and had sex with her. Eventually, we each...got together with Judy."

"How did you feel about Judy?"

"I'm not sure I know what you mean?"

"It's a pretty straightforward question. How did you feel about her?"

"Okay, I guess. She was a great piece of ass. What do you want me to say? Beyond the sex, there wasn't much. I certainly had no real feelings for her." Woodbridge sipped his merlot and, for a moment, seemed elsewhere.

I was deeply in love with Judy.

She first approached me in January of this year. Justin was in Russia on business. I remember that first night. She asked me to meet her for a drink at the Holiday Inn. She was in a corner booth in the bar and she was wearing sunglasses. I thought that was weird, but she looked very sexy.

We talked for a while. We knew each other from parties and fundraisers we'd attended. We had a few drinks. We talked about Palos Verdes and about my work—she actually liked politicians. She thought they were the only people who really could make a difference. She compared me to John Kennedy. I know I'm not in that league but I was flattered.

We were having such a good time we decided to have dinner. She said Justin was going to be gone for a few days and asked if it was okay to call me.

I said that would be okay.

The next couple of nights were amazing. The way she spoke, the way she laughed, her ability to listen as well as talk...

But of course she was Justin's wife.

A few nights later, we'd been drinking and she touched me with her leg under the table. At first I thought it was an accident, but then after a while it was plain as day: she wanted to have sex with me.

I told her I could get a room and she said she would like that. But...

She said she couldn't do that to Justin. Then she took my hand in hers, looked me in the eye and begged me not to judge her. She said that Justin had become obsessed with watching her have sex with other men and that he was putting together a weekly "private swing club." She said she went along with it because she felt obligated to Justin. She explained that Justin had a list of men he wanted her to have sex with but that she would try to manipulate him into asking me to join the club. If I joined, she said, at least she would be able to "make love" once a week. She begged me to think about it.

The whole thing really freaked me out. Still, I have to admit I was intrigued. The truth was that I was hooked on Judy.

My marriage was in limbo. The sex wasn't good, but the rest wasn't too bad. We weren't thinking about divorce. I decided that such an arrangement might work out well for everyone.

The following week, Justin, Judy and I went out to dinner and he invited me to join their group. I actually think he believed it was his own idea.

Making love with Judy was incredible. Each week she always whispered in my ear—so the others couldn't hear—that she loved me.

"So, you weren't in love with her then."

"Absolutely not," said Woodbridge. "But the sex was good. That's really about all there was to it. I mean, who passes up free sex?"

Sawyer thought of a few clever things to say, but he kept them to himself and paid for the drinks.

Chapter Twenty-seven

How long was long enough to stay in a loveless marriage? For years Sawyer's friends, both male and female, had posed that question to him when their relationships were falling apart. In the past that question had little relevance to him because he never believed he would find himself in that situation.

Yet here he was, meeting his wife in a restaurant because she wanted to avoid the awkwardness of speaking in their home.

Sawyer sipped a Blackstone Merlot in a corner booth at Chez Melange. It was 6:55, five minutes before their meeting time. Sawyer knew that most married couples went through rough patches. They either got through them or got divorced. Some chose a kind of slow motion suicide: They figured out how to live together...without really living together.

Rebecca had been living with her sister in Manhattan Beach for the past few days. No one at her Palos Verdes real estate office knew that she and Sawyer were having problems—at least that's what she had told him. They both knew that once you started telling friends and family about your private business there was no going back.

When Sawyer saw Rebecca he stood and waved her over to the booth. She sat down and forced a smile.

"Hi," he said simply.

"Hi. You look well."

"Thank you. So do you. You hungry?"

"Not really. I just wanted to talk and I thought this would be a good place."

"In public so nothing terrible can happen?" said Sawyer, only half joking.

"I'm taking the next step in the separation."

Sawyer noted that she didn't say, "I'm *thinking* about taking the next step..." Rebecca had made up her mind and she was moving, if not forward, at least in a different direction. Away from him.

"What does that mean?"

"I have a client who needs her house looked after while she's in Europe. It's furnished and there's no long-term commitment. This way I get out of my sister's spare room and I know where I'm going to be for a month, at least."

"I see."

"I wanted to arrange a time with you when you're not going to be home so I can come by and get enough things for a month."

"Sounds like you're moving out."

"It's just the next step."

"But it's a step away from me."

"Can I get you something to drink?" said the waitress to Rebecca.

"No, thank you," she said in a way that was not impolite but it let the server know that she was dismissed.

"What exactly is going on here?" said Sawyer when the waitress was out of earshot.

"What do you mean?"

"You know exactly what I mean. You're my wife and I'm your husband. You decided to move in with your sister, in the middle of the Christmas holiday season, and now you won't even come home to have a conversation with me about moving your things out."

"You must know that things haven't been good between us for at least a year. Until now we haven't even talked about it."

Sawyer couldn't argue with that. The past year things just hadn't been right. They had major disagreements about minor things. It wasn't even *what* was said; it was more *how* it was said. The attitude. It seemed as though they had suddenly lost respect for each other.

Sawyer considered himself to be a sensitive guy. He held doors open, didn't interrupt his wife, worked around PMS without ever daring to utter an opinion, and even convinced himself to be grateful that his wife at least still "participated" in their sex life in order to accommodate him after menopause. Still, he couldn't help noticing that sex for her was clearly a chore, like vacuuming once every two weeks. There was no passion or intimacy. Yet until now he was willing to live with it all.

Until she no longer wanted to live with him.

"Look Rebecca, I'm not even saying that things have to be the way they were. I think most married couples realize things change after a while. I'm willing to carve out a future we both want, starting from where we're at now. But I get the distinct feeling that you're already gone."

Rebecca said nothing for a moment. "You might be right. I'm not saying you are, but I don't feel the same way I used to."

"What exactly does that mean?"

"I'm not sure."

"It sounds to me like you've already made up your mind."

"This is a big decision in our lives and I know you over-react to everything I say—"

"*Over-react!*" said Sawyer, reacting.

"See, there you go."

"Listen to yourself. You're accusing me of over-reacting to you telling me that our marriage is over. Don't you think I'm entitled to a little reaction?"

"Whatever you say."

"You seem so matter-of-fact. Apparently our marriage means a lot more to me than it does to you."

"Are you going to get angry and make a scene?"

"I'm going to be real. I'm your husband, you're my wife and you're leaving me. Excuse me if I get a tad excited." Sawyer paused and took a deep breath. "So, what do you want?"

"I want to come by in the next day or two and pick up enough things for a month's stay. I don't want you to be there. We don't need more confrontation."

"I guess you think we need more prolonged disengagement."

"Sawyer…"

"Sorry. Don't mean to be emotional when my life is melting down."

"You're being sarcastic."

"Sorry," said Sawyer. But he wasn't.

"Can I come by around five tomorrow?"

Sawyer thought about it and decided that was as good a time as any. "Sure."

Both were silent for a moment. Sawyer toyed with his wine glass and finally said, "Are we getting divorced?"

"I don't know. It's a possibility."

That was the first time the D-word had been said aloud. Both Sawyer and Rebecca were tough people and street-smart. Neither had wanted to be the first to use the word, because when it was officially out there it redrew the boundaries.

"Is there someone else?" he asked. It was a question that haunted him at night in his empty bed. The main reason he had refrained from asking it was because he was afraid she might tell him the truth. And that was a truth he wasn't sure he could bear.

"Why would you ask that?"

Sawyer knew that was not an answer and that fact alone sent a chill through his body.

"It's a logical question. You're moving out and leaning toward getting a divorce—"

"I didn't say that."

"Not those exact words."

"I'm not in love with another man," she said finally.

Again, Sawyer knew that was not an answer. She hadn't said, *Sawyer, how could you think I'm sleeping with someone else? You know I'm not interested in sex.* She simply had said that she didn't love anyone else. People had sex with people they didn't love all the time.

"Because if you are having sex with someone else..."

"Yes?"

Sawyer didn't know how to finish the sentence. He really didn't know how he felt. Should he feel angry? Should he feel relieved that things at least had been resolved? He didn't know how he felt so he said nothing.

"So, five o'clock tomorrow. I'll pick up a few belongings and be gone by six," said Rebecca, picking up her purse and preparing to leave.

"You don't want dinner?" was all Sawyer could think of to say.

"No, I've got to show a house."

"This late?"

"A condo in Manhattan Beach overlooking the ocean. Four million dollar property. The buyer's leaving town tomorrow and couldn't get away tonight till seven-thirty."

Sawyer didn't know whether to believe her or not. In the end, he thought, it didn't really matter one way or the other. She was going.

And she was probably already gone.

Chapter Twenty-eight

Suddenly Sawyer was free for dinner. He called Tony Arquette and asked him to meet him at Chez Melange—what the hell, thought Sawyer, I've already got a table. He didn't need to explain what he wanted to talk about and it sounded as though Arquette was looking for a reason to get out of the house.

"I appreciate you meeting with me, Tony."

"You're welcome," said Arquette, taking a sip of his Grey Goose martini. "If it was anyone but you, I wouldn't be here. But I trust you. You're Justin's friend and so am I. He helped me out a couple of times, so if there's anything I can do to help him, I'm happy to do it. Off the record, of course."

"Of course."

"We *are* all friends here, right?" asked Arquette.

"I'm not wearing a wire or anything, if that's what you mean."

"That's not what I mean," said the ex-cop. Arquette, more than most people, knew what to say and what not to say. He would never tell Sawyer anything that could possibly hurt him. Friend or no friend.

"What happened that night, Tony?"

"Nothing out of the ordinary."

"What's an ordinary night like, having sex with your friend's wife?"

Arquette thought about getting angry, but he didn't take the bait. "We all arrived around eight. We drank—as you know, Justin always has the best liquor. Then we played some poker."

"We?"

"Danny, Jake, Robert, Justin and me. Then about nine Judy came into the library. Oh man, did she look great. She wore high heels, a T-shirt…and nothing else. You've seen her body…" As soon as the ex-cop said it, he regretted it.

"Yeah, I saw her body."

"I know you saw her *dead* body. I was referring to…"

"I know what you meant. So what happened next?"

"One of us—I'm not sure exactly who went first—'got together' with Judy in the private bedroom just off the library. Have you ever been in there?"

"No."

"Huge California King bed, mirrors on the ceiling, lots of pillows, the whole nine yards."

"You said 'private.' Did you shut the door?"

"No. Sometimes Justin liked to watch."

"So everything went according to plan that night…"

"It was like any other 'poker night.' We passed some money back and forth—I was up about five hundred. We had sex with Judy, then we all left around midnight."

"I've got to get a better feel for this thing. You started having sex with Judy about nine and you all left at midnight. She had sex with you guys for three straight hours?"

"No, it wasn't like that."

"You gotta help me out here. I need a timeline."

"Judy would have sex with each of us for about twenty minutes to half an hour. I know that sounds like a long time for a bunch of old guys, but some of us popped Viagra with our first round of drinks. It not only gets you hard, it makes you last longer. Sometimes it's actually difficult to come."

"Really? I wouldn't know."

"Hey, don't knock it. It's a recreational drug now."

"I'll take your word for it. So, the timeline…"

"Like I said, I'm not sure who went first, but I went last— that was about 10:30. When we were done, Judy came out and played cards with us. Justin was in another room watching TV or something. All I know is that he excused himself because he was feeling tired."

"And you didn't see him again before you left?"

"No. But that wasn't unusual. Justin's in his seventies. It's amazing he keeps up as much as he does."

"I have to ask you something…"

"Okay."

"You say you 'went last'…"

"Yes?"

"Wasn't that a little…"

"I wore a condom."

"Then how did DNA from your sperm get in or on Judy's body?"

"When I had an orgasm, I usually removed my condom."

"I'm lost here. I don't mean to be insulting, but you've got to walk me through this."

"Okay. First and foremost, we trusted Judy and Justin. I know this sounds crazy, but we all believed that they were monogamous—except with us. In fact, all members of the Club had to present a recent blood test to make sure we were all free of any STDs. If you were the person who went first on a given night, you might not wear a condom. Even if you weren't, it was your choice, but none of us were concerned about disease.

"However, Judy—how do I put this delicately?—provided a number of ways for each of us to have an orgasm. We could come in one of two other…places. We could come on her back or between her… I know this sounds bad, but it wasn't. Really, it wasn't."

"So you and Judy came back into the library and played poker with the other guys until a little after midnight."

"That's right. We all left at the same time."

"Tell me about your relationship with Judy," said Sawyer.

"Nothing special, really. There was the sex. Of course you know that already. Beyond the sex, there wasn't much. Certainly no real feelings…" Arquette looked at his drink as though it were a crystal ball.

Judy loved me. And, if truth be told, I loved her too.

She first approached me in February of 2006 when Justin was in Australia on business. She asked me to meet her for a drink at the Marriott. We knew each other from social gatherings. After a few drinks we weren't feeling any pain. We talked about Palos Verdes and about my work—she liked cops, I can tell you that. She compared me to Rudy Giuliani—you know, the whole tough on crime thing. I know I'm no Giuliani, but I was flattered.

We were having such a good time we decided to have dinner. She said Justin was going to be gone for a few days and asked if it was okay to call me.

I said yes.

A few nights later we'd been drinking a bit and I felt her leg touch mine under the table. At first I thought it was an accident, but then after a while it was clear: she was giving me a sign that she wanted to have sex. Which was incredibly exciting.

I told her I could get a hotel room and she said she would like that. But...

She said she couldn't do that to Justin.

Then she said something I'll never forget. She took my hand in hers, looked me in the eye and begged me not to judge her. She said that Justin had become obsessed with watching her have sex with other men.

I couldn't believe it—it sounded so wild. Still, I was interested because I was so attracted to Judy.

She said she would try to manipulate Justin into asking me to join them once a week. She explained that she felt obligated to Justin because he had given her so much. Then she broke down and started crying. She said the weekly sex parties made her feel bad about herself. They were so demeaning. She said that if I would join the club at least she would be able to "make love" once a week. She begged me to think about it.

My marriage wasn't bad, but the sex part of it had been missing in action for a long time. Judy didn't have to work that hard to convince me. I was falling in love with her and if this was the only way we could be together, then so be it.

The following week, Justin, Judy and I went to dinner and he invited me to join their group. I actually think he believed it was his own idea.

The first time I made love with Judy at their house, it was incredible. And each week, when I finally had an orgasm, she

would always whisper in my ear—so the others couldn't hear—
that she loved me.

"So you had no romantic feelings at all toward Judy, is that right?" said Sawyer, trying to bring Arquette back into the moment.

"No. No romantic feelings at all. But the sex was good."

Suddenly Sawyer recalled a lyric from a song he couldn't quite place:

Love makes you stupid/Sex makes you blind
Searching for a lover/You ain't never gonna find

The tune was for there for a moment.

Then it was gone.

Chapter Twenty-nine

Sawyer arrived at Admiral Risty around 9:30. He stuck with the Blackstone Merlot as he watched and listened to Michael perform "Clocks," a Coldplay song that Sawyer liked.

Sawyer wasn't focused on anything besides how to deal with what was left of his marriage. Did he really want to salvage it? Was there anything left to salvage? Could he still make it work if Rebecca had given up? He knew that the answer to the last question trumped everything else.

And there were no signs of reconciliation or compromise in Rebecca's demeanor tonight.

And he wondered why. He knew that was a mind game that could drive him crazy. If she wouldn't tell him why she was leaving, then he had to fill in the blanks. Such self examination rarely yielded accurate information, merely echoes of a person's insecurities. *Was there another man? Had he done something to cause this? Had he let his appearance go? Or was it simply that she no longer loved him?*

There were no good answers to these questions.

And if he reconciled himself to the fact that she no longer wanted him, what then? It was a question he had never planned to answer.

"If all people wanted from sex was an orgasm, restaurants would go out of business."

"What?" said Sawyer incredulously. He looked at Michael Hall who was sipping a Sam Adams and grinning.

"I mean, what would be the point of getting take-out when you've got everything you need at home... Self-contained, if you know what I mean."

"Where do you come up with this stuff?"

"You keep forgetting, Sawyer, that I'm a 'Tantric Master.'"

"I wish I *could* forget it."

"Now, now... I mean, think about it. After you've had kids, sex is purely recreational. I know that people think of it as 'intimacy,' but it's really more like mutual masturbation, or a sport that requires very little time, equipment or preparation."

"It's always refreshing talking to you, Michael."

"You don't mean that."

"You're right, I don't. But it *is* always entertaining. And speaking of entertainment, you must hear a lot of gossip."

"I get more dish than a hairdresser. People speak to me openly about sex all the time—that's my business."

"Kind of a 'Have Gun, Will Travel' type of thing."

"Sorry?"

"Before your time, maybe." Then Sawyer had a disturbing thought. He rarely came down to see Michael play without Rebecca. He now realized that Michael hadn't asked about her. Maybe he was just being paranoid, but it seemed that Michael knew about everyone's sex life. Maybe he knew about Rebecca's.

"I noticed you didn't ask where Rebecca is," said Sawyer diving off the deep end.

"And...?"

"She and I usually come down to see you play."

"I figure she's busy."

There was something in Michael's answer that seemed "off" to Sawyer. "Rebecca and I are separated."

"You're kidding."

Sawyer tried to gauge the level of sincerity in Michael's response. He couldn't get a handle on it. "No. And there's nothing funny about it. You're the 'sex guru to the rich and famous.' You hear anything about my wife?"

"Of course not."

"Would you tell me if you did?"

Michael didn't answer immediately. "What do you want me to say? If I heard a rumor about Rebecca screwing around, that I'd call you right away? Play that out, Sawyer. What if I was wrong?"

"What if you were right?"

"Even if I was right, is it right for me to call you? If someone tells me you were all over some hot blonde at the Red Onion last night, you think I should call Rebecca and tell her? These aren't easy questions to answer when you find yourself in the middle."

"Are you in the middle?"

"Do I know something about Rebecca fooling around? No."

"Have you *heard* something?"

After a moment, Michael said, "People talk. People know I'm your friend and they tell me you've bedded at least four women in the past two years. Is that true?"

"No. I haven't had sex with anyone besides Rebecca."

"See? Would you have wanted me to call Rebecca and tell her every rumor I heard? Gossip is nasty stuff."

"So you've heard things about Rebecca." It was not a question.

Michael sipped his beer, then said, "This is not someplace you want to go, Sawyer. Trust me. Especially if things aren't good between you two. I'll make you a deal, okay?"

"I'm listening."

"You admit all the things I've heard about you with other women over the past two years are untrue, right?"

"If they involve me having sex—of *any* kind—with them, they're absolutely untrue."

"As your friend, I'll look into anything I hear about Rebecca. As a friend, I won't pass along anything unless I'm sure it's more credible than the things I heard about you."

Sawyer thought about that for a minute and looked into his friend's eyes. He realized that was as much as he was going to get from Michael tonight. Because they were friends.

"Okay. But you'll ask around? Discreetly."

"I'll look into it. My gut feeling? It's all gossip. In fact, I got the 'information' about Rebecca from the same person who said you were sleeping with Ginger Sanborn."

"Ginger Sanborn? Are you kidding me? We met a few times because she wanted to ask me to find out if her husband was cheating on her."

Sawyer's cell started vibrating. He looked down and saw Veronica Mays' name on his caller ID and flipped open his phone. "Sawyer."

"Hi. You busy?"

"I'm in a meeting," he said.

Michael nodded, stood and went to the bar for another beer.

"When can we meet?" she said.

"I'm open."

"Tonight?"

Sawyer looked at his watch, and then laughed slightly. He had no plans. "Sure."

"Okay. Where?"

He thought a moment. "My place."

"That okay with Rebecca?"

"She's, ah…visiting her sister."

"Great. Give me the address."

He gave her directions and hung up. Sawyer figured that probably the safest place in Palos Verdes to meet with a woman who was not his wife was at his own home.

Chapter Thirty

It was an odd feeling entertaining a woman other than Rebecca in his home. *Their* home. He wasn't comfortable with it. But he knew Rebecca wasn't going to walk in on them—she had made a point of not wanting to be in their home…with him…when she came by to "pick up a few belongings." *Belongings*… Sawyer thought about the word. He didn't know what belonged to whom anymore.

He wasn't even sure where *he* belonged anymore.

The doorbell rang, Sawyer answered it and ushered Veronica Mays into the living room and to a large couch. He offered her a drink and she asked for a martini. He made them each a Grey Goose martini, neat. He delivered hers and took his drink back to a black leather Lazy-Boy directly across from his guest.

"I hear you're a star these days," said Sawyer, raising his glass in Veronica's direction.

She raised her glass and sipped. "Thanks to you."

"Glad to be of service."

"Really…" she said with a skeptical smile.

"What does that mean?"

"Don't get me wrong. I appreciate the scoop, but I'm the one who did *you* a favor."

"Haven't you got that backward? I did *you* a favor. I needed the information out and I could have given it to anyone. I gave it to you."

"Okay, I'm in a good mood. You win. Where do we go from here?"

"Justin's my friend. I do what's best for him."

"Even if he killed his wife?"

"He didn't."

"Great. Let me make the announcement and we can all go home."

Sawyer didn't say anything. He knew he didn't have to. She had called him and she had something to say.

"We can help each other," she said finally.

"Nothing wrong with that."

"You made me look like a hero and I'm grateful. I don't mind getting used when I get something out of it. Just don't feed me something that isn't true just to make your client look good."

"He's not my client. He's my friend."

"Whatever. Just so we're clear on that."

"I've never done that, Veronica. You know me. But so far it sounds like a one-way street. Not much incentive for me to move you to the head of the line."

"I hear a lot of things before you do."

"Many of those things don't turn out to be true."

"But they get on the air anyway and the way I look at it, it's worth something to know when the sky's about to fall."

"I'm listening."

"That's it. I'll keep my ears open and I'll be like a spy in the enemy camp."

Sawyer knew the media was Justin's enemy and their main job seemed to be attacking and convicting him with nothing but innuendo. Every day the media broke speculative stories to which St. James needed to respond.

"Okay," said Sawyer. "Let's give it a try. Either party can back out without notice. So, I'm still waiting to hear what you've got for me."

"I thought you might say that," said Veronica with a sly grin. "Friend of mine said he's working on an angle that Judy had a lover. Not like the multiple kind, but a single lover she was in love with. My source said she was supposed to have a 'love nest' somewhere."

"Does this 'lover' have a name?"

"I'm sure he does, but I doubt that my source would have told me even if he knew. And the 'love nest'…sounded very speculative to me. Could be some by-the-hour motel for all I know. But I thought you might want to know that's the scent the hounds are following."

"Thanks. I don't have anything I can give you. Not tonight anyhow. I'm seeing Justin tomorrow and if I have something I'll call you. And I'll pass along your information."

"Good. So, you mind if I get personal?"

"I'll let you know."

"I heard that you and your wife are getting a divorce."

Sawyer was stunned. Even *he* didn't know that. But he knew the press usually got the story wrong a few times before they got it right. "Where in the hell did you hear that?"

"As you can imagine, the press has been camped out in Palos Verdes for a couple of days now. People talk. And you're one of the people we talk about. You're famous—locally anyhow. You visited Wright the night of the murder. And you've been seen coming and going from the house. People want to know who you are. More people in this town know you—or *think* they know you—than you realize. For example, we bought dinner for one of the women who works in the same real estate office your wife does. She says Rebecca moved out a few days ago and all her calls have been going to her sister's house in Manhattan Beach."

Sawyer tried his best not to look surprised, but he couldn't pull it off.

"It helps to know the 'little people.'"

"Especially little people with big mouths."

"If it's any consolation I told them I knew you from my days working downtown and that you're 'good people' and to lay off."

Before his marriage Sawyer and Veronica had dated. They slept together a few times and, from what he remembered, nobody demanded a refund. And she was right about keeping her mouth shut. He had told her lots of things off the record when he worked downtown and nothing he told her ever made its way onto the evening news.

Veronica downed the last of her martini, stood, walked over to Sawyer and gave him a peck on the cheek. "Thanks for the liquor and the deal. I like doing business with you. Always did," she said with a smile.

Sawyer showed her to the door, walked her to her car and watched her drive away. He locked the door, turned off the lights, undressed, retrieved Judy's diary and went to bed. He put on his reading glasses and continued reading. He had read about ten pages earlier in the Whale and Ale and nothing stuck out. There were notations scribbled around drawings, random thoughts about a particular type of painting or about what an instructor had said.

Then there were the occasional verses like the first one he read. Clearly, they were romantic, even sexual, in nature. But they weren't attached to anyone or any event he could determine.

He was nearly halfway through when the sheer weight of the day's events kicked in. He put the diary on the table beside his bed, looked briefly at the empty side of his bed, and then snapped off the light.

Sawyer didn't want a divorce, but he knew that if Rebecca wanted one there was nothing he could do about it. He also felt something he had never felt before. He was tired. He was tired of fighting, tired of trying to keep track of what to say or not to say. Tired of trying to figure out who was really right and who had simply been misunderstood.

He was older now. Not old, but older in the sense that he was pretty much set in his ways and wanted a companion even more than a lover. He wanted that too, but he had wanted a lover more when he was younger. Now he wanted someone he could laugh with, someone to hang out with, to travel with. He didn't want to be judged anymore, nor did he want to judge. He wanted to be accepted and to accept someone on her own terms.

And if he couldn't have that, he felt that he could learn to get along on his own. The price paid for what he received in return didn't seem worth it anymore. And he knew Rebecca felt the same way.

He began to swim in that state between consciousness and unconsciousness, the place between reality and dreams. And for an instant his mind filled with pictures of women: Rebecca, Judy…and Veronica.

Chapter Thirty-one

Sawyer was awakened about seven by the sound of his ringing phone. He answered it groggily.

"You awake?" said a voice.

"Not yet."

"That never gets any funnier, by the way," said Noah St. James. "I've rented a suite of offices just above the Bank of America in Malaga Cove. Furniture's being delivered at nine sharp and I've already got people working here on their laptops and cells phones. Can you meet me here in about an hour or so? I've got Crispy Crème."

"Magic words. I'll be there about 8:30."

"See you then," said the lawyer and hung up.

Sawyer breathed deeply and tried to shake the martini dust out of his head. He had been in charge of a number of high-profile homicide cases when he worked for the LAPD. He knew some journalist or attorney was always pouring gasoline on the fire, coming up with crackpot what-if scenarios that could only happen in a cartoon. The thinking was, if O.J. got off, anything was possible.

Cops lived in the real world and they usually got it right. Writers and reporters had too much time on their hands or airtime to fill and they filled it with speculation, out-of-context "evidence," and often just plain lies. Once this speculative stew got served to a public hungry for information, it became difficult for even a fair person to distinguish truth from fiction.

He brewed some fresh coffee and showered. He shaved, put on his robe and his "shower slippers." These were slippers that were used when stepping out of the shower only. He had another nice pair of "house slippers" for wearing around the house—he and Rebecca usually took off their shoes at the front door or when they came in from the garage. House slippers that started to show wear and tear were demoted to "shower slipper duty." And so the cycle of slipper-life went.

Sawyer poured himself a cup of his custom-blend boutique coffee, added some half-and-half and walked outside to the pond in the backyard.

The koi pond was the centerpiece of the house. It had been built by a "professor of Japanese gardens." On Christmas day, a few weeks after it was completed, the professor showed up with thirteen fish. Seven years later there were more than one hundred. And the original koi were big, one nearly three feet long.

Sawyer sat down on a rock near the edge of the pond and the fish swam toward him. The biggest one, which Sawyer had named Ace Junior—in honor of his beloved and departed Chinese Shar Pei, Ace—stuck his head up out of the water and waited to be petted. Sawyer reached down and stroked the fish's head. Several other fish got the same treatment. Koi were very friendly and social creatures.

Rebecca had fed them all kinds of things, from tiny shrimp or shrimp parts to pasta and even tiny watermelon pieces. The fish seemed to be willing to try anything.

Sawyer tossed Ace Junior a couple pieces of fish food. The fish sucked in the food, rose up out of the water toward Sawyer, until Sawyer petted him, then swam away.

Suddenly Sawyer was overcome with a feeling of sadness. His life was changing. And he couldn't shake the feeling that one way or another all this was going away.

Chapter Thirty-two

Malaga Cove was supposed to be the jeweled hub of Palos Verdes Estates when it was built back in the mid-1920s. No money was spared on its design or construction. It was supposed to not so much *resemble* as it was to actually *be* an Italian *piazza*. Noah St. James' temporary home was in the Syndicate Building, the cornerstone of Malaga Cove Plaza.

Sawyer pulled his jade green Lexus LS 430 up in front of the Neptune statue, a replacement of the original statue put there in 1926, which was a replica of the original statue in Italy. Its current incarnation was the direct result of the Beautification Committee that had resurrected the *piazza*, and the statue specifically, from a state of embarrassing disrepair.

Sawyer ascended the stairs to St. James' second-floor office as a couple of movers in overalls were coming down. He heard St. James barking orders and followed the sound.

"Sawyer!" said the lawyer when he spotted the ex-LAPD detective. "Come in." He waved Sawyer into an office and shut the door behind them.

"Looks like you've been here for years," said Sawyer, looking around the room that was filled with boxes and a large mahogany desk.

"This store's open 24/7 while Justin needs me."

"You wanted to see me?"

"Few things. First, I've heard from various sources that the press and even the cops think Judy had a lover. I mean the specific, one-on-one traditional kind. They located a studio she had in San Pedro and went through it thoroughly."

St. James paused and Sawyer said nothing. They looked at each other to see who would speak first.

Finally St. James said, "One of my guys just happened to be hanging around outside Judy's studio when the cops were leaving. He talked to the manager and a guy matching your description talked to the manager and went into Judy's studio yesterday."

"You don't say."

"You don't owe me an explanation. I understand you're Justin's friend. I'm counting on that, Sawyer—that you're his friend, that you know your way around a high-profile investigation like this, that you know what to tell me and what not to tell me."

"You seem to know a lot."

"If there's anything I should know I'm sure you'll let me know."

Sawyer decided not to tell St. James about the diary. At least not yet. When he finished reading it he would be able to make a more informed decision. He also knew that Riley Gaines wouldn't be pleased when he found out Sawyer had been at Judy's studio. Right now no one knew about the diary except him. And Judy and Justin. Judy was dead and Justin wouldn't be saying anything to Riley Gaines in the near future.

"This angle about Judy having a lover can cut both ways," said St. James. "Of course, we'll spin it that the lover is now the prime suspect. The cops will say it's an even better motive for Justin to have killed his wife."

"Anything else?"

"You know Justin's ex-wife Natasha?"

"I've met her a few times socially. She's kind of a loose cannon."

"So I've heard. She leaves a pretty long paper trail, but you can go where my people can't. People in Palos Verdes know you and like you. If Natasha decides to turn this into her 'fifteen minutes of fame' and hammer Justin, then that could be a problem."

"Is she planning to do that?"

"Not so far, but I need to be prepared. I need some leverage with her. Something that doesn't show up in a credit check or a LexisNexis search. You know what I mean?"

Sawyer knew what he meant. "Getting dirt on people isn't part of my job description."

"All I'm asking is to help me understand the ex-wife better so I can keep her off balance if she goes on the attack. I want to give her some incentive to 'play nice.'"

"You want dirt."

"I just want some live ammunition to fire back if she starts using a machine gun on us."

"Farm that out to one of your other guys. If I run across something, I'll let you know. But I'm not in the smear business."

"Fair enough. There's one other thing. Justin's son, Nathan."

"Yeah, I saw him at the house yesterday."

"Could you nose around a little about him, too?"

"You don't suspect him of—"

"No, of course not. I just want to get a feel for who this kid is. He's lived with his mother more than with his father since the divorce. If he's going to go negative on us when someone sticks a microphone in his face and start talking a lot of trash about his father and late-stepmother, I need to be prepared."

"I met him. He seems really to care about Justin. I don't think there's anything to worry about on that front."

"Okay. Finally, I want you to know how much I appreciate your help. I owe you. What I mean by that is specific. If you ever need me, you got me. First hundred grand is on me. Understood?"

"That's one debt I hope I never need to collect."

"Me too," said the lawyer with a wry smile.

Sawyer thanked St. James and left. He realized that if he ever got in a serious jam, he probably *would* call St. James. But a hundred thousand wouldn't get him more than a week of the great man's time. The funny thing, thought Sawyer, as he pulled his Lexus out of the plaza, was that even so it would probably be worth every penny.

Chapter Thirty-three

Sawyer dropped by Eric Gregg's office unannounced and found his ex-partner cleaning up some spilled coffee from his desk.

"Better my desk than my lap. Or my laptop."

"Am I disturbing you?"

"No, have a seat."

Sawyer sat down, declined a cup of coffee, as Gregg shut the door and resumed his seat behind his desk.

"Your ears burning?"

"Yeah, and I can imagine who's been talking about me, too."

"Riley Gaines is not a big fan of yours."

"What does he know?"

"It isn't so much what he knows, but what he suspects. He knows you were at Judy's studio in San Pedro yesterday. What he doesn't know is exactly what you were doing there and if you tampered with, or removed, evidence."

"Okay," said Sawyer, giving nothing away.

"Now, as your ex-partner I assured him that you would never, under any circumstances, do anything like that. And if you did...I'm sure you wouldn't tell me."

"You didn't tell him that last part I hope."

"No, but I think he guessed it. I imagine you can expect a phone call or a visit from Mr. Gaines in the next day or two. So, be prepared."

"Thanks. I'm sorry if you're getting in the middle of this."

"Don't worry about it. I have no idea what you're doing and I don't want to know. But if you need any help..." said Gregg with a sly grin.

"Thanks."

"So what can I do for you?"

"I'm trying to get a handle on the Wright clan—Justin, Judy, Natasha, and Nathan. Most people don't feel compelled to reveal any brushes with the law. Even to their friends. DUI's, domestic violence calls, you know... I just wondered if you knew anything that might come up in the course of an investigation."

"Because..."

"Purely 'defensive' purposes only. You know me."

"Since I've been here, we've been called out to Justin's house three times and to Natasha's place twice. Two of the three times we went to Justin's were for noise complaints. We just told him to keep it down and that was the end of it."

"The third time?"

"Domestic violence. About two weeks ago."

Sawyer shook his head. This was not good. "Who was beating on whom?"

"You know the drill. By the time we got there it was hard to tell. But Judy was the one who called 911. They weren't exactly lovey-dovey when we got there, although they seemed to have made some kind of agreement to keep things 'unofficial.'"

"Did she look roughed up?"

"She had the makings of a shiner. But with Wright's money and lawyers, and her unwillingness to cooperate—no matter what the law says—that case wasn't going anywhere. And dragging Wright in at 3 a.m. with an I'm-only-doing-my-job disclaimer didn't seem like a smart career move."

"Natasha?"

"She hosts parties almost every weekend. If it isn't some charity event, it's a dinner party. She's got enough space between her house and her neighbors that we rarely get any complaints."

"You said you had two."

"Right. One was a knock-down, drag-out fight. A Rolls-Royce backed into a vintage Jaguar and the two drivers started going at it. We gave them both city accommodations for the evening."

"The other call."

"Now that was interesting. Natasha was hosting a very wild party at her place."

"How wild?" said Sawyer.

"Let's just say it was 'adults only.' Seems one of her neighbors didn't like the inconvenience—or didn't like not getting invited—and decided to report Natasha for illegal parking violations. Usually we just let that kind of thing go. But this neighbor was determined to make us do our duty."

"When was this?"

"That was about three weeks ago. The front door was wide open and I walked in. The real action seemed to be around the pool. Some people wore swimming suits, but there were more than a few skinny-dippers. Everyone was boozed to the gills. One woman, who wore only a bikini bottom, looked at my uniform and thought I was the entertainment."

Sawyer smiled as he ran a version of the story in his head. "So what did Natasha have to say for herself?"

"She acted offended that I'd been called. She kept saying that 'sex wasn't illegal between consenting adults,' something like that."

"Technically, she's right."

"She's right technically *and* legally. And it wasn't like she was charging at the door and no money exchanged hands. I didn't see any drugs; just a helluva lot of skin and high-end booze."

"So what did you do?"

"There wasn't a whole lot I could do because, like she said, sex isn't illegal and the nudity was in her home. But having cops at the party was kind of a 'buzz kill' and the party broke up shortly after we arrived. I ended up citing her for a parking violation, and that was it."

"That's it?"

"Not exactly," said Gregg with a knowing smile. "I sat outside for about an hour to make sure people moved their cars. I was on the clock, so what the hell... Two former city councilmen and their wives were there—I recognized them from meetings I'd had with them. There were two other couples there whom you know. I'm not going to tell you who they are because it doesn't pertain to the matter at hand and it would be a breach of ethics. There was also a famous movie actor and his date, and a local TV news anchorman with his hands all over some woman, maybe his wife. And..."

Sawyer could feel something coming and he knew it wasn't good.

"Judy was there."

"With Justin?"

"No. She was on her own. She came out alone toward the end of the party and tried to hide her face. I knew who she was because she had answered the door when we went out for one of the noise complaints."

"Thanks, Eric."

"There's more. And you're not going to like it either."

"Okay."

"The night of Natasha's party there was one car left on the street an hour after everyone left, and I ran the plate."

"Let me guess. Nathan Wright."

"I didn't see him inside. All I know was that a car registered to him was on the street after everyone left."

"Why didn't he park in the driveway?"

"My guess is that by the time he got there, there wasn't anywhere else to park."

"Not exactly the Partridge Family," said Sawyer.

"More like the Addams Family. That kind of money does something to people."

"I wouldn't know."

"You got more money than most people, Sawyer."

"Not that kind of money." The way Sawyer figured it, you've either got *fuck you* money or *fuck me* money. If you don't have *fuck you* money you were going to get fucked sooner or later.

Sawyer thanked Gregg and left. He called Justin and set a meeting for noon. Which would give Sawyer enough time to finish Judy's diary. He drove to the library on Silver Spur, found a little corner away from everyone and sat down to read.

Chapter Thirty-four

There was no smoking gun in the diary. No phone numbers or names, but the poetry became more intense, more erotic and more explicit as he read deeper into the book. Clearly Judy was speaking about a lover and that lover appeared to be a man. A man who was not her husband.

When he finished he wondered why Judy had been so guarded with her diary entries. It was almost as though she thought it would be found one day and she didn't want to incriminate herself or anyone else. Sawyer was a veteran detective and after reading the diary he was no closer to determining who her lover was than before he found the book.

The only thing he saw that got his attention were the letters "BK" in the margins, not in the main body of text. They appeared a total of seventeen times over 64 pages. He had no idea whether they were a person's initials or an abbreviation of something else.

Sawyer needed to prepare himself for his meeting with Wright. He needed to take the gloves off. Sawyer didn't feel deceived that he didn't know all these things Eric Gregg had told him about Wright's past—such details were usually on a need-to-know basis. For lawyers. Or lovers.

Still, Sawyer knew that Wright had to be made to understand that he needed to know everything. Wright needed to know that it was up to Sawyer to determine what was important and what was not. He couldn't help him otherwise.

Sawyer needed to know why Wright gave his wife a black eye. He needed to know if Wright really believed Judy was having an affair.

These were things friends didn't like to talk about with friends.

Justin didn't look well. He looked nervous and tired. A TV was on in the library, but the sound was down. Sawyer declined a Bookers, but Wright poured himself a half-glass and sat down in a chair opposite Sawyer, so that he could watch the plasma TV screen out of the corner of his eye. Sawyer figured that for Wright it was like watching a car accident—it was awful, but he couldn't take his eyes off it.

"You okay?" said Sawyer.

"No. You have any good news?"

"Frankly, no. In fact, just the opposite."

"Terrific." Wright let his head fall back on the chair and exhaled slowly and deeply. "Let's have it."

"Were you aware that Judy was having an affair?" Sawyer held up his hand. "Before you answer, I want to tell you something. If you lie to me I can't help you. I don't want you to parse words or get cute. You're not on the witness stand and I'm not interrogating you. I'm on your side, but I can't, and I won't, help you unless you level with me."

Wright took a dose of bourbon and exhaled deeply again. "I suspected."

"Knowing you, Justin, if you suspected, you'd do something."

"I tried. I even hired a detective."

Sawyer saw the train wreck clearly up ahead. He could already picture the private detective talking with Larry King, giving out his website address for a free download of a photograph of Judy Wright walking hand-in-hand with her lover.

"But he didn't come up with anything. He followed her for a couple of weeks and got nothing."

"Really?"

"Really."

"What did you make of it?"

"Judy was about as street-smart as they came. She was very careful. We had a pre-nuptial agreement that stated if she cheated on me, I would cut her off with only one million dollars—which would never have supported her lifestyle."

"I hate to split hairs but wasn't she cheating on you every week with four different guys?"

"That wasn't 'cheating' *per se*."

Sawyer made a mental note to pick up a copy of the *Rich and Promiscuous People's Dictionary* on the way home.

"My guess is that if she were having an affair she would be very careful. She would always suspect there was a chance she was being followed. I checked her cell phone and there was no unusual activity to any specific number. Knowing her, if she was calling a lover, she used a cell phone I never knew about. That would have been easy. Her lover could have provided her with one. I checked her credit cards. Again, no unusual activity. I checked her closets and her car. Nothing unusual."

"You ever go down to her studio in San Pedro?"

Wright exhaled deeply again. "I sat outside all afternoon a couple of days. Nothing. But then, there was a back entrance to the place and I couldn't be both places at the same time."

"Did you ever think about having your private detective bug her studio?"

Wright laughed. It was not a happy laugh. "You and I think alike. You're damned right I did."

"And?"

"Nothing. For two weeks the only time she spoke in her studio was when she answered a cell phone call from me."

"Maybe she was just painting. After all, it was her art studio."

"It would have been just like her to find the bug and play it that way."

"So, your detective found the diary?"

"Yes. I assume you did, too."

"Yes." Sawyer didn't know whether or not to tell Wright that he had taken the diary. "What did you make of it?"

"I don't know. Nothing incriminating in there. There were some passages in the book that made it sound as though she was having an affair, but you could make the case that they were just artistic musings or else they could be explained in some other way. No names, no phone numbers, no meeting places."

"If she knew you were bugging her studio, why leave the diary at all?"

"I don't know."

Sawyer didn't either. "You ever get physically abusive with Judy? This is truth-telling time, Justin. Don't think about sugar-coating it."

"It's hard to explain."

"Try me."

"Judy was a unique character. The easiest thing for her to get was a compliment. She was beautiful. What got her attention was someone who treated her differently."

"Someone who would smack her around?"

"No. Someone who would stand up to her. She was used to twisting guys around her little finger. A body like hers made smart guys stupid. Including me."

"So you stood up to her."

"Yes. And she liked that. That and the money, of course. She looked at herself as a prized creature that needed to be disciplined now and then. Nothing that left a mark, but she wanted to *feel* that I was stronger than she was. She said it made her feel protected."

"Things ever get out of hand?"

"No."

"Don't stop now, Justin. You were doing fine. I'm thinking of a time when Judy called the cops."

"Yeah, there was that..." Wright took another pull of bourbon. "Things did get out of hand that night."

"Why?"

"We had a disagreement. Things were tense between us. I'd found out something that upset me."

"About her going to a wild party at your ex-wife's house?"

"Palos Verdes is a small town, isn't it?"

"It gets really small when big things happen. So what upset you so much about Judy going to Natasha's?"

"A couple of things. First, she went without me. My understanding was that the party was pretty wild. We don't have sex with other people behind each other's back. She had never broken that rule. She swears she didn't break it that night, but I guess I was just jealous. Second, it was at Natasha's house. Natasha hates me. Having Judy there just gave Natasha another weapon to use against me."

"Didn't Judy see that? If she's so street-smart I'd think that would be pretty obvious."

"Exactly. That was what the fight was about. I couldn't understand why she did it."

"What was her explanation?"

"She said Natasha had asked her to stop by, that she was having a few friends over. She said she thought Natasha was extending an olive branch."

"Why didn't Judy tell you before she went?"

"She said she thought I might be angry. She said she wanted to try to get along with Natasha, if only for Nathan's sake."

"How did you feel about Nathan being there?"

"I'm sure it was just a fluke he was there that night. These days he lives most of the time at his own place, but he lived most of the past decade in the guesthouse behind Natasha's main house. He still has a lot of his things there and he stays there often, particularly on weekends. He told me that when Natasha entertains he just 'gives her space.' He didn't have to go through the house to get to the guesthouse—there's a private entrance. Quite a place, really. Nothing but ocean for as far as the eye can see. "

"The bottom line is that you didn't believe Judy."

Wright thought about that for a moment. "I guess not."

"And that was why you hit her."

"Yes."

"Did you ever hit Judy again?"

"Like I say, she liked me to stand up to her. It was never anything serious. A slap here, a slap there. Nothing like the night she called the cops. I was really angry then."

"How did Judy react when you slapped her?"

"You really want to know?"

"Tell me."

"She got aroused by it. Became very loving. Like I said, she told me it made her feel protected. Like she was being taken care of."

"Okay," said Sawyer, but what he was really thinking was that it was hard for him to believe. If he had ever slapped Rebecca she would have tossed his stuff out on the front lawn and they would have been talking through attorneys by the end of the day. Then again, as a former cop he had seen hundreds of dysfunctional relationships built on things that made other relationships crumble.

"Any other humiliating questions?"

"Do you think Judy was having an affair?"

"As I said, I thought she might have been. She was the kind of person who could pull it off. She was very clever."

"And if you had to put money on a likely suspect, whom would you choose?"

"I don't know."

"I know you don't know. But of all the candidates, who would be the most likely?"

Wright thought a moment, and then said, "Danny Rosenberg. But I have no proof."

"Okay."

"You know," said Wright, suddenly sounding melancholy. "You find yourself in a situation like this and you start thinking that juries can be wrong. They often are. They might hate me because I'm rich and convict me of killing Judy even though I didn't. Where do I go from there? What can I do from a prison cell? I'm starting to appreciate the little things, including friends. I won't forget what you're doing for me, Sawyer. Lots of 'friends,' who were supposedly closer to me than you, aren't returning phone calls."

"You're welcome," said Sawyer. "By the way, can you get me a couple of samples of Judy's handwriting?"

"Sure. What do you want?"

"Letters, cancelled checks, anything she made notes on, scribbled on… That kind of thing."

"How about a day planner?"

"That would be perfect."

"No problem. I'll have something ready for you the next time we get together."

"Great."

Sawyer drove home with the radio off. It was about three o'clock when he tossed his keys down on the marble island in the kitchen. He needed some sleep.

And he had to be out of the house before five o'clock.

Chapter Thirty-five

Sawyer had just fallen into a deep sleep when the doorbell rang. People rarely dropped by unannounced. Most of the ones who did were selling something he had no intention of buying. He tried to go back to sleep, but the doorbell kept chiming.

Finally he got up, peered out a side window and saw Riley Gaines standing in the courtyard. He didn't look happy. And it didn't look as though he planned to go away.

Sawyer opened the door. "I was expecting you."

"I'll bet you were. Mind if I come in," said Gaines as he walked past Sawyer and into the living room. It wasn't a question. "Nice place. Guess writing about cops pays better than being one. I should really have taken that typing class in junior high."

"All right, all right. You want something to drink?"

"No thanks. I just came by to carve you a new one."

"What exactly are you talking about, Riley?"

"Don't even start. I'm assuming that you didn't forget everything about being a cop and that you weren't stupid enough to pilfer anything from the studio—or leave any prints behind if you did. But I've got to say…with all due respect…what in the *fuck* did you think you were doing?"

Sawyer decided to come clean. Sort of. "I told you Justin's a friend of mine. He's on the rack now and I know that, if he's innocent—as I truly believe he is—you wouldn't wish that kind of pain on anyone."

"You going somewhere with this?"

"You sure you don't want something to drink?"

"Hell, you're rich. You got any Scotch I can brag about to my friends?"

"I have just the thing. Be right back."

Sawyer returned with two half-glasses and a bottle of a 25-year-old Bowmore Single Malt Scotch. He poured them each a small glass and handed a glass to Gaines. "This is about $250 a bottle. It was a gift from a movie producer who optioned the rights to my last book."

Gaines sipped the alcohol as though he were partaking of some spiritual herb, nodded slowly and breathed the aroma out his nose. For a moment he was somewhere other than in a place where he was kicking Sawyer's ass. But the mood passed quickly. "You were telling me some story…"

They both sat down in the living room, Sawyer in a chair, Gaines on a couch opposite him.

"So, Justin told me about a studio in San Pedro he paid for so that Judy could paint. I had no reason to believe that the studio or anything in it had anything to do with her murder."

"Do you think this stuff up as you go along or did you write it down and rehearse it before I got here?"

"Anyhow, I went down there to see if there might be something that could prove potentially embarrassing to Justin."

"Like what, a murder weapon?"

"I had no idea. I just knew the press has been dancing on his grave. I figured there was no need for the media to get their hands on any other dirty laundry that had nothing to do with the case. And I knew it was just a matter of time till they found Judy's studio. The way I looked at it, it was 'no harm, no foul.'"

"Really… You gotta be fuckin' kiddin' me…"

"It wasn't a crime scene, Riley. I had no idea you would ever consider it part of the investigation," said Sawyer trying his best to keep a straight face.

"I think I'm gonna explode from all the smoke you're blowing up my ass. I know you didn't have a key to get in there and that you browbeat some poor schmuck into letting you in."

"That's not true."

"I can make it sound that way."

"And your point is?"

"Why didn't Wright have a key to his wife's studio?"

"I don't know."

"My guess would be that she didn't want him to have access to it."

Gaines rolled the amber liquid around in his glass and took another sip. When he exhaled again he said, "Cop to cop... You take anything?"

"No," said Sawyer. It was a calculated risk. If he burned the diary, no one would know about it. And even if someone knew about the book, no one could prove he took it. The bottom line as far as Sawyer was concerned was that there was nothing truly damaging in the book—nothing he had found anyhow. But the media could shape every paragraph into something salacious and detrimental to Wright. Sawyer worked hard at convincing himself he did the right thing.

"Look Sawyer, I like to think of you as one of us. But you do this shit, you put yourself in an adversarial position—you know what I'm saying?"

"Yes."

"We think the wife had a lover. I'm not giving you anything you don't already know."

"So that gets Justin off the hook?"

"You really ought to consider a career in comedy. The way I look at it, it sinks the hook in deeper. Oldest motive in the world. Guy finds out his wife is cheating on him, he kills her."

"So you really think my instincts are that bad?"

"You're too close to it. *You* know what happens when you get too close."

Neither man said anything for a moment.

"This is going to get worse before it gets better," said Gaines finally. "Fact is, it might never get better for Wright. I'm looking for a sign that you're ready to join the team again, Sawyer. I don't like you pissing all over my turf. I'll only take so much of it till I push back. And you won't like it."

"Okay. Message delivered. If I get anything I think you need to know, I'll give you a call. But honestly, Riley, even though I know this guy's no angel, I don't like him for Judy's murder."

"You might be right. I don't think so." He finished the last of the Scotch, stood and walked to the door. "I don't mind being wrong. You know that. I don't want to put an innocent man in jail. But I won't let a guilty man walk...no matter how much fucking money's he's got."

And with that Riley Gaines was gone. Sawyer closed the door and went back to bed, setting the alarm for 4:15. That would give him time to get up, pull himself together and get out of the house by 4:45.

Sleep came quicker this time. Probably because of the Scotch.

Chapter Thirty-six

The alarm went off at 4:15. He was dreaming about a painting of Judy Wright's nude body. The "J-Lo part" was all he could remember.

He threw some cold water on his face, put on a black high-neck sweater, black slacks, a gray sport jacket and a pair of black Mephisto shoes. He ran a brush through his hair, brushed his teeth and he was good to go.

It was 4:47 when he pulled the Lexus out of the driveway.

He parked a couple of blocks away. There was only one entrance to their development. He noted that Rebecca drove in, alone, at 5:16. He settled in for at least a thirty-minute wait.

At 6:05 she drove out of the development and headed north. Sawyer followed at a safe distance. He was good at this.

As he followed his wife Sawyer felt his heart beating fast. He wasn't sure why he was doing this, and he was sure that it was a bad idea. But he couldn't stop himself.

He listened to the songs on the radio and they all seemed to know his story and eloquently expressed the sadness in his heart. He followed his wife down the hill, the back way, through Lunada Bay, Malaga Cove, and into Redondo Beach. She turned east just before Torrance Boulevard, onto a quiet residential street about five blocks from the ocean. He drove past the driveway where she parked. He circled back around the block and parked halfway down the block, turned off his lights, took a pair of night binoculars from the glove compartment and focused them so he could see Rebecca unload her car.

She had help. A man who looked to be around forty and fit helped her carry boxes into a house. He wore a t-shirt with a logo on it that Sawyer didn't recognize, jeans, and tennis shoes.

The man laughed occasionally and Rebecca seemed to be comfortable with him.

Sawyer knew that he was on dangerous ground. The man could easily be someone from work or just someone she knew who volunteered to help her with the move. He wasn't necessarily her lover.

But he could be.

Sawyer's heart beat faster. He thought about Justin who was clearly excited about his wife's affairs, who enjoyed watching his wife have sex with other men. Even provided the venue. And the booze.

Yet even Justin drew the line at his wife doing things behind his back. Without him.

Sawyer knew that Rebecca was leaving him. She was not trying to work things out. She was not asking him to attend marriage counseling with her. She was not asking him to read a book that would help save their marriage. She was boxing up her stuff and, with the help of a good-looking younger man, setting up housekeeping elsewhere.

He wondered why she would do such a thing. He knew they had problems but he didn't understand why she was committed to such a dramatic step.

Was it about sex or love? Not enough sex? Not enough love? Sawyer believed that anyone who paid attention realized that sex and love were separate things. It was nice when they showed up at the same "meeting," but they were not the same thing. Sawyer loved Rebecca even when he was not sexually attracted to her. And there were many, many times when he was sexually attracted to her that love was not even in the same zip code.

He believed that separating sex and love was a sign of maturity. Because at some time, for some reason, sex would eventually end. And what would be left? If a person didn't know how to love without sex, the last part of his or her life was destined to be very lonely.

When the car was empty Rebecca hugged the man and gave him a kiss. Sawyer wasn't sure if the kiss was on the mouth or not because they were turned away from him. The man got in his car and drove away while Rebecca went inside the house and closed the door.

At least Rebecca wasn't moving in with the man, thought Sawyer. He wasn't sure of that, but it didn't look like it tonight. Should he camp out there all night? What for? If Rebecca was with a man, or even if there was a steady stream of men, what could he do? Sex between consenting adults wasn't illegal—even if one or both of them were married.

But it could still end up getting you killed.

Sawyer's cell phone rang. He answered it and said, "Hello."

"We just caught a break."

"What?"

"I take it you're not near a TV and you don't have your radio on."

"No. What happened?"

"Danny Rosenberg just committed suicide."

"You're kidding!"

"This is great news, Sawyer. We're at the office. Can you swing by?"

"I'm on my way."

"See you soon."

When Sawyer hung up he was thinking about how a man killing himself could be such good news to so many good people.

Chapter Thirty-seven

Sawyer had always felt that suicide was the easy way out. But over the years he had tempered that view. Often it wasn't easy to pull the trigger or leave loved ones behind. To those left behind it might seem cowardly, but every scenario had a context and suicide was not always the worst option.

Sawyer started working the puzzle of the hour, the one every TV and radio talk show host would be doing for at least the next twenty-four hours: What drove Danny Rosenberg to kill himself? The media was now reporting Rosenberg's name in connection with the Wrights' private sex club—Sawyer figured one of St. James' people was responsible for that. There were rumors that Judy had a lover. Was Rosenberg the unnamed lover? Had he wanted more from her than a once-a-week, take-a-number relationship? The press would tear the accountant's life apart like a pack of starving dogs working on a very small piece of fresh meat.

Sawyer pulled into a parking space, again near the Neptune statue, parked and locked his car, then made his way to St. James' offices.

When Sawyer entered the offices the mood was festive. People were laughing. They were relaxed and drinking freely from several bottles of chilled champagne. He noticed the label. St. James had no problem spending other people's money.

When St. James saw Sawyer he greeted him, handed him a glass of champagne, led him into his office and closed the door.

"Looks like a party."

"This is good news, don't you think?"

"Why?" asked Sawyer. Not because he didn't know what St. James was going to say. He just wanted to hear him say it.

"Well, it's obvious. Rosenberg—the man we all knew wanted more from his relationship with Judy—killed himself…apparently after he killed her."

"Sounds like you're reading from a press release."

"I'm just summarizing."

"Any suicide note?"

"I don't know."

"The only things you don't know about are things that haven't happened yet," said Sawyer. He knew that St. James' connections within the LAPD and the press were better than his. In some ways better than almost anyone except the police chief himself. And even that was debatable.

The lawyer cleared his throat and tossed down a dose of Cristal. "No note."

"Don't you think that's strange? A man tries to clear his conscience and yet takes no responsibility or even acknowledges what he did or why?"

"You know what they say about looking a gift horse in the mouth…"

"You know what they say about counting your chickens before they're hatched."

"Come on, Sawyer. You have to see that this can only be a good thing, if only from the point of view of reasonable doubt if we wind up going to trial."

"I see how you can spin this and I'm not discounting that this can work in Justin's favor. But…"

"But what?"

"How did Rosenberg die?"

"Slit his wrists and bled to death in a bathtub. More than that, I don't know."

"So, where do we go from here?"

"That's up to Riley Gaines."

"He came by my place this afternoon."

"That's what I hear."

Sawyer nodded and decided not to ask how he knew. "He knows I got to Judy's studio before his people did. He wasn't happy about it."

"That's why Justin trusts you—you're one step ahead of your old team."

"If I ever become convinced that Justin killed Judy or Danny, I'm not on this 'team' anymore."

"Does that mean you would tell Gaines what you know?"

"It means I wouldn't lie to him and if I'm on the witness stand I'd tell the truth."

"I know, Sawyer. I know all about you. I also know that Justin didn't kill Judy and so do you. Together I think we're an unbeatable team."

"And I know all about you, Noah. The only thing we really have in common is that we both believe Justin didn't do it and he needs our help. You get paid for it. I don't." Sawyer tossed back his drink and stood. "I gotta go."

When he was almost out of the room, St. James said, "Sawyer..."

"Yes?"

"About Rebecca... I'm sorry—"

Sawyer turned suddenly and fixed the lawyer with a hard stare. "You stay the fuck out of my private life. I don't need or want your help. And if you have anyone watching her, or me, call him off right now because if I spot him—and you know I can do that—you and I are going to have a big problem. Are we clear?"

"Right. Okay. No problem," said St. James. He didn't scare easily. This was as close as it got.

Chapter Thirty-eight

As he got into his car Sawyer's cell rang. He saw Veronica's name on the Caller ID, flipped open his phone and said, "Hi."

"I might have something for you."

"What time is it?"

"About ten."

"Palos Verdes isn't a late-night town. Most of the restaurants are closed by now. You know the way to my place. I'm ten minutes away."

"See ya."

Veronica was parked in front of Sawyer's house when he pulled up and parked next to one of the angels. He got out of his car and the two of them walked into the house together.

He fixed them each a Grey Goose martini and led her into the living room, where he lighted the gas fire. She kicked off her shoes, sat down on the couch and put her bare feet up on the coffee table. Sawyer took a seat in an overstuffed chair opposite her.

"So, what have you got?"

"Big news all around. Of course, you know about Danny Rosenberg."

"Of course. So, I suppose this gets Justin off the hook," said Sawyer just to test the waters.

"Give me a drag off whatever you're smoking," said Veronica with a smile. "I haven't been that high since college."

"Now, now... It's only logical."

"Really... People I'm talking to don't buy the suicide angle."

"By people, you mean professional media vultures who will try with their last breath to keep this story alive."

"That's harsh."

"That's the truth."

"Anyhow, most people aren't buying it. I heard there wasn't a note. You'd think he'd leave a note to cleanse his conscience and grease the skids to the next life."

Sawyer knew that was a problem, but he said, "This isn't a movie, Veronica. Not everyone who commits suicide leaves a note. You got a read on how this is playing downtown?"

"Word is Riley Gaines thinks this just makes his case against Wright stronger."

"I don't know how." Sawyer knew how, but he wanted to hear her say it.

"The way he sees it, Rosenberg was the boyfriend and Wright killed them both. Maybe he killed Judy and paid someone to kill Rosenberg. The two of them dying within days of each other is too much of a coincidence."

"Unless you believe Rosenberg committed suicide. In which case it makes even better sense. He killed Judy and couldn't live with himself. Besides, how can you stage a suicide?"

"Don't you watch TV? Professional killers—even amateur ones—stage 'suicides' all the time. They cut brake lines—"

"That only happens in movies, by the way."

"Whatever... They slit people's wrists and drop the blade nearby—with the victim's prints on the knife. They shoot someone at close range and put the victim's prints on the weapon. They get people drunk and pour sleeping pills down their mouths. And those are just the obvious ones. Gaines believes that the absence of a note is important."

"I don't," said Sawyer, even though he did. "Maybe Rosenberg was too depressed to write anything or he didn't know exactly what to say."

"Maybe... But in this case Gaines believes that the person who killed Judy felt so passionately about her that he used a knife to carve her up. Why does he suddenly run out of steam? Gaines thinks the person who killed Judy made a statement by killing Judy the way he did and that such a person would certainly leave a parting-shot note if he took his own life."

"That's weak."

"Maybe. He thinks that if Rosenberg was having an affair with Judy, then it explains both murders."

"If Justin did it. But why not kill Rosenberg first? Or kill them together?"

"I don't know. Neither does Gaines, from what I hear. If he had all the answers your buddy would be in jail."

"So, even if Justin was locked away in his house at the time of Rosenberg's...death, and could prove it, Gaines still likes him for both murders."

"Rich people hire people to clean their toilets. They sure as hell can hire someone to kill people they don't like."

"I'll be honest with you, Veronica," said Sawyer, even though he was not so inclined, "I don't see it that way. Rosenberg was putting the wood to Judy once a week for about eight months. Why go crazy now?"

"Maybe she was going to leave Wright and end the fun and games."

Sawyer felt a sensation in his stomach. It wasn't a pleasant feeling. Rebecca was leaving him and he was starting to feel his life drifting away. Into the unknown. Somewhere that seemed more dark than light. He knew people did things under such circumstances that they wouldn't do otherwise.

"I happen to know that Justin had a pre-nup and if Judy 'cheated' on him she walked away with only a million dollars," said Sawyer.

"That's real money to most people."

"Judy hadn't been 'most people' for a long time."

"There's more to life than money, Sawyer," said Veronica. She just let it hang there between them, not taking her eyes from his.

Finally Sawyer looked away and sipped his drink. "I'm not buying it. Justin doesn't rattle easily. His lawyers could handle the divorce and he's away clean. Over and done. Killing his wife and murdering her lover is way too messy."

"You mix sex, emotion and betrayal... Isn't that the famous drink: The Moron Cocktail? Even people like Wright get tipsy when they drink a pitcher of that. Maybe *especially* people like Wright."

"What do you mean?"

"How many people in the last thirty years do you think said no to him? How many times has he wanted something and not got it? How many people walked out on him and lived to tell the tale? Rich people *are* different, Sawyer. But then, you'd know more about that than me. I guess I should say 'more than I,' but I figure I'm among friends."

"Don't worry. Colloquial English is spoken here. I even know a little Ebonics."

"Yeah, that's right, you're a writer."

"I can even sign a book if you want to impress your friends."

"I'm kind of like you. I don't have any friends." Veronica paused, sipped her drink and looked at Sawyer. "I don't know whether you remember this or not, but I had the 'hots' for you way back when."

"I don't know whether you remember this or not, but the feeling was extremely mutual."

"Before you married Rebecca."

"Right…" The mention of his wife's name ricocheted him somewhere else. Her arms around another man, kissing him on…was it the cheek or the lips?

"Sawyer?"

"Yes?"

"Thought I lost you for a minute."

"No. Still here."

"Look, I don't want to seem like an opportunist. I know things aren't good between you and Rebecca right now. But I was there before Rebecca. You chose poorly, in my opinion," she said with a little laugh. "All I'm saying is that I always felt something between us and, for me, it's still there. If things don't work out with you and Rebecca, I want you to know I'm still interested. Have I humiliated myself enough yet?" she said with a nervous laugh.

"Not yet. But you're close."

They both laughed.

"Thanks," he said. "This is a tough time for me. I don't know what's going to happen. I know Rebecca doesn't seem to be interested in working things out. I don't know why. All the answers I come up with make me feel like throwing up. I don't know how I feel and I don't know where things are going to be in a month. All I know is that I feel like shit."

"Well…" said Veronica, lifting her glass in Sawyer's direction, "If you ever want to feel really, really good again, you know my number."

Sawyer looked at Veronica. She was not drop-dead gorgeous. But she was very attractive. She was slim. She worked out five times a week to make sure she was ready for her next shot at the big time. Her hair was the latest style and dyed the latest color, which just now, apparently, was auburn. She had the nose Michael Jackson paid for but never got—small and just ever so slightly upturned. She looked almost elf-like. Her teeth were shiny white and perfect, like every TV anchorperson. Her breasts were perfect and, he had it on good authority, were on display on a famous plastic surgeon's website. Her eyes were big, brown and bright, like a Japanese *manga* character. But her best feature was her butt. It could still draw a parade on a deserted street.

"Thanks," said Sawyer. "That's the nicest thing anyone's said to me in a long time." And that was the truth.

"I'm serious, Sawyer. We had a shot once. I never forgot that. Neither one of us is twenty-five anymore. We've each got another chapter left. If Rebecca's out of the picture, then I'm interested. And, if I may be so bold, I'll bet you are, too."

"I am but I can't get ahead of myself here. I'm still married."

"You know, maybe I'd better be going." Veronica finished her drink and stood.

Sawyer walked her to the door. Before he opened it, they turned toward each other. Veronica put her arms around Sawyer's neck and kissed him on the mouth. Slowly. Purposefully.

"I'm not playing, Sawyer," she said. "And this has nothing to do with the Wright story." She smiled, opened the door herself and walked out.

Sawyer watched her go. Watched her walk away. Veronica Mays was definitely prime time.

Sawyer fixed himself a nightcap, turned off the lights and went to bed. He was thinking about lies and love. Had Judy lied to Justin? Was Justin lying to Sawyer? Was Rebecca lying to Sawyer? Had Justin loved Judy? Had she loved him? Did Rebecca love Sawyer? Did he love her anymore?

And where did Veronica fit into this puzzle?

Sleep came easier tonight...

And for that Sawyer was grateful.

Chapter Thirty-nine

Sawyer awoke to a ringing phone. He no longer needed an alarm. The Caller ID registered Robert Sanchez' name. He hit the talk button and said, "Sawyer."

"Feel like a little tuna fishing?"

"Robert?"

"Boat's leaving in about… How long will it take you to get here?"

"What time is it?"

"About nine-thirty."

"Where are you?"

"On my boat."

"I can be there in about an hour."

"Add fifteen minutes to that and stop somewhere and pick up a bottle of Herradura Anejo. I'm out." Sanchez didn't wait for a reply.

Sawyer staggered out of bed, started the coffee machine, plugged in the hot water machine, took a shower, brought in the paper, grabbed a cup of coffee, read the sports pages, did the Jumble and the Sudoku.

Rebecca had bought him an herbal tea he used to drink every day. Thirty herbs, no caffeine and it was supposed to be good for detoxification. He put the bag in a large cup, hit the button on the hot water machine and filled the cup halfway. He also tossed in a bag of green tea—which seemed to be the cure for everything these days—and walked outside to the pond.

The fish were frisky this morning. He brought a cupful of fish food with him and he sprinkled it liberally onto the water's surface, paying special attention to make sure Ace Junior got his fill.

It was a clear morning and Sawyer could see Catalina Island in the distance. When he moved to Palos Verdes with Rebecca he was aware that he had achieved the "good life." Wealthy friends, parties, being able to afford the best restaurants, receiving invitations to this, invitations to that. Travel—where and with whom - became important. How much it cost really didn't matter. Life *was* good.

Yet here he sat, feeding the fish, looking out upon the kind of view that only money could buy, his life spinning out of control. He knew many couples with a lot less money and no view at all who looked at their future and saw something bright. Something better than an ocean view.

Sawyer could barely remember that feeling.

Sanchez was a lone wolf and a tough guy's tough guy. He was also mega rich. Owning a fleet of ships and various other businesses made him that way. He was listed in *Forbes' Top 200 Wealthiest Men*. His father, Gilbert, had been a gardener. Not a poor gardener. Eventually his father built one of the biggest landscaping companies in the South Bay that grew into a multi-million dollar a year business. Gilbert sent his son to Stanford—an opportunity the son could have earned on his own with a 4.0 grade average and three major schools, including Stanford, offering a full athletic scholarship to the all-city linebacker.

Sanchez's roommate at Stanford came from a prominent East Coast shipping family. Over several summers Sanchez had become close with his roommate's parents and the young Sanchez was welcomed into the family business when he graduated from Stanford.

Sanchez had learned well and when an opportunity to buy a small shipping business appeared, he arranged the financing—with his roommate's father's help—and built the company into a success in ten years.

But that was just the beginning. He leveraged his successful, but small, shipping company to buy a distressed mid-level shipping company and made that work too. That was harder, much harder than his first venture. The thing that made it all work for him was his toughness—a toughness learned from spending time on the streets…in places his father had never gone.

In 1983 Sanchez' business was on the ropes. If he could bring in a major contract, which was on the table, his business could survive. However, the unions weren't cooperating. There was a famous meeting that was rumored to have taken place at the eleventh hour. Sawyer had heard the story but didn't know how much of it was true.

Supposedly Sanchez set a meeting with two union bosses in the back room of a popular Boston blue-collar bar. The men came alone and Sanchez brought only one person. And it wasn't his lawyer—which surprised the union guys. The man who sat next to Sanchez that night was Irish, as were the union reps. The man said nothing during the entire meeting. He didn't have to.

While the man was virtually anonymous in the United States, he was well known in Ireland. The two union reps would later say that they thought the man was either dead or in jail.

Yet that night he was alive and mute and sat expressionless across from them.

The meeting was short. Sanchez had slid an envelope across the table to each man. It did not contain money. But there was an address in each envelope and a photograph. They were addresses and photographs of the men's parents who still lived in Ireland.

Sanchez explained to the men that he only wanted what was fair.

And he got it.

His business exploded exponentially after that and while unions didn't much like Sanchez, they respected him. And he did his best to be fair with them…as long as it was in his best interest.

Chapter Forty

Sawyer pulled up in front of his favorite liquor store, went inside and spoke with Rudy, the owner. He was always there. If there was a liquor equivalent to the head of the Medellin drug cartel, Rudy was that man. He had the usual beer, wine and liquor, but he had several high-end single malts and special orders, as well as a cigar room in the back where he sold Cuban cigars to trusted customers.

Sawyer purchased a bottle of Herradura Anejo, per Sanchez' instructions, and was on the road again in five minutes. He checked his watch, hit the CD button, turned right on Pacific Coast Highway and headed toward Redondo Beach. The car was filled with the sounds of the Hendrix' classic "Castles Made of Sand."

A year ago Sawyer's life was on track. He was married. He was okay financially and opportunity knocked. When your marriage was bad, it spilled over into your life and poisoned everything else.

Sawyer wasn't sure when things started to go bad between him and Rebecca. She obviously started keeping score before he did. But clearly, things were not right and she showed no signs of wanting to make them better. He wondered why that was.

And why she was kissing another man. On the cheek...or was it on the lips?

It was starting not to matter.

Sanchez welcomed Sawyer and took the tequila as two dark-skinned men untied a couple docking ropes. The engines rumbled to life and soon they were headed out into the Pacific. Sawyer wasn't sure why he had been summoned, but he knew there was a reason. And he also knew that the reason was not fear. Sanchez was not the kind of man who responded to fear. He believed that fear—his own and others'—was a weakness that could be exploited. And when he saw a weakness in himself he stared it down.

Even though Sanchez was not afraid, thought Sawyer, there *was* a reason he wanted to speak with him. Privately.

"I get away by myself more these days," said Sanchez, sipping the Herradura like it was a fine cognac. "You like time alone?"

"I like time alone. I just don't like *being* alone."

"My sons are grown and they call me only when they need money. My wife hates me—and, I suppose, if I were her, I'd hate me, too. The business can pretty much run itself now and I've got more money than I can spend if I live to be a hundred."

"And now you're once-a-week sex party's gone."

"I don't mean to sound like a victim. My wounds are self-inflicted. Most of them, anyhow. I was just taking stock. You lose close friends, it makes you think about what's important."

"You know, Robert, you seem to be the kind of person who can find out anything about anyone with a phone call or two. Who do *you* think killed Judy? You must have thought about it."

"Damned if I know. Believe me, if I knew, I'd turn the bastard over to the cops in a heartbeat. If—or *when*—my name gets out there, my reputation will be destroyed." He paused and sipped his tequila. "It's bad for business. It's bad for me personally."

"Robert, I love the boat ride, the tequila, and the ocean breeze in my hair, but I know there's a point here somewhere."

"It's a good thing you're not working for me."

"You'd fire me?"

"Worse than that. I'd promote you."

Sawyer smiled.

"I know the media seems to be trying to create this big affair between Rosenberg and Judy, but I don't believe it for a minute."

"Why?"

"Judy and I saw each other now and then."

"Besides the once-a-week party?"

"Yes. But we didn't have sex on those occasions. We only had sex once a week, in Justin's house. Not that I didn't want to. But those were the rules."

"So, she talked about Rosenberg?"

"His name came up every once in a while. She didn't think that highly of him."

"She thought highly enough of him to invite him to have sex with her once a week."

"She didn't think highly of him as a man. She certainly never considered him a serious lover or potential husband. She told me that he had approached her about something 'more serious,' but she told him that she wasn't interested."

"How did he take it?"

"You either took it or you stopped having sex with her every week."

"Sounds like a subject you know about."

"I know Judy liked money, and lots of it. I didn't know the specifics of her arrangement with Justin but I got the distinct impression that he had some kind of a financial collar on her. So I made her an offer. One hundred million in an offshore account and a million dollars spending money a year for as long as we stayed together."

"What makes a woman worth that much money?"

"Everything's relative. I could afford it. For some people, it would be like giving a mistress five hundred a month. But Judy was unique. She was smart, sexy and she had one quality in a woman I'd never experienced."

"What was that?"

"She was unobtainable. There's nothing more attractive than something you can't have."

"So she turned you down."

"Of course. And I knew that upping the ante wouldn't make any difference, even though I tried on a number of occasions. I knew I had more money than any of the others—except Justin—and, if money was what she wanted, then, by God, I'd have her."

"You'd own her."

"No one ever owns the wind. She was like that. But in the end, it was clear to me that she wanted something more than money. And someone other than me."

"And you don't think it was Rosenberg."

Sanchez coughed a dismissive laugh out his nose. "Rosenberg had no idea who he was. He was an accountant whose second and much younger wife had cut off his balls years ago. He was excited to be invited to the once-a-week party, but he was in over his head. You know Danny. He was not a particularly attractive man. And he was extremely self-conscious. I know he always popped a little blue pill an hour before our weekly parties. He told me. He was always afraid of failure, yet he courted rejection like a teenager pursuing his first love."

"So he pursued Judy."

"Almost from the first night he was invited to the club."

"If she wanted someone other than Justin and it wasn't Danny, who was it?"

"I have no idea. You could never get Judy to reveal anything she didn't want you to know. It was odd really... I mean, it would appear to an outsider that she laid herself bare, literally. Yet I don't think any of us, including Justin, really knew her at all."

"Who was the first member of the club?"

"I was. One night last December I met Justin and Judy for dinner and they asked me to join their...private club."

"Didn't you think that was odd?"

"Of course. But I'd seen Judy a couple of times before and I got the impression that she and Justin had some kind of 'open marriage thing' going. And my marriage hadn't been good for some time. Frankly, it sounded like fun."

"Who was second?"

"Woodbridge was invited in January, then Arquette in February, and Danny was invited in April."

"Why do you think she picked you four specifically?"

"I've thought about that. I think she liked having control over people who had control over others. Danny managed hundreds of millions of dollars for his clients. Jake used to run this city like he was king, not just a city councilman. Lots of people think he has even more power now that he's out of office. As a former police chief Tony used to impress the hell out of the people with his war stories."

"What about you?"

"She got me to beg her to leave her husband and she turned me down... I think she liked that."

"And that made you want her even more."

"Life isn't logical. Maybe that's what makes it so exciting."

"Judy was exciting..."

"Most exciting woman I've ever known. She not only knew the game, she made the rules. Other people could win, but she could never lose."

"Looks to me like she might have miscalculated."

"Everybody dies, Sawyer. Some just do it sooner than others."

"Being stabbed that many times wouldn't be my idea of a graceful exit."

"Maybe not graceful but it sure as hell was dramatic."

Sanchez sipped his premium tequila, stared out at the Pacific, and pondered questions for which there were no answers.

"Who do you think killed Danny?" said Sawyer finally.

"I don't know. My guess is he killed himself. Isn't that what the papers say?"

"Some people think Justin killed Danny—or had him killed—because he was jealous."

"Yeah, well, some people will say anything. But like I told you before, Justin had no reason to be jealous of Danny. Judy would have never left Justin for Danny."

"You willing to say that in court?"

"I'm never seeing the inside of a courtroom unless I'm on jury duty. That's why we're having this conversation privately."

"So the point of this is..."

"I don't think the people in the once-a-week party group had anything to do with Judy's murder *or* with what happened to Danny."

"Which lets you off the hook."

"I know it sounds self-serving, but I'm just telling you what I know."

"You're telling me what you want me to think."

"It's the same thing."

"Which puts it all back on Justin."

"I didn't say that."

"You didn't have to."

"What I'm saying is that I think Judy put Justin in the same category as the rest of us—he's rich and powerful, and she was never going to end up with him..."

"But she *was* with Justin. She married him."

"She was married to him, but she wasn't *with* him."

"What do you mean?"

"It was a feeling I got whenever I was around them—even more than the once-a-week parties. She loved being adored and he loved watching people adore her. But I never got the impression they were particularly close. I never saw her show him affection. She gave him sexual attention, but not affection.

"In the end, I think Justin was like the rest of the group—he wanted her but knew he could never truly own her body and soul, which is, I think, what he really wanted."

As Sawyer looked out at the Pacific he was thinking about how ownership of anything was an illusion time eventually destroyed.

And that nothing lasts forever.

Chapter Forty-one

Sawyer called Noah St. James on his way back to Palos Verdes and asked if he could stop by the office and use the lawyer's LexisNexis connection to do a little research. Many big-time lawyers paid for access to the enormous database. A person could find out a lot about someone using the Internet, but the LexisNexis database contained much more information and fantastic search tools. Noah said he would be out, but that Sawyer was welcome to come by and use the office computer and his password—which his office manager knew—to connect to the database. Sawyer said that he would call him later.

Sawyer poured a cup of fresh-brewed Starbucks, got the logon information from Nellie, St. James' office manager, who showed him to an unoccupied office where he closed the door and started trolling through Judy Wright's life.

People who had never been arrested or who'd never seen their names on the front page of the *LA Times* usually thought they flew under the radar and that no one really knew that much about them. Sawyer knew that most people would be shocked to see what came up about them on LexisNexis by simply punching in their social security number or other identifying information.

Judy's maiden name was Alexander and she was born in 1955 in Columbus, Ohio. Her mother's name was Alma and, apparently, Alma was a single parent. Judy graduated from Franklin County High School and attended Ohio Northern University. She left after two years and never attended college after that.

She was arrested for marijuana possession in Santa Monica, California, in 1975. The charges were later dropped after she completed a drug program.

She married Terry Clark in 1977 in Venice, California. They were divorced in 1978.

In the late seventies Judy had a series of dead end jobs, including "waitress," "cashier" and "telemarketer."

In the early eighties she opened an aerobics dance studio in Marina Del Rey, where she lived in a condominium. The other name on the lease was Jeanie Sachs. Sawyer jotted down the name and did a quick supplemental search. Nothing came up on Sachs.

Business at Judy's studio must have been good because the former waitress/telemarketer paid cash for a new Mercedes 450SL in 1982 and then purchased a new SL every three years…without taking out a loan.

In 1987 she bought a condo in Venice where she lived until she married Justin seven years later.

She had a few parking tickets since then but nothing stuck out.

Except for the fact that her life changed dramatically in the early eighties.

Back in his car, Sawyer called Justin Wright on his private cell number. "I was thinking of stopping by this evening about eight."

"That'd be fine," said Wright.

"Oh, by the way… What kind of alcohol did Judy drink?"

"Wine."

"No vodka or any hard stuff?"

"I saw her have an apple martini once. She liked it…until she threw up all over a friend's bathroom floor. She wasn't much of a drinker. And when she drank, it was always wine. Why?"

"No reason," Sawyer lied. He was thinking about the half-finished bottle of Ketel One vodka in Judy's San Pedro studio refrigerator.

"I found some canceled checks and even a couple of receipts from the guy Judy took art lessons from. His name is Vincent Insenga. Phone number is 310-555-9799."

Sawyer scribbled down the name and number and said, "Thanks." He hung up and push-buttoned Insenga's number and a man answered.

"Vincent Insenga?"

"Yes."

"My name's Sawyer Black. I'm a friend of Judy's—Judy Wright—and a good friend of her husband. He gave me your number and I'd like to stop by and ask you a few questions."

"I don't know... This whole murder thing is creeping me out."

"Yeah, well, I'm sure you'd like to help find the person who killed Judy any way you can. You might know something that could be important. Could I come by now? I won't need more than ten or fifteen minutes of your time."

"I dunno..."

"I could meet you at a neutral spot. You're in the San Pedro area, right?" Sawyer could tell where the man lived from the phone number's prefix.

"Yes."

"You know the Whale and Ale?"

"Of course."

"I could meet you there in about fifteen minutes. Mr. Wright would really appreciate any help you can give him during this terrible time."

"Okay. It'll take me about ten minutes to get ready. I'll see you at the Whale and Ale in a half hour."

"Thanks, Vincent," said Sawyer, purposely calling the man by his first name. Once a cop, always a cop.

Chapter Forty-two

Sawyer was early. He wanted to pick the table. He recognized Insenga when the man walked in. The ex-cop could tell it was the art instructor because he was trying his best not to look nervous…and doing a lousy job of it. Sawyer waved him over to the table and sat with his back to the window so the sun was in the artist's face.

"Thanks for coming, Vincent. Like I said, Justin really appreciates any help you can give."

"I read on the Internet that the cops think *he* might have done it."

"If that were true, he'd have been arrested by now," said Sawyer, even though he knew that wasn't true. "Justin's a friend of mine and we've known each other for a long time. I don't believe he's involved in his wife's death in any way."

"And who are you exactly?"

"As I said on the phone, my name's Sawyer Black and—"

"Oh yeah, I know who you are," said the man. "I read a story about you in *Palos Verdes Style*. You're an ex-homicide cop who writes books."

"Guilty as charged. Call me Sawyer. Everybody does. So, you were Judy's art instructor…"

"Yes."

"She any good?"

"It's hard to define good."

"You're in a position to know. You're a professional art teacher and what we call in my business an 'expert witness.' You're entitled to have an opinion."

"Well, she had promise."

"Look, all I'm trying to get at is, was she serious about her art or was she a dilettante?"

"I don't want to speak ill of the dead…"

"I think you just did."

"Really?"

"Just kidding. How did she end up hiring you?"

"We met about a year ago at a fundraiser at one of those big houses overlooking the ocean."

That narrowed it down to about half the houses in Palos Verdes, but Sawyer said, "Who introduced you?"

"I was there trying to sell my paintings. I was one of about five artists showing that day. She introduced herself and said that someone told her I taught at Angel's Gate. She said she was interested in taking some abstract classes and I told her that was my specialty. Between you and me, whatever she would have said she was looking for I would have told her it was my specialty. I don't live in one of those mansions. I need to work for a living. And people like that don't argue about the price of art lessons."

"Did she start right away?"

"About two weeks later. She asked me if I knew where she could rent a studio in San Pedro, and I turned her on to a place."

"She asked if you knew of a studio or a studio specifically in San Pedro?"

"Yes. She wanted San Pedro specifically. She said she had friends with studios down there and that it would be convenient if they all wanted to get together."

"How did she do?"

"She wasn't that bad. Apparently she painted in high school or in college—or at some time. She had some basic skills."

"Some people have natural talent."

"Let's just say she was one of those people who had to work at it."

"Is it common for a student at her level to rent his or her own studio?"

"At her talent level, no. At her income level, yes."

The waiter came to the table and Sawyer told Insenga, "It's on Wright. Order whatever you want."

"Okay. I'll have a Ketel One on the rocks with a twist."

"Sam Adams," said Sawyer and the waiter disappeared.

"I'm sure you've thought about Judy's murder since you heard the news... You have any idea who might have killed her?"

The painter didn't answer immediately.

"Relax, it's a logical question. I've considered it myself. Can I be honest with you?" said Sawyer, lowering his voice and doing his best to sound conspiratorial.

"Sure."

"Justin had never been to Judy's studio. I think she wanted it that way."

"You think she was having an affair?"

"I didn't say that."

"But that's what you're implying."

The waiter delivered the beer and vodka and took Sawyer's credit card.

"Why do I get the impression you're trying to get me to say something I don't want to say?"

"Is there something you don't want to say?"

"I didn't mean it that way."

"I know. Relax. I look at you as a window into a world, or a part of Judy's world, that Justin and I know nothing about. From what I hear, the South Bay art scene is a pretty close-knit family."

"Not really. I mean, the major players all know the other major players. But there are a lot of peripheral players, like Judy... People might know who she is and she might be able to sell some paintings to her friends, but the people who count didn't take her all that seriously."

"So, if she's such a marginal talent, and she had the money and connections to do whatever she wanted to do, why do you think she decided to take up painting and rent a studio in San Pedro?"

"I told you—she had friends who had studios down here."

"Did she ever tell you her friends' names?"

"No."

"You know what I think?"

"What?"

"I think she took that studio so she could use it to be alone with her lover."

Insenga shook his head and started looking uncomfortable. "I wouldn't know anything about that."

"I'll bet you do."

"Why would you say that?"

"I saw that bottle of Ketel One she had at her studio…just for you. She doesn't drink hard liquor. And I spoke to a guy who had a studio on the same floor and he described a guy who looked a lot like you coming out of her studio," said Sawyer, taking a shot. Actually, the guy Tony described was bald and Insenga had a full head of hair. The way Sawyer looked at it, you rattle a tree sometimes something falls out.

The ex-cop could almost see the blood rushing from Insenga's face. "Okay, okay… Judy knew I liked that kind of vodka. She said it would be more convenient for her if I came to her studio to give her lessons instead of coming to my studio at Angel's Gate. She provided the vodka as an extra enticement. But that's it."

"That's it?" said Sawyer with a dismissive laugh. He had the guy on the ropes…without a lawyer.

"Am I in trouble here?"

"Depends on what you did?"

"I didn't kill her. No fuckin' way! I'm ready to take a lie detector test right now. Any time, any place! You can't pin her murder on me."

"Calm down. I just want you to tell me the truth. That's all."

"Bullshit! You're trying to keep your friend out of jail."

"That too."

Insenga took a long drag off the Ketel One.

"Did you have sex with Judy?" asked Sawyer.

"No. Absolutely not!"

"She was pretty good looking."

"I'm gay, okay?"

It was okay with Sawyer, but it wasn't the answer he wanted to hear.

"Look, I gotta go. I've got a lesson in fifteen minutes. I probably said too much already."

"You did fine."

"I'm sure you and I have different ways to judge that. Thanks for the vodka. I think I'm gonna switch to Grey Goose." He stood and was gone.

Sawyer's cell vibrated. It was St. James.

"You free for dinner?"

"I was planning to drop by Justin's place around eight."

"I've asked him to join us for dinner. Pacific Edge at seven?"

"Okay."

"Why don't you and I meet a few minutes before Justin gets there? I'd like to talk to you about a few things."

"I can be there by six-thirty."

"See you then."

Sawyer closed his phone, paid the bill and left.

Chapter Forty-three

Pacific Edge was a beautiful restaurant overlooking the ocean from the Redondo Pier. Sawyer had eaten dinner there a couple of times with Rebecca. Each dinner was excellent and the service was even better than the food. This latter detail was the direct result of having been served by the same waitress, Tatiana, on both occasions. She was as charming as she was efficient and seemed to anticipate their every wish.

Sawyer arrived ten minutes early. Tatiana spotted him and seated him at a corner table that provided a grand view of the moonlight that began its journey about a quarter of a million miles away and skid to a flickering halt on the waves of the beach below the restaurant. He ordered a split of champagne.

As he sipped his champagne he toyed with the idea of swinging by Rebecca's new place and parking outside. Just to see what was going on. He knew that such behavior bordered on stalking and, depending on what he observed, things could get really bad really fast. Yet he sensed that he was going to do it even though he would advise anyone else against it.

"Thanks for coming, Sawyer," said Noah St. James as he sat down opposite Sawyer at the table for four. Not waiting for an acknowledgement, the lawyer continued. "Justin will be here in a few minutes. We need to talk."

"I'm listening."

"My contacts downtown tell me that Rosenberg's timely demise didn't help us as much as I hoped it would."

"That was always wishful thinking, Noah."

"Even though Justin has an iron-clad alibi for the time of Rosenberg's death, the DA figures Justin has more than enough money to hire someone to kill Rosenberg."

"I thought Rosenberg's death was being billed as a suicide."

"As you predicted, the fact that no note was found makes it suspicious. There's no doubt his wrists were slit and that his fingerprints were on the razor blade, but Riley Gaines isn't ready to put a suicide stamp on it just yet."

Sawyer knew this was the way it was going to play out. "The DA's spinning it that Justin's motive for killing Rosenberg was the same as for killing Judy: Jealousy. I know that's absolute horseshit. Proving it, however, is another matter. Robert Sanchez says that Judy didn't think much of Rosenberg and turned him down flat when he made an offer for a more 'permanent' relationship."

"Will Sanchez say that on the witness stand?"

"Not in this lifetime. My guess is that he won't 'recall' ever telling me anything like that. But he gave me a heads-up. Which means that if Justin actually killed Rosenberg then he was misinformed and killed a rival who was no rival at all. Or, if Justin *was* informed, then he didn't kill Rosenberg. At least not out of jealousy."

St. James shook his head and sighed. He got Tatiana's attention and ordered a Bloody Mary. When the drink was delivered and the waitress was out of earshot, the lawyer said, "You did a LexisNexis search in the office today?"

"Yeah. I was trying to find out who Judy was before she became Mrs. Wright."

"And?"

"No smoking gun. But I want to ask Justin a few questions."

"Anything else?"

"Not much. I spoke with a guy who gave Judy art lessons."

"And?"

"He's gay."

Noah shook his head again. "Judy's a hard person to get a handle on. I mean, I didn't know her all that well, but I've known Justin for a few years. I'd dined with the two of them on a number of occasions and we served together on a couple of fundraising committees. To me she seemed...perfect."

"No one's perfect, Noah. You probably know that better than most people."

"Okay. Perfect's the wrong word. She seemed so buttoned up. Careful. I still have no idea who the hell she was. I feel like I'm missing something."

"Yeah, me too," said Sawyer. "She had money. She had offers of more money from other men if she left her husband. Yet she turned them down and continued her weekly parties. Why didn't she take the money and run?"

"Maybe she was in love."

"Maybe. But not with Justin—at least that's the way Sanchez sees it."

"Then what did she really want?"

"I'm thinking more 'who' than 'what.'"

"How did she find time for a romantic relationship?" said St. James. "Seems like her dance card was kind of full."

"Yeah, I know. But I keep thinking... She's got offers of more money than she can ever spend. She's having more sex in one night than most people her age have in a decade. So what does Judy want that she doesn't already have? Who or what does she turn everyone down for? What was her passion?"

"Looks to me that the woman was 24/7 passion," said St. James.

"You're talking about sex, not passion. I still haven't met anyone who I believe really knew her."

Just then Sawyer looked up to see Justin Wright walk into the restaurant. He said something to Tatiana and she led him to the table. A man in a dark suit who had accompanied Wright into the restaurant took a seat at a table so that he could see the door.

Everyone exchanged greetings and Wright ordered a bottle of Cristal for the table—because he saw that Sawyer was drinking champagne. Wright also ordered crab cakes and shrimp cocktail as appetizers...without asking Sawyer or St. James if they wanted them. When you were used to running things, there were certain chores you didn't delegate. And it was clear that Wright looked at Sawyer and St. James as working for him.

"Did you bring a sample of Judy's handwriting?" asked Sawyer after Tatiana had opened the Cristal, poured their drinks, and left.

Sawyer watched St. James' expression. He said nothing. He may not have been clear on exactly why Sawyer had requested the sample, but he knew that if it helped his client, Sawyer would let him know. If it didn't... He didn't want to know about it.

"Yes. I tore out a few pages from her day planner/calendar," said Wright and he handed Sawyer an envelope, which Sawyer stuffed in his jacket pocket.

St. James told his client essentially what he told Sawyer but with enough spin so that Wright stayed "positive."

"I'd like to ask you a few questions, Justin," said Sawyer.

St. James coughed and tossed his napkin on the table. "I'm gonna hit the head."

When he was gone, Sawyer said, "On a scale of one-to-ten, how well do you think you knew your wife?"

"I don't know... What husband really knows his wife?"

The rhetorical question resonated somewhere inside Sawyer and he suddenly felt uncomfortable. He thought he knew Rebecca. Obviously he didn't know her as well as he once thought he did. In the end no one really knew anyone but himself. And a lot of that, he realized, turned out to be wrong.

"Most husbands don't know their wives as well as they think they do," said Sawyer. "That's not a crime. On the other hand, there are clues that people are unhappy even though we might be oblivious to those clues at the time."

Both men were silent for a moment as they danced with shadows that came in and out of view.

After a while, Wright said, "I wasn't sure, but I felt that Judy wasn't happy."

"You indulged her every wish and fantasy. She had money, prestige, position, and all the sex she could possibly want. What was missing?"

"I really don't know, Sawyer." Wright tossed back his Cristal and poured himself another glass. "I could never figure Judy out. She kept changing."

"When did you meet her?"

"I met her in 1982 at a night club in Marina Del Rey. It was a big pick-up joint at the time and Judy and I hit it off right away. We saw each other pretty regularly after that and I decided to help her with her business."

"An aerobics studio."

"Yes. How did you know that?"

"I'm a smart guy. And you also paid for a condo."

"Not exactly. I made sure my name wasn't on the lease, but I gave her the cash every month. She shared a place with a roommate for a few years, then I bought her a condo. Again my name wasn't on any paperwork."

"So you were her 'benefactor' for years before you married her."

"Nothing illegal about that."

"No, but you were married to someone else at the time."

"I didn't invent adultery."

"No, but you and Judy seemed to have perfected it."

"What difference does that make if I set up Judy for a few years until I got a divorce and married her?"

"None. Except that you might soon be on trial for murder, and a lot of the men and women on that jury might not like the idea of a rich guy leaving his wife for a younger woman."

"That was years ago. The only thing that really matters is that I didn't kill Judy," said Wright.

"That's all fine and good. And if the court would allow you to get up on the stand, make that statement and then sit right back down in your chair, that'd be just great. But it doesn't work that way. When you're done exonerating yourself, the prosecution gets its shot at turning over all the rocks in your life and showing the jury what an asshole you are."

"You asked me about rating how well I knew Judy on a scale of one-to-ten. I'd say it was a nine."

"Don't get caught in that trap, Justin. I asked you that question for a reason. The prosecutor will bring up a dozen things you didn't know about Judy that every husband on the jury thinks you *should* have known. In the end everyone will believe you didn't know your wife at all. And if they believe that, and the prosecution can show that you found out 'something that changed everything'…some event that sent you over the edge… Then you're screwed and you're probably headed for life in prison unless some hotshot prosecutor can figure out a way to stick a needle in your arm."

Wright rolled the champagne glass between his fingers. "I trust you, Sawyer. That's why you're on the team. What do you recommend?"

"I recommend that you tell me everything you know and give me everything I ask for. I'm starting from the premise that you're innocent, but you can't be afraid to answer questions from me that any prosecutor will ask you on the stand."

"Okay."

"Was your wife affectionate toward you?"

"I was affectionate toward her."

"But she was not affectionate toward *you*?"

"Not overly. No."

"Why do you think that was?"

"I don't know. It bothered me," said Wright with frustration and some pain. "I gave her everything she ever wanted."

"Maybe what she wanted was something you didn't have to give."

Wright sighed deeply. "Maybe. I tried not to think about that."

"But you sensed it."

"Yes."

"Did you think she was going to leave you? The truth."

"I don't know. I focused on catering to her desires. I figured that might work. And...I figured that what I didn't know wouldn't hurt me. As long as she didn't want a divorce."

"Did she ever talk about getting a divorce?"

"Every once in a while in the heat of battle. But never seriously. At least I don't think she was serious."

"When she spoke of divorce, what did she say?"

"I'm not sure I understand what you mean?"

"Did she say she wanted a divorce because you were a lousy lover, a philanderer, wife-beater, a wimp, too old? You get the idea. What was her reason for wanting a divorce?"

"Like I said, what she said was always in the heat of battle. It wasn't logical."

"What wasn't logical?"

"She just said something like she was sick and tired of not being able to 'connect' or 'communicate'—I'm not sure which word she used. The feeling I got from her was that life wasn't as exciting as it used to be. I just figured she was going through a stage. Maybe menopause or something."

"She seemed to be pretty 'active' for someone going through menopause."

"I know of several women older than Judy who found a lover and suddenly the 'juices starting flowing' again. I suppose that was one of the reasons I went along with the weekly sex parties. I felt she was getting bored with me and I am twenty years older than she is…was. I didn't want to lose her to some younger guy she found more exciting. This way, I thought she could have her cake and eat it, too. And I wouldn't lose her."

"Okay, but if I'm a prosecutor I'm going to hammer you about the parties being more for you than for Judy."

"You have to understand what she was going through at this time in her life. Men have knelt at her feet since she was a teenager. Now she was in her fifties and, even with her cosmetic touch-ups, she seemed to need 'reassurances.'"

"Okay, so your wife needed to bolster her self-confidence by banging a bunch of your friends every week while you watched. What did *you* get out of it?"

"I don't know."

"That's not gonna cut it. You need to know the answer to that question."

"I have to admit that I enjoyed it," said Wright after taking another sip of Cristal. "I'm in my early seventies and I've got this woman everyone wants to have sex with and she's so beautiful… It makes me feel good that I have something so valuable…that they can't have."

"But four other guys *did* have her. Once a week."

"They had her sex. I had *her*. She would never leave me for any of those guys. I know it. For us, sex was recreation. As bizarre as it sounds to an 'outsider,' the parties were something we did together."

"Well, all the people on a jury are going to be 'outsiders,' so you might want to get that explanation into a couple of well-phrased sentences that don't offend most people's values."

"You asked me why Judy wanted a divorce. I think she had simply fallen out of love with me. I don't think she hated me. I think she still liked me. I know she respected me. But I don't think she loved me anymore. Some people just get tired of each other.

"Things changed about a year ago when I retired. Before we were married it was always fun seeing each other on the sly. Risking so much for each other. Looking forward to getting married someday. Even the first few years of marriage were new and exciting. She loved being my wife and not my lover. She liked playing the part of a society wife. She loved handing out checks to foundations, chairing fundraisers, that kind thing.

"About a year ago, I started staying home almost every day. Suddenly she wanted to cultivate 'other interests,' but I got the feeling that was just an excuse to get out of the house. To get away from me."

"You ever ask her why she wanted to spend so much time...pursuing 'other interests'?"

"No," said Wright with a wry smile.

"Why not?"

"Because she might've told me the truth."

Out of the corner of his eye Sawyer saw St. James returning from a leisurely trip to the restroom. He sat down next to his client, opened the menu and said to Sawyer, "What's good here?"

"Just about everything. I can recommend the rack of lamb and the filet mignon."

Nothing else very important was said during dinner or afterward, but everything had been accomplished.

Chapter Forty-four

Sawyer didn't fight for the check. St. James picked it up but everyone knew that Wright would eventually get the bill.

As Sawyer pulled out of the parking lot and turned right on Catalina, he realized that he was only five or six blocks from where Rebecca was staying. In fact, he had thought of little else for the past hour while he was eating. And drinking.

He turned left onto Rebecca's street, found a parking place across the street from the house where she was staying and parked the car. He turned the engine and lights off. As he sat alone in the darkness he was aware that nothing good could come of this. As a cop he'd seen hundreds of situations like this—husband follows his wife or sits in a car outside a building where the wife or girlfriend is supposed to be… None of those scenarios ever ended well. Even as he sat there, feeling his heart beat faster, he knew this night would be no different.

Sawyer's imagination was on fire and out of control. The fact that he'd had almost an entire bottle of Cristal only served to fan the flames. Rebecca's car was in the driveway, which meant that she was either inside or someone had picked her up and she was out. There was a light on in the living room and the porch light was on. To Sawyer, this meant that either she was not home and wanted the lights on when she returned, or she was home and expecting someone. At nearly ten o'clock. If the porch light was on at ten, Sawyer reasoned, there would be some further activity.

Most of the scenarios playing in Sawyer's head involved Rebecca ultimately in bed with someone. He was not Justin Wright. It didn't turn him on to think of his wife with another man. It made him feel sick. It made him feel a lot of things he didn't want to feel. Didn't want to believe he was capable of feeling.

He took a deep breath and tried to concentrate on an interview on the radio with a college football player he had never heard of. The words seem to blur together.

A white Lexus SC 430 pulled into the driveway behind Rebecca's car. Rebecca got out of the passenger side and the man he had seen earlier got out of the driver's side. They were laughing and Rebecca carried a small sack in one hand. She handed him the "doggie bag," fished around in her purse for her keys, and unlocked the door. The two of them went inside.

Someone turned off the living room and porch lights.

And Sawyer's heart began to beat faster.

He had been on stakeouts before but none where the outcome had been so important to him. He was glad he had left his gun at home.

What should I do? What can *I do? What were the laws governing such situations? It wasn't like I'm catching my wife with some guy in my own bed. This is her place. She moved out. It's* her *property. Property! She's my fucking property! No, not property. No, that's wrong. Fuck it! It might be wrong but that's how I feel. If I go in there, could I get sued? Fuck it! Let it go to court. I'd never lose. I* could *lose. They could say I was a loose cannon. Some drunk stalking his ex-wife... No, not 'ex' wife. Not yet. Still, she moved out. It* could *look like I'm stalking her. But this is my wife! It's not stalking if you're following your own wife.*

Sawyer could sense his brain short-circuiting. He knew he wasn't making any sense. He wasn't thinking clearly. He was only feeling. And all the feelings were bad.

He saw a light go on in the back of the house. *Probably a bedroom. Oh God, can this really be happening?*

Sawyer thought that he should give it some time. Maybe it was all very innocent and the guy would walk out the front door in a few minutes and drive away.

Ten minutes passed. The last light went off. The house was dark.

Sawyer's breathing became labored and, after a few minutes, he knew what he was going to do.

He got out of the car, checking to see if there was anyone else on the street. He saw no one. He walked up the sidewalk to the front door and used his pick set to unlock the door. He quietly turned the handle and opened the door slightly. There was no chain. He walked inside, gently closing the door behind him.

He heard sounds coming from somewhere in the house and he followed them. At the end of a hallway, a room was dimly lit. The light flickered. Candles, he thought. He felt as though things were moving in slow motion, as though he were slowly diving into a dream.

The scene was surreal. He recognized his wife's naked body. He had seen her naked hundreds of times. But never with another man. The fact that she moved in a way that showed she felt pleasure from another man being inside her reminded Sawyer of feelings and sensations he had experienced when we had been shot.

He had taken a bullet in his left calf during his second year on the job. He hadn't felt the pain immediately. It was like it was happening in slow motion. Not to someone else—he knew it was happening to him. Yet he felt somehow removed from his body. From the pain. For a while.

As he watched his wife writhe in pleasure it was as though he were being shot...over and over again. He felt the sensation, knew it was pain, but felt nothing. There was so much sensation that the overload caused a part of him to shut down. It was not natural for someone to feel this much. His brain seemed to sense this and limited what he could feel.

He heard himself say, "What the fuck..."

The two lovers were jolted by the intrusion. The man rolled out of bed on the side away from Sawyer, who could not help but notice the man's erection and make the obvious comparison. Sawyer filed that image away for another sleepless night. The man grabbed his clothes, scurried into the bathroom and locked the door. Sawyer could hear the man throw his weight against the locked door. Just in case.

Rebecca quickly recovered and pulled the blankets up over her nude body.

"What the fuck are you doing?" said Sawyer.

Rebecca breathed deeply and stared him down. And said nothing.

"Aren't you even the least bit embarrassed?" he said finally.

"Not really. I'm unhappy, Sawyer. I've been unhappy for a long time. I'm not a slut. I haven't cheated on you constantly. This isn't the first time, but it *is* only the second. And both have been in the past week with the same person."

"Is that supposed to make me feel better?"

"Neither one of us seems to care much about how the other one feels these days."

"At least one of us doesn't."

"Don't be glib."

"Don't tell me how to feel. I caught *you!*"

"Bullshit! Don't pretend you care that someone stole something you threw away a long time ago," said Rebecca.

"So this is a cry for help?"

"I really don't care if you hear me anymore. This is just me doing what's best for me. You took me for granted. Not just for a few weeks or a few months. It's been years. I used to love you so much I ached for you when you were away even for twenty-four hours. But things have changed."

Sawyer didn't know what to do first: Kick down the bathroom door and beat the shit out of the guy who was fucking his wife, read the riot act to Rebecca, or engage her in a conversation about his alleged failings in their marriage.

"Look, Sawyer, I'm not trying to hurt you…"

"Yeah, well, you couldn't have done a better job."

"This is not about you. This is about me. I'm doing this for me. I'm not doing this to hurt you. There's a difference."

"Maybe someday I'll see it." After a moment, he said, "Do you want a divorce?"

"I think so."

Her response was yet another bizarre detail in the scene playing out before him. "This is so awkward," he said finally as he collapsed into a chair opposite the bed.

"Our life has been awkward for a long time. You just didn't notice."

"Was I really that bad?" he said.

"It isn't that you're bad. You're oblivious. And I'm not a bad person either, by the way. I just want someone to care about me and love me. I want someone to make me laugh. I want to be around someone who thinks I'm smart. I want someone who looks forward to getting between my legs. Those aren't bad things, Sawyer."

"I thought I was that person."

"You used to be."

"So, just because I'm busy, you use that to justify an affair?"

"If you think I'm doing this just because you suddenly got busy, then you have no idea what I'm talking about. And you apparently know less about yourself than I thought."

Sawyer thought about saying something mean, but he didn't. She was right. Rebecca was not a tramp and her libido was not out of control. At least he didn't think it was.

But things *had* changed. And not just in the way that things changed as relationships "matured." Over the past year or so there had been a noticeable drop off in their intimacy. It hadn't bothered him, but apparently it had bothered her. And he hadn't noticed.

"I didn't want the moon and the stars, Sawyer. I just wanted you."

He sat there looking at his wife propped up on a couple of pillows, nude under a sheet stained with another man's sweat. That man sat silently behind a locked door, listening to the sound of a marriage falling apart.

Sawyer stood. "You ever coming home?"

"I don't know," she said.

Sawyer just nodded and walked out of the room, closing the door softly behind him.

Chapter Forty-five

Sawyer passed by the angels in the front yard and parked the car. Inside he went to the liquor cabinet and scanned it for the proper medication. After a moment, he decided there was nothing inside that cabinet strong enough to kill the pain.

He went out to the pond. The underwater lights were still shining. He took off his shoes and socks and put his feet into the water. The fish swarmed toward him and, even when they realized he had brought no food, they stayed with him, letting him pet them as they rubbed up against his legs.

He needed to touch. Needed to *be* touched.

Sawyer now knew that his life was out of control and that he was just barely holding on. He was afraid to go to sleep because when he awoke he would have to deal with the reality that what he had seen tonight was not a dream. It was real and it scared him. Made him feel lost. And he had no idea how to make the images and the pain go away.

As he sat there with the fish nibbling on his toes, he realized none of it was going away soon and that he needed to get used to living with that sick feeling in his stomach. For a while.

He recalled from a seminar he took twenty years ago that most things you fear don't happen. But sometimes things worse than what you fear happen. He also recalled from the same class that when something terrible happens you try to envision something even worse happening and, by comparison, what's just happened seems less horrible. Sawyer wasn't sure what would be worse than seeing his wife making love with some guy, but whatever it was, he couldn't think of it tonight.

The pond lights went off and Sawyer walked inside. His answering machine, as usual, was full. He fast-forwarded through all but one. Veronica had called about an hour ago and said that she would be up late, and to feel free to call no matter when he got in.

Sawyer thought about it. But he didn't call. He wouldn't be any good for Veronica tonight.

He wouldn't be any good for anyone tonight.

Chapter Forty-six

Sawyer awoke at 4:40. He couldn't sleep. All his dreams were nightmares. The *Times* wouldn't arrive for at least another hour, so he couldn't occupy his mind with the daily Sudoku puzzle. He brewed a fresh pot of coffee, downed a cup with a shot of half-and-half, donned his sweats and running shoes and took off.

He enjoyed running in Palos Verdes. Every trail and almost every street had a view. It felt good to run. He started to sweat out some of the alcohol, and the endorphins eventually kicked in. He had to deal with what happened with Rebecca and he knew he would. He just didn't know how. Not yet.

Sawyer had been married and divorced once before. When his first wife left him he thought he would go mad. Sawyer had thought that because he still felt like killing himself after the first month, after the second, and after the third. It seemed that feeling of hopelessness might never go away. But it did.

And now, as he ran down Crest Road toward the ocean, he reminded himself that "this too shall pass."

Sawyer picked up the *Times* from the driveway when he got back from his run. He read the sports pages and the Calendar section. He did the Jumble in thirty seconds and the Sudoku in a little over six minutes. It was still only 6:30. He took a long, hot shower, had another cup of coffee, checked his email and put together a list of things he had to do.

As he sat at his desk putting together his list, he noticed the framed honeymoon photograph of Rebecca and him taken in Venice. They both were smiling. He picked up the photograph and stuck it in a drawer.

He looked at the clock, which read 8:00, and called Veronica.

"Hi," she said.

"You free for breakfast?"

"Sure. What time do you want to get together?"

"Nine. Too early?"

"No problem."

"Coco's is good for me. The one on PCH near Hawthorne."

"See ya," said Veronica and hung up.

Sawyer push-buttoned another number. "Larry?"

"Yes. Who is this?"

"Sawyer Black."

"Long time, no talk."

"You still in business?"

"Until my wife dies. Then I can buy a dog and work out of my home office."

It was an odd thing to say, except that Sawyer knew exactly what the man meant. Larry Waters was a retired handwriting analyst whose wife would not permit him to have a dog. The most she would ever allow was a fish. And only one. And that was in a bowl in the garage.

Waters rented an office a few years after his retirement because he couldn't stand being cooped up with his wife all day.

"I've got something I'd like you to take a look at. You still at the same place?"

"When was the last time you were in?"

"It's been about three or four years."

"I moved. I'm in an office building at the corner of Hawthorne and Indian Peak Road, near the Peninsula Center."

"Yeah, I know the place. I've got a nine o'clock breakfast. I'll be to you around eleven."

"Look forward to it."

Sawyer sat in front of the computer, looking at his list of things to do, his feet up on the desk. But his mind was elsewhere.

Coco's was going strong for nine in the morning. Sawyer took a booth, ordered an orange juice, and waited for Veronica. She arrived ten minutes late.

The reporter looked at Sawyer with some concern and sat down. "You look like hell."

"I had a tough night."

"That's what I hear."

"What?" said Sawyer incredulously.

"Just as I was leaving I got a call from a local hairdresser. She said you walked in on Rebecca and her new guy."

"But how... It's only 9 o'clock the next morning."

"News travels fast. One of the two of them told someone."

"I know it wasn't Rebecca," said Sawyer. Even though he knew no such thing.

"Whoever... Somebody told somebody and somebody told me. People talk a lot about you, Sawyer. Or didn't you know?"

"You'd think people would be a little more discreet. Besides, I'm really not that interesting."

"You are now. You're a hot topic because of your connection to Justin Wright, and everyone knows I'm collecting information on anyone even remotely associated with Judy's murder. That's why my source called me. My boss pays well for facts or hot gossip. That creates a very active and motivated underground information network."

"But who could know this so fast?"

"My hairdresser source was told by a woman who works in the same real estate office as your wife. I've already given my source seven hundred and fifty dollars for tips about various people involved on the periphery of Judy's murder."

After a moment Sawyer said, "Do you know who the guy is?"

"Yes. You want a name?"

Sawyer thought about it, then said, "Not really. What can I do? It's not like he broke into our house and raped her. She invited him into her bedroom. And asked *me* to leave." He paused. "What does he do?"

"He's a contractor."

Despite his pain, Sawyer coughed a little laugh. "Of course. Contractors get more action than James Bond."

"I hope you know I don't take pleasure in any of this, Sawyer. And don't worry, I'm not going to run with the gossip about you and Rebecca—because we're friends."

"Thanks."

"I'd like to win you fair and square, not off of some desperate rebound. I really think I'm better for you than Rebecca and that we're better for each other. But I know that's hard for you to see right now."

"It's getting a little easier," he said as he sipped his juice. "Let's change the subject."

"It's even money on the street that Wright's going to be arrested any day now."

"With St. James standing in the way, they better be prepared to back it up with something more than what I hear they've got."

"Yeah, maybe. Maybe the bigger the target, the more a politically-motivated DA might be willing to take a risk. And this DA is pretty political."

"You got anything for me?" said Sawyer.

"This relationship is starting to be a one-way street."

"I'll give you what I can the minute I can give it to you. You know that."

"I know you'll feed me information so that you and St. James can get out in front of something."

"Now, now... It's not that bad, is it? I promise you that when this thing starts to wind down and I can give you something really strong that no one has, I'll give it to you first."

"That's a big 'if.' Because if Wright is actually guilty, at the end of the day, I've got nothing."

"I really believe Wright's innocent."

"Too bad you won't be on the jury. You ever hear the name Zona Day?"

"She's a real estate person here on the Hill."

"Right. Zona used to be Judy's best friend. I hear that they used to know each other before their current Palos Verdes incarnations. Zona's kept a low profile since the murder and hasn't spoken with anyone, according to my sources."

"Why not?"

"That's a good question. Zona's the queen of PR and you would think that she would milk this for all it's worth."

"If she was Judy's best friend, why wouldn't every other reporter know that? Why wouldn't Justin give me her name?"

"My guess—and this is just a guess—is that Judy didn't talk much to Justin about Zona. Like I said, they were friends from way back. I think they stayed in touch but they didn't publicize their friendship."

"How did you find out?"

"I'm a brilliant reporter."

"No, really."

"Really. I did some digging. In the years leading up to her marrying Justin, Judy used to have a roommate named Jeanie Sachs."

Sawyer recalled the name from his LexisNexis search.

"Sachs changed her name to Zona Day in the late 80s when she changed her profession to real estate."

"From what?"

"That's a good question," said Veronica. "When you find out, let me know."

"Maybe I should speak with Ms. Day."

"And you can tell me all about it."

"You got anything on the Rosenberg murder?"

"Hey, you're the cop."

"Judy wasn't leaving Justin for Rosenberg. From what I hear she didn't even like Danny much."

"She liked him well enough to have sex with him once a week."

"I'm starting to think that Judy didn't think that highly of any of the guys she was having sex with."

"Including her husband?"

"I don't know. She seemed to be able to separate sex and love pretty cleanly—if that's the right word."

"Then whom did she love?"

"It's easy to say that she only loved herself. But that doesn't seem right either. She's a mystery. Every time I find out something about her she seems to move further away."

"Does Justin know who Judy loved?"

"I don't think so. And I think he's having doubts that she loved *him*."

"Ain't love grand…"

Sawyer downed the rest of his juice and took her point. Apparently dozens of people knew more about Rebecca and his marriage than he did.

"You feel like a little company tonight?" said Veronica.

"I don't know. I've got to play this thing out my own way. I might call you, I might not. Don't read into it either way."

"Either way?"

"Either way," said Sawyer. "I might just need some company, I might just need some space. I'm not someone you can depend on emotionally right now."

"I understand."

They were both silent for a moment.

"Let me know what happens with Zona."

"I will," said Sawyer. "You'll be the first person I call."

"Probably the second. But that's okay. She might not know who killed Judy, but my guess is that she knows something."

Sawyer walked Veronica to her car. As he watched her drive away, he was aware of the feeling that it was nice to know that *someone* wanted him.

Chapter Forty-seven

Sawyer arrived at Larry Waters' small office a few minutes before eleven. The four hundred square foot office was as much a refuge as it was a working environment.

Waters was born in Japan, immigrated to the United States in the seventies and went to work as a computer programmer for a large software developer. By the mid-eighties he had devised a handwriting analysis program so precise that hundreds of police departments around the world used it routinely.

In 1990 Waters left the software firm and started his own company, which essentially refined the same handwriting analysis techniques he had developed earlier.

In the late nineties, ready to retire, Waters made a deal with his old company and agreed to return as a consultant, for which he was paid three hundred thousand dollars annually. Waters had told Sawyer all this one afternoon over a leisurely lunch while Sawyer picked his brain about a scene in one of his novels. The reason for the office was the same reason he traveled out of the country at least once every three or four months. He wanted to get away from his wife.

After some small talk, Sawyer handed Waters an envelope containing the pages from Judy's day planner. The pages contained notes and lists in Judy's handwriting. He also gave him the diary he found in Judy's studio.

"I need to know if the handwriting in the day planner matches the handwriting in the diary."

"When do you need it?"

"Yesterday would be good."

"Let me do a couple things," he said. He picked up the material, took it to a large flat-bed scanner, positioned a day planner page and a diary page carefully, and then pressed a few buttons.

Sawyer watched as a large wide-screen monitor filled with the image of the day planner page Wright had given him on the left, and the image of a page from the diary on the right.

"Whoever wrote this is quite successful," said Waters pointing to the side of the screen displaying the diary page. "Very decisive and used to telling others what to do."

Sawyer believed one hundred percent in Waters' ability to tell a forgery from the real thing, but when he started rattling on like a psychic reader, Sawyer remained skeptical.

"The person who wrote this is very deceptive. See the way these letters are alternately capital and lower case—no rhyme or reason. The writer not only purposely deceives others, but unwittingly himself or herself as well."

"I'll save my tea leaves so you can read them after lunch."

"You'll see I'm right. And this person has low self esteem in spite of many accomplishments."

"Well, I know you're wrong there."

"I doubt it. The writer may come across bold and brazen, but he or she feels bad about himself or herself. The personality the writer presents to the world is forced. And..." said Waters, turning to look at Sawyer, "he or she can be very dangerous."

"Not anymore. She's dead."

"Hmmm... Maybe she was so dangerous that someone killed her."

"Nice try. Anyhow, thanks. The thing I need to know is whether or not the day planner handwriting samples and the diary match."

"I can never say that anything is a one hundred percent match. You can sign two checks, one right after the other, and chances are they will not match 'one hundred percent.' But the computer program says it's a match based on patterns and probabilities I've programmed into it. Then as I look at it..." Waters paused, turned back toward the computer screen, and cocked his head this way and that as he compared the check and the diary. "I can spot things the program can't."

"Like what?"

"It's not enough to look just for similarities. You also have to look for dissimilarities. But sometimes less obvious similarities are overwhelming. Take a look at these capital J's. Even though one's capital and one's lower case, the hook in the letter has a slight wiggle or crook in it at the bottom just as it comes back up to the left. I feel extremely confident saying that the person who wrote the J's in the day planner wrote the J's in the diary entry."

"Then you earned your lunch at Fu Yuan Low."

"You still have your koi pond?"

"Yes."

"I'm thinking about putting a pond in the backyard."

"I thought your wife wouldn't allow it."

Waters made a face and shook his head. "That's over. She wanted a new Lexus and I wanted a dog in the house. We compromised. She got the Lexus and I got a small fish pond behind the garage."

"You drive a hard bargain."

Chapter Forty-eight

Zona Day's office was located in the Peninsula Center within walking distance of the restaurant where Sawyer and Waters had lunch. Sawyer walked in and was greeted by a woman who looked to be in her mid-fifties. She smiled widely and Sawyer recognized the unnaturally even bite of dentures. White dentures. Really white.

"May I help you?"

"I'd like to see Ms. Day."

"Do you have an appointment?"

"No. But I live up here and I'm thinking about selling my house."

"I'll let Ms. Day know you're here, Mr. ..."

"Black. Sawyer Black."

"I know who you are—you're that writer. Just a sec." The receptionist pressed a button and spoke into the phone. She looked up at Sawyer and said, "You can go on back."

"Thank you."

There was only one office in the back—plus a general-purpose room on the left as he waked down the small hallway. He walked in and shut the door. Zona stood when Sawyer walked in, waved him to a seat in front of her desk and they both sat down.

Zona Day was a serious real estate agent. Engraved plaques on the wall. Pictures of her with anyone who was anyone at every social function in the past ten years. Lots of framed "Number One Agent" certificates starting from 1994 and running consecutively through last year.

Zona told people that her father was related to Doris Day and that her mother, who was part Cherokee Indian, named her for a bright Arizona morning the day she was born.

Of course, none of it was true. Her father's last name *was* Day, but Doris Day's real last name was von Kappelhoff. Zona's mother, Ruth, was not Indian, but Jewish, and hailed from the Bronx. But in the Palos Verdes real estate market a memorable name was an edge. Five to ten times a week people asked about her unique name and she told the same bogus story. In fact, she had told it so many times that when one of her clients asked her to join a native American Indian organization Zona had not only agreed, but actually went on to become the fundraising chairperson.

Zona had been a blonde for twenty-seven of her forty-eight years. Her third husband had paid for her second round of plastic surgery, and was the first to sample the goods. A year ago he was replaced by a fourth husband who lived life one fifth at a time. She put up with the drinking because he was old, rich and usually too drunk to keep track of her lies. Zona figured she had nine lives when it came to marriage and even more if you included affairs lasting more than two weeks. She had a sixth sense about men and could always tell from a first meeting whether or not she would sleep with that person.

She looked at Sawyer and knew immediately that he would not be one of her conquests.

"I wondered when you'd be by," said Zona.

"Well, here I am."

"Can I have Sandy get you anything? Coffee, tea…or something stronger?"

"That's very politically incorrect."

"I think you'll find I'm not very politically correct—when I'm not working, that is. And I doubt you're here about selling your house."

"I'll have what you're having."

She hit a button on her desk and said, "Sandy, bring us both a cup of the 'special blend.'" She looked at Sawyer and said, "Hope you like bourbon."

"I do actually. And I haven't had any for hours."

They made small talk till the drinks were delivered. Sawyer sipped his and figured there was a good shot and half of bourbon in the coffee.

When Sandy left, Sawyer said, "I hear you and Judy were pretty tight."

"We used to be. Very tight, actually."

"Yeah, I saw your name on a lease in Marina Del Rey, along with Judy's," said Sawyer recalling his LexisNexis search. "But it wasn't Zona Day back then; it was Jeanie Sachs."

"Those were good times. We were young and wild. *And* good-looking." Zona paused and looked up at Sawyer from the lip of her cup. "I'm not that young anymore."

"Were you around when she met Justin?"

"Oh yeah. Justin fell hard for Judy and he couldn't get enough *of* her or do enough *for* her. But he was married and there wasn't anything he could do about it till his kid was grown and out of the house. Least that was what he said."

"You didn't believe him?"

"I've heard enough stories from cheating husbands to fill a fairy tale book. The most common thing they say is that they can't leave their wives for some reason that can only be solved in the course of time. Like waiting for the kids to grow up and get out of the house, or the wife's got some illness that she's almost cured of, or he's planning to sell his business and that we should wait so that the money will go to me instead of the wife. Believe me, that's just chapter one of a very long book."

"So you didn't believe him."

"No."

"But Justin *did* leave his wife and marry Judy."

"Only after he thought he was losing her to another man. Works all the time," said Zona as though touting some miracle drug that everyone needed to know about.

"Was she going to leave Justin for another man?"

"Now that's complicated."

"I've still got a half a cup of bourbon left."

"This was in the early to mid-90s, probably about a year before Judy and Justin got married. We weren't roommates anymore. I'd been married and divorced, but we kept in touch and were still good friends. There was a guy. Some musician who used to play in one of the South Bay clubs. He was a guitar player. He didn't have a pot to piss in."

"You remember which club?"

"It was one of the clubs on a small street that dead ends onto the beach. I think it was in Hermosa Beach, but I'm not sure. It was a long time ago."

"Was Judy serious about the guy?"

"Hard to say. She didn't let me too close to that relationship. Which was one reason I thought it might be serious. I think she felt that if I knew too much about it I might slip up and spill the beans some night to Justin when I had too much to drink."

"Maybe she was afraid you'd steal her man."

"I like the way you think," said Zona with a wide smile. "But that definitely wasn't it. I think she had something special with this guy that she'd never had with anyone else."

"A penniless musician is quite a change of pace from Justin Wright."

"Musicians are fun. They put your dreams to music. And they're usually good-looking."

"Sounds like you've been with a few music men in your time."

"A few. Bottom line is that they make great lovers and lousy husbands."

"Why?"

"Because most people's dreams don't come true. And if you're stupid enough to marry a musician, when it becomes clear that the dreams aren't coming true, you're not left with much."

"Are you sure you can't remember the name of the guy Judy was dating?"

Zona thought for a moment while she sipped her special blend. "For some reason it seems to me that he had one of those 'one-word' names. Like Dylan, Donovan, or Slash."

Sawyer thought about reminding her that Dylan actually had a first name but he knew what she meant. "Do you have any pictures of him? Maybe some you took when you and Judy lived together?"

"You know, I just might at that. I don't know where the hell they are right now, though. I just moved. Everything's in boxes. And any photos from that period would still be in boxes I haven't unpacked from the last two moves. I hate moving!" Zona paused and sipped her coffee. "Do you think this guy had something to do with Judy's murder? Because I don't. As far as I know they haven't been in touch since Justin busted them up years ago."

"How did he do that?"

"Well, Justin noticed that Judy wasn't quite as available as she used to be. They would usually get together on weeknights, but rarely on weekends. Married men usually reserve those nights for their wives. Every wife knows that the only business their husbands are up to on Saturday nights is monkey business."

"How did he find out Judy was seeing this other guy?"

"The old fashioned way—he had her followed. He confronted her with some photographs of her and the guy together. Judy told Justin they were just friends—Justin didn't have any pictures of them in the act, but he had a strong circumstantial case."

"Like?"

"Like the detective following the two of them to her condo at two in the morning and watching the guy come out at noon the next day."

"What did she say about that?"

"She danced around it. Of course, Justin didn't believe her. Still, they weren't married and he could only push it so far."

"So what happened?"

"Judy's a smart cookie. She turned it all around on him. She said it was *his* fault. Can you imagine?"

Unfortunately, Sawyer could imagine the scene all too clearly.

"Judy said she was tired of waiting around for Justin to get a divorce. She even said—I overheard the whole thing—that she was tired of him lying to *her*. Judy had balls. She said Justin had told her he was going to leave his wife for about ten years and he hadn't done so. She gave him an ultimatum. She wanted a *real* relationship where the two of them went out on weekends together, spent their birthdays and holidays together. And if she couldn't have it with Justin she would have it with someone else."

"How did he take it?"

"He filed for divorce within a week and they were married less than a year later."

"And you never saw the musician again?"

"No. Like I said, she kept that part of her life to herself."

"That's quite a story. Did you two remain friends when you both moved to the Hill?"

"We saw each other once in a while, but I know Justin wasn't crazy about Judy seeing me. I believe he thought I knew a lot about Judy he didn't want anyone else to know and he didn't want to be reminded of."

"You think you could look through your boxes and see if you've got an old photograph of the guy Judy dated?"

"Sure. Give me a day or two."

"I'll call you."

"I know you will. Men always call back when they haven't gotten what they want yet. You might ask Justin if he still has those photographs the detective took."

"I'll do that. You said Justin fell hard for Judy. How did she feel about him?"

"She knew a good thing when she saw one. Don't get me wrong, it wasn't like she was playing Justin. Judy genuinely liked Justin, but he was about twenty years older than she was and, at that time, Judy was a star—at least on the nightclub circuit. Velvet ropes disappeared whenever she wanted to get into a club. We had fun."

"Who got up to the Hill first—you or Judy?"

"I did, actually. I met a guy—CEO of a Fortune 500 Company. He used to live in Rolling Hills. He was in the middle of a divorce and I made him happy...for a while. We were married for a few minutes and I got enough money and real estate connections to last me a lifetime when we split up. I got no complaints. Neither does he, by the way. We still travel together now and then—when his new wife's out of town."

"Old habits die hard."

"Hey, good lovers are hard to come by. Particularly good lovers who also pick up a check."

Chapter Forty-nine

Sawyer called Justin from his car and arranged a 6 p.m. meeting at the Morning Glory Coffeehouse in the Peninsula Center. That gave him about three hours to go home and relax or take a nap.

He checked the answering machine. There were three messages—all from reporters. None from Rebecca.

The phone rang. He looked at the Caller ID, punched the Talk button, and said, "Hi."

"Just thought I'd give you a call and see how you were doing," said Veronica.

"I'm okay. I saw Zona Day this afternoon," he said, purposely changing the subject.

"How'd that go?"

"She's an interesting person."

"Yeah, I know. I talked to her at a party a couple of years back. She's a trip. Anything there?"

"Maybe. Too soon to tell. She's looking into something for me. If it pans out I'll let you know."

"Care to speculate with me over dinner?"

Sawyer was about to say no, but he caught himself. *Why not? "*I'm available."

"Great. How about the Bull Pen? I could use a good steak."

"Sounds good. Eight o'clock?"

"See you there," said Veronica and hung up quickly before Sawyer could change his mind.

Sawyer hadn't been on a "date" in a long time. He wasn't sure he looked at it that way, even though he knew Veronica did. He knew she wanted to be with him.

He just didn't want to be alone.

The Morning Glory Coffeehouse was quiet at six o'clock. The music didn't start till about seven. People were sitting on couches and in stuffed chairs drinking coffee, tea and a couple of esoteric cider drinks, reading books or magazines. A guy in the corner was pounding away at a laptop.

Sawyer ordered a tea with a Chinese-sounding name and grabbed an overstuffed chair in the corner away from the door.

Wright arrived on time, joined Sawyer in a chair next to his and ordered nothing. He was in the mood for something stronger than caffeine.

"How did the handwriting samples work out?"

"No problem. They match the diary. The same person who wrote the sample also wrote the diary."

"I guess that's good."

"I just wanted to make sure that her diary wasn't forged."

"You thought the diary could have been a fake?"

"I had to be sure."

Wright let that sink in. If the diary was a fake, then a reasonable person might conclude *he* had faked it because he was the one who guided Sawyer to it. "Well, good. At least we're past that."

"Who was the guy Judy was seeing just before you asked her to marry you?"

"I don't know—"

"I know you hired a detective who took photographs of the two of them together."

"I was going to say that I don't know the man's name. But you're right, I did have her followed and she was seeing someone. I confronted her with the photographs and we...came to an understanding. I think she was just trying to force me to get a divorce. And I saw her point. I'd been promising her I would get a divorce for over ten years."

"You still have the photographs?"

"She made me burn them as part of a condition for us getting married."

"The detective... Think he kept the negatives?"

"No. Judy and I went to his office and we watched him burn the negatives."

"You remember the detective's name?"

"Thomas Sanders. He had an office in Torrance. He'd done some work for my company a few times—background checks, that kind of thing. I knew I could trust him. I read a few years ago that he died. Heart attack, I think. Is it important?"

"I have no idea."

"How could something that happened so long ago be relevant?"

"Has she seen the man in the photograph since that time?"

"Not to my knowledge, no. I can't imagine how this could have anything to do with Judy's murder."

"Did you ever hire a detective on any other occasion to follow Judy—before or after your marriage?"

Wright did not respond immediately.

"I can find out, Justin. And if I can find out, others can, too. And there's the possibility that if you did hire someone, that person might want to cash in. It's better to stop these kinds of things before they get started."

"I hired a detective last summer…about six months after Judy got her studio in San Pedro. As I've already told you, it occurred to me that she might be having an affair."

"It 'occurred' to you. That's an odd way to put it. It's also odd that you don't consider the fact that she was having sex with four other men on a regular basis an affair. Or four affairs."

"I know it doesn't make sense to most people, but when she had sex in our home, even if it was with other men, it wasn't as though she were cheating. I knew about it, I was there. It seemed safe. If she were to see someone else, behind my back, and lied to me about it…well, that was simply unacceptable. I would have felt betrayed."

"So, you suspected that she was seeing someone."

"Yes."

"What did the detective turn up?"

"Absolutely nothing. He said the studio thing seemed to be on the up and up. He said that her art teacher sometimes came by to give her lessons, but the detective didn't think she was fooling around with him. And that was it."

"And you didn't suspect the art teacher?"

"No. The detective checked him out and he came up clean. In fact, he said he thought the guy was gay."

"What's the detective's name?"

"Hank Simpson. He's retired LAPD."

"How can I reach Simpson?"

"When I go home, I'll call you with his number."

"If I'm not there, leave a message. I'll count on getting his number tonight when I get home."

"You'll have it."

"I don't mean to come down on you too hard, Justin, but better me than someone else." Sawyer paused and sipped his tea. "So, how you holding up?"

"This is the worst time of my life. I know it's a cliché, but I really do keep thinking that maybe this is just a dream or hallucination I'll wake up from. It's all too terrible to fully comprehend. Not only is the love of my life for more than twenty years gone, brutally hacked to death in our home, but I'm being blamed for it! I just can't believe it's really happening sometimes."

"What about Nathan?"

"He's doing as well as can be expected. I know he didn't get along too well with Judy when we were first married. Most of that I blame on Natasha brainwashing him night and day. But they buried the hatchet over the past couple of years. Being away at school, out from under Natasha's constant influence, helped him develop a broader perspective."

"How did Natasha take the news?"

"We still haven't spoken since Judy's murder. But then, we hadn't talked for more than a year before that."

"Natasha wouldn't have any motive for killing Judy, would she?"

"Not if you exclude the fact that she's an evil bitch."

"Divorce doesn't bring out the best in people, does it?"

"Not usually. On the plus side, as long as the checks clear, Natasha does her best to stay out of my way."

"Then what makes her so 'evil'?"

"Immediately after the divorce, and for several years after that, she did her best to poison Nathan against me. Whenever he and I got together my whole focus was on trying to undo the damage she'd done. Also, Natasha sits on many boards of community organizations. Therefore, she influences lots of people, many of whom used to be 'our' friends. After listening to her version of the truth, day after day, many of those people no longer speak to me. What the hell," said Wright. "Who needs those people anyhow? They were only nice to me because I gave them money and now they hate me because my wife's giving them money and she hates me. *My* money! Life's pretty fucked up sometimes, Sawyer."

"I hear it's still better than the alternative."

"I'll let you know in a few years," said Wright with a smile. He looked at his watch and stood. "I gotta see Noah in about thirty minutes." He extended his hand to Sawyer and said, "I won't forget this."

"Don't worry. I won't let you."

Wright smiled again and then he was gone.

The sun had set more than an hour ago and the fog was so thick he could hardly see the parking lot, which was only about thirty feet from where he sat.

"Hey, Sawyer."

Sawyer looked up to see Michael setting his guitar case down in front of a microphone set up on a small stage.

"Hey... What are you doing here?"

"I play a set down here once in a while. It's a nice crowd. Very appreciative of original songs, and they listen to the lyrics."

"You look kinda' glum," said Michael as he sat down in the chair recently occupied by Justin Wright.

"Let's just say I'm not in the holiday spirit and leave it at that."

"I heard about what happened with you and Rebecca."

"Yeah, I think I saw a piece about it in the *Times*," said Sawyer drolly.

"Palos Verdes is a small town. Rich but small."

"Especially, if you're a Tantric yoga teacher."

"People are handy at different things. Did I ever tell you I self-published a manual on Tantric sex?"

"No. And I think I'd remember that."

"I did. I wrote the book on sex. Man, I love saying that."

"Does it work—the stuff in your book?"

"Yes. I have sex with a partner at least every other day, but I only have one orgasm a week."

"Bullshit."

"Swear to god."

"You ever have a woman cheat on you?" asked Sawyer, changing the subject to a topic on which *he* was an expert.

"What do you mean by cheat?"

"That's usually not a word that sends people running to the dictionary."

"No, I mean I've had a number of 'open relationships' with women in which we each had sex with other people during the time we were 'together.'"

"I'm talking about someone you were committed to—by that I mean you vowed to be exclusive to each other. Have you ever had a person in that kind of relationship have sex with someone else and found out about it?"

Michael thought about that a moment, then finally said, "Yeah. And it's a bitch."

"Tina?" asked Sawyer, referring to Michael's second ex-wife.

"Yeah, I didn't tell you everything."

Nobody ever tells anyone everything, thought Sawyer.

"It was a strange time in both our lives—Tina's and mine. 2000 and 2001 transformed me from a 'financial genius' into a bum. I felt pretty bad about things and about myself. Things got pretty tense between Tina and me. Sex became like something I remembered from a past life.

"I still knew some people who didn't think I was a slug and I started hanging out with them more and more. I was at a strange place in my life: The person who thought the least of me was my wife. I couldn't shake the feeling that the person who knew me best thought I was a loser, while people who didn't know me as well thought I was okay. Even better than okay. Who should I believe? I finally came to the conclusion that I didn't do anything bad. At least not on purpose. I didn't murder anyone. I didn't steal anyone's money. I really wasn't such a bad person. And if Tina couldn't be a member of the team that thought I could succeed, then I should start hanging out with people who did."

"Uh...Michael. This story was supposed to be about someone cheating on *you*. Not the other way around."

"Four years ago I'm sharing an office with a real estate agent over on Silver Spur. I leave the house every morning about eight. One morning I tell Tina I've got a noon lunch meeting in Beverly Hills. A few minutes before I was supposed to leave for Beverly Hills, I realized I'd left something at home. I didn't call ahead, like I usually would have, because Tina told me she was having lunch with one of her friends in Long Beach. So I go home and walk in on Tina and some guy I'd never seen before."

Sawyer breathed deeply and finished his tea. "So, what did you do?"

"I went outside and threw up in the driveway."

"Well, at least I kept my dinner down."

"I know it's tough, Sawyer. But you get over it. I know it doesn't seem like you will—"

"No, I know I will. I'm a homicide cop—least I used to be. I've seen worse. I know I'll get over it and I know that the more honest I am with myself about what I'm feeling, the quicker those feelings will work themselves out."

"Sounds like you've been there before."

"I'm fifty years old. I've been married twice. I was a homicide cop for twenty years. I've made a few bucks from a couple of Hollywood studios and lived to tell the tale. There isn't much I haven't seen."

"The voice of experience..."

"Experience means nothing unless you're paying attention."

"How true."

"I know that I must have played *some* part in what's happening between Rebecca and me."

"Don't go 'Oprah' on me, buddy."

"I'm just saying that there's a context to everything. Rebecca having an affair didn't come out of nowhere. I'm not blaming myself for what she did. She did what she did and she's responsible for her actions. So am I. But I don't get anywhere sitting around with my friends talking about what a scumbag she is."

"So what *do* you do?"

"Feel pretty bad for a while. Then figure out where I'm at and move forward from there. Right now I have no idea what that means. I don't want to go through another divorce, but I don't want to stay in a loveless marriage. I'm really not sure how I feel about Rebecca and I don't know how she *really* feels about me."

"You got plans for tonight?"

"I'm having dinner with a friend."

"Anyone I know?"

"Probably." Sawyer didn't volunteer any more information. Instead he changed the subject. "I've talked to Judy's friends, people close to her, and I get the distinct feeling that she might have been having an affair, but no one knows with whom."

"Some people are more clever at covering their tracks than others."

"Some people have more to lose."

"That too."

"You seem to be the closest thing there is to an expert on people having affairs on the Hill."

"Thank you. I'll take that as a compliment."

"If you like. What's the best way to pull off an affair without anyone knowing?"

Hall pondered the question for a moment. "First, you tell no one. Not your best friend, not even your dog. No one. Then, when you're out in public with your lover, act politely toward each other, but never touch. People pick up on affection. Lots of people miss affection more than sex if both go away, and people notice what they want and don't have. Also, when you're in public don't lean close and whisper to each other like you're sharing a secret you don't want other people to hear."

"If the two people—one being Judy—were as smart as you say, and neither told anyone, how can I find out who her lover was?"

"You might not be able to."

That was not the answer Sawyer wanted to hear.

Sawyer and Michael talked for a few minutes more. Nothing changed. Sawyer knew that whatever pain he came in with, he would take with him when he left. And it would be there again in the morning. But he also knew that eventually it would fade.

That was the thought that kept him sane.

Chapter Fifty

When Sawyer walked in to the Bull Pen Restaurant in Redondo Beach, Veronica was already seated in a booth sipping red wine. She waved him over and Sawyer sat down opposite her.

"I started without you."

"Hope you don't make that a habit," he said, with the hint of a smile. He ordered a glass of merlot and a plate of calamari.

While they ate the appetizer he told her about his meeting with Zona Day.

"I hope she can find a photograph of Judy's old lover," said Veronica.

"Even if she does, there's no indication that the guy has anything to do with Judy's murder. Justin says she hasn't seen her old beau since before they were married."

"Did you get the detective's name?"

"He's dead," said Sawyer.

"Least that's what Wright told you. And a husband who hires a detective once, might hire someone again. Especially if he thinks his wife is cheating on him. And everyone seems to think Judy was cheating on Justin with someone."

"Maybe. He says he didn't hire another detective." It was a small lie that Sawyer could rectify later. He wanted to check out what Justin had told him with Hank Simpson, the second detective, before he gave the information to Veronica. If there was nothing there, then it didn't matter. If there was something there, and it could hurt Wright... Well, that was different.

Sawyer wouldn't protect Justin if he found out his friend had killed his wife, but he didn't want to help the media put a rope around the neck of an innocent man. Also, he knew that Sanders, the first detective, was a dead end. He had called Nellie at St. James' office on his way back from seeing Zona Day. She did a quick search that confirmed that Sanders had, in fact, died in 2003. Either Justin was telling him the truth or, if he was lying, he had given him the name knowing that Sanders was dead. Either way, there was nothing there for Sawyer. But Hank Simpson was another story.

Sawyer ordered a very rare prime rib, while Veronica opted for a porterhouse steak.

"Got anything for me?" asked Sawyer as he refilled Veronica's glass from the bottle of merlot he had ordered with the meal.

"I just might." She paused. "Oh, you mean about the murders," she said with a smile.

Sawyer smiled back. It felt good.

"I've been thinking about the 'other man' angle," said Veronica. "If there *is* another man, then either he's married or he isn't. If he's married, maybe there's a 'love nest' somewhere."

"Yeah, that narrows it down."

"If he's not married, then they could meet at his place."

"I've been thinking too. This was definitely a crime of passion—the choice of weapon, so many stab wounds. Someone felt the kind of rage that can only come from a strong emotional attachment. Most likely a jealous lover."

"Though not always," said Veronica. "It could be simply a person who felt rejected by her even though she might not have known that he existed."

"Still, in the mind of the perpetrator there was a strong emotional attachment. So we're looking for someone who, if we looked close enough at Judy's life, we'd see, even if he's on the periphery of her life."

"So what about Rosenberg? Why would Justin kill him if Judy wasn't interested in him?"

"I don't know," said Sawyer. "It's obviously connected. I'm missing something. I'll find it, but I just can't see it now. I've had cases like this before. When it's over I'm always amazed I didn't see it sooner. It seems so obvious when you know the answer."

Sawyer and Veronica skipped dessert and polished off the remainder of the merlot.

"You got any after-dinner plans?" asked Veronica as she finished the last of her wine.

"Not really." Sawyer knew where this was going. His first instinct was to respectfully decline and go home alone. But he didn't really want to go home alone. Yet he didn't want to take Veronica back to his house. At least Rebecca hadn't taken her lover to their home, thought Sawyer. Sawyer almost laughed at himself: Suddenly there were rules and gradations of infidelity.

"I'm not looking forward to the drive home," she said.

"You ever been to the Porto Bella Hotel in Redondo Beach?" said Sawyer finally.

"No. You?"

"Never stayed there. Might be fun. I hear they have rooms right on the ocean. This time of year it shouldn't be a problem to get one."

Sawyer paid the bill and walked Veronica to her car.

"I'll follow you," she said and kissed him lightly on the lips.

Chapter Fifty-one

Veronica checked in using her corporate credit card—she had stayed in the South Bay a couple of nights since Judy's murder, but not in any hotel as nice as this one. She went to her room, called Sawyer's cell and gave him the room number. Five minutes later Sawyer hung the "Do Not Disturb" sign on the doorknob and double-locked the door.

He had never done this before—he had never cheated on Rebecca. Was this really cheating, he thought, when his wife was screwing some guy and talking about getting a divorce?

Many years ago Sawyer had a relationship with Veronica. The sexual spark was still there. Maybe it was the alcohol, maybe it was a need to feel desired, maybe it was just a fear of being alone, but Sawyer felt a kind of attraction to Veronica that he had not felt for any woman, including his wife, in a long time. It was not love. But it sure as hell *was* passion.

He embraced her and she kissed him with open lips. His hands slid down her back below her waist and he discovered that she wore no panties. She was ready. Had she planned this, he thought? It didn't matter. He felt himself getting hard against her thigh. He guided her down onto the bed, lifted her skirt, removed his pants and underwear.

"Looks like you're happy to see me," she whispered.

He positioned himself between her legs and experienced a rush of pleasure as he felt himself slip smoothly inside her. She groaned and wrapped her arms around his neck. "Fuck me," she said. "Fuck me like you've missed me forever."

Sawyer was amazed at the heat of his passion. He remembered that sex with Veronica had been good, but he did not remember that it was *this* good.

He moved his left leg outside her right and leveraged himself in a way so that he began to make a circular motion. Veronica began to moan. The motion caused him to rub against her clitoris in a rhythmic motion…and she began to moan louder and louder until she finally had an orgasm.

And another.

And another…

Afterward, as they lay in bed, Veronica's head on his left shoulder, Sawyer exhaled deeply.

"You remembered," she whispered.

"Some things you never forget," he whispered.

"Why are we whispering?"

They both laughed.

Sawyer knew why he whispered. He was having sex with someone other than his wife. He had reasons for doing so, but then everyone, including Rebecca, had reasons for their infidelity. He did not believe that Rebecca's reasons justified what she did.

Were his any better?

He didn't know. He could only feel. And he felt better than he had felt in a long time. Did Veronica love him? He had no idea. It was too early to think of such things. He had no idea if Veronica would be his next wife or just a former lover with whom he had a one-night stand.

"Want a nightcap?"

"I'm a little worn out. Maybe in the morning," said Sawyer.

"I'm talking about a drink."

"Oh… Sure. What the hell."

"Besides, it's on the company."

Fifteen minutes later there was a knock on the door and a bottle of Cristal was delivered to the room. Veronica, wearing a hotel bathrobe, signed the bill at the door and added a twenty-five-dollar tip.

"You think your boss is going to spring for a two-hundred-dollar nightcap? I know the department wouldn't."

"The LAPD isn't as profitable. Besides, if I get hit with an extra hundred bucks, it's worth it," she said, sitting down on the bed with the champagne. She popped the cork, poured him a glass, and kissed him gently on the lips.

They drank champagne and watched Jay Leno while they let everything sink in.

"I don't want you to—" said Sawyer finally.

"Don't," she said, gently putting a finger to his lips. "I know what you *don't* want... You don't want me to read too much into tonight. You don't want me to feel too much for you. You don't want me to get hurt. You don't want me to think you're a jerk for fucking me if you wind up getting back together with Rebecca."

Sawyer smiled. "Well, I guess that pretty much covers it."

"But I know you, Sawyer. You wouldn't have slept with me...again...just because you're wounded. And if you did, that's on me because I know that you're vulnerable. Personally, I think we have a future, but I'm not a 'home-wrecker.' If Rebecca were still in your bed you wouldn't be here and I wouldn't have invited you in."

Sawyer sipped his Cristal. He knew she was right, but he said nothing. Finally he said, "It's too soon. Not for this, but for what comes next. I really don't know what's happening in my life. I don't know what Rebecca wants. I don't know what I want."

"I know what I want. But I also know that you don't. I'm just telling you that I believe I'm better for you than Rebecca. You know me. I don't sit at the back of the room and hope the teacher doesn't call on me. I speak up. If you get back together with Rebecca, that's life and I'll live with it. In the meantime, she's chosen someone else. And even if that person is a fling, she didn't choose you. I'm not trying to be mean, but that's the truth. She's moved on."

Sawyer thought about that for a moment. He knew Veronica's assessment was self-serving, but there was a lot of truth in it. "This is where I want to be, and you are the woman I want to be with...tonight."

"Tonight...the present moment...is all we have Sawyer. All anyone ever has."

"Yeah, well, that sounds pretty metaphysical, but tomorrow morning—or later this morning," said Sawyer, looking at the clock, "we get up and the world goes on. I have no idea what's going on with my marriage. I'm in the middle of a high-profile murder case that can work for both of us or make us both look really bad."

"I look at it like this: You and I have found each other again after many years. Screw Justin Wright and his promiscuous wife. One way or the other this will be over some day. When it is, everyone moves on to the next big thing. I want us to move on together."

"I can't promise that."

"I know. But the difference between now and any time in the last ten years is that we're both thinking about it."

Sawyer thought about what she said. Veronica was not a desperate woman. She was very attractive and he knew that Veronica was pursued by many men. Men with money. Men with power. He also knew Veronica well enough to know that she wanted something more. And he was more than a little flattered to hear that she believed she had found what she wanted in him.

Sawyer's cell phone rang and he picked it up off the side table next to the bed. He checked the caller ID. It was Noah St. James. "I gotta take this," he said and pressed the Talk button.

"Yeah."

"Thanks for picking up. We need to meet."

"Not tonight."

"Tomorrow. Early tomorrow."

"Okay. Where?"

"My office."

"What's the big deal?"

"I don't want to talk about it on the phone. There's nothing we can do about it tonight. Eight o'clock?"

"You get up early."

"It gets easier when you're making six hundred dollars an hour," said St. James and hung up.

"Who was that?"

"St. James." There was no point in lying. He gave nothing away.

"He's an asshole."

"He's a lawyer," said Sawyer. He had a lot of friends who were lawyers. Most of the ones who became criminal defense attorneys took the mirrors out of their homes after their first year in practice. The ones with consciences.

"Where were we?" said Veronica as she repositioned herself in the crook of Sawyer's left shoulder after he lay back down on the bed.

"I think we're finding our way," he said and turned off the light.

"That's good enough for tonight," she said. She kissed him gently on the lips and snuggled closer.

Chapter Fifty-two

Sawyer was up by six. He kissed Veronica—who was used to getting up around eight or later—and said goodbye. And that he would call her. They both knew that was true.

Sawyer checked the hallway for a security camera, found it and looked away. *What the hell... I didn't kill anyone. What difference does it make?* Still, he felt a twinge of guilt.

He was home by 6:30. He checked the answering machine. Rebecca still had not called, but Justin Wright had left Hank Simpson's number. Sawyer wrote down the detective's number, then showered, shaved, brewed and drank some coffee, changed clothes, did the Jumble and the Sudoku and set off to see St. James.

St. James brewed some coffee and offered Sawyer a croissant. The two men drank coffee and ate pastries while they talked.

"So, what's the big news?" said Sawyer.

"I spoke with someone I know on the inside. He pulled the LUDs from Justin's cell phone. And from Judy's cell phone. They both called the same person after midnight the night she was murdered."

"And who was that?"

"Nathan. Judy called him first, about one. Then shortly before three Justin called him."

"What do you make of it?" Sawyer already had a few ideas.

"I'm not sure."

"How long were the calls? Maybe they both just left messages."

"Both calls were in the three-minute range."

"Let me speculate here a minute, Noah. Anyone who watches 'Law and Order' knows that their phone calls, especially from their cell phones, are going to be on record with the phone company and that the police have access to those records. Why make a phone call you know is going to be incriminating—given the fact you know you're going to kill your wife in a few minutes, or have already done so?"

"I like the way you think. Still, Justin needs a good explanation for that call to his son, which I calculate to be a few minutes after he discovered Judy's body."

Sawyer noticed that the lawyer didn't say Justin needed to tell the truth about the call, only that he needed a "good explanation."

"Any ideas why Judy might have called Nathan the night she was murdered?"

"I have no idea, Noah. I'm more interested in why Justin called Nathan."

"The guy I spoke with said Judy's LUDs were pretty clean. Her personal cell and their home phones turned up no red flags."

"Yeah, but if she knew Justin might have hired a detective, she wouldn't make any incriminating phone calls on her cell."

"What *could* she do? Hypothetically…"

"She *could* get a cell phone that couldn't be traced back to her—even by a detective. That way she could call her lover anytime she wanted to. She could have her lover buy her a phone in his name, or he could buy an untraceable phone on the street."

"That sounds like a lot of work."

"For some people it's worth it."

"Can you speak with Nathan today?"

"Okay."

"Good," said St. James as he wrote something down on a pad in front of him. "I'll call Nathan and tell him you'll be stopping by. He wants to help his father any way he can. Here's the address and phone number of his kayak shop in Redondo Beach." St. James slid a piece of paper across his desk and Sawyer pocketed it.

St. James' phone rang and he nodded at Sawyer, who took another croissant and left.

Chapter Fifty-three

Sawyer went back home and petted the fish.

His life was spinning off its axis. Petting the fish helped. As much as anything he couldn't put in a glass.

The phone rang and he went inside. The caller ID read "Private Number." He picked up and said, "Yes?"

"Hi." It was Rebecca.

Sawyer felt as though he'd been kicked in the stomach. "Hi," was all he could think of to say.

Neither knew what to say next. Intuitively, Sawyer knew that the next words should be Rebecca's. She was the one who had called.

"You okay?" she said finally.

"Yeah. How about you?"

"I'm okay."

Silence.

"That was uncomfortable...the other night," said Rebecca.

Sawyer had felt many things, and uncomfortable was one of them. But he had felt much, much more than that.

"Yeah," he said. He was determined not to drive this conversation. She had called and he wanted to hear what she had to say. Anything he said might sound silly and weak until he knew where she was coming from.

"I think we should talk." She paused. "About us."

"Okay. When and where?"

"Sooner the better. How about tonight at Restaurant Christine?"

"Okay. Seven o'clock."

"I'll see you there."

And then she was gone.

Sawyer had no idea how he felt. Partly because he still had no idea how Rebecca felt. How could he respond? He knew he should have his own feelings, independent of his wife's, but he knew that his feelings would be shaped by how she felt. Was she remorseful? Did she have regret? Or did she want a divorce?

He had no idea and, therefore, no plan.

Just dinner at seven. And the rest of the day to wonder what she was going to say.

Sawyer put down the phone, which he just realized he still held.

Nathan's kayak shop was located on the Redondo Beach Pier, not far from a place where Sawyer and Rebecca used to go in the summer for fresh crab. About a dozen kayaks hung on the wall or were suspended from the ceiling. Prices ranged from $600 to about $2000, depending on the brand and whether they were single or tandem. There were rows of bright colored paddles, vests and helmets. According to a sign behind the counter, kayak rentals ranged from $35 to $100. Lessons were available at a rate of $65 per hour.

Sawyer spotted Nathan standing in the corner talking with two men who looked like surfers and seemed to be about the same age as Nathan. After a couple of minutes the men shook Nathan's hand and left.

"Morning, Nathan," said Sawyer.

"Hi."

"You got a few minutes?"

"Yeah, sure. Let's go next door and grab some coffee," he said. "Things are kind of slow this time of year anyhow." He grabbed a jacket, picked up a small sign with a clock's face on it, set the hands for eleven o'clock, put the sign in the window, and locked the door as they left.

The coffee place was nothing special, but it had a view of the Pacific. Redondo Beach cafes with an ocean view charged four bucks for a cup of nothing special. More if you called it something that sounded French.

"My dad's in trouble, isn't he?" said Nathan after putting some real sugar in his coffee.

"Yes, he is."

"I've never seen him in trouble before. He's always been this kind of invincible character. He always takes care of everybody and everything."

"Some things money can't fix. Even your father's kind of money."

Nathan nodded absently. "He looks older, you know. He never looked his age. I know he's an old guy, but he never acted that way or looked old. He looked old the last time I saw him."

"This kind of thing wears you down. I've seen it do more than that to some people. But your father's strong."

"I hope so. I don't know what I'd do without him. I know most people think I need him for the money. But I could make it on my own. I've got my degree and I know what I'm doing. But it wouldn't be the same without having him around to share it with. He's my best friend."

"Really…" said Sawyer.

"I know that sounds lame. But it's true."

"So, why did you go live with your mother after the divorce?"

Nathan smiled. "You know my mom?"

"Not well, no."

"The bottom line was that I didn't have a choice. Not really."

"I hear she talked bad about your father to you every chance she got."

"That's true. And in the beginning, I have to admit it affected me. But as time went on, and I matured, and spent some time away at school, I began to understand both my parents more. My dad never said anything bad about my mom. I noticed that and I admired that. I love my mother, but she can be petty and mean. I know she felt hurt when my father divorced her and she has a right to her feelings. But my father never left *me*."

"Sounds like the two of you have a mutual admiration society."

"Yeah, well, I don't apologize for having a good relationship with my dad. So, how can I help?"

"I'm not sure you can, really. There are a couple of things… Judy called you the night of the murder."

"As a matter of fact she woke me up."

"What did she say?"

"Nothing much. She said she wanted to take me to lunch the next day. She said she had something important she wanted to talk to me about."

"Did she say what it was?"

"No. Her idea of something important was planning a surprise birthday party for my dad or introducing me to someone who might be able to help me with my business. We went to lunch probably once a month."

"Did she usually call at one in the morning and ask you to lunch?"

"To be honest," said Nathan with a slight grin, "it wasn't that unusual. Judy and my dad drank a lot. They know I stay up late. So sometimes they'd get loaded and call me. No big deal."

"Your dad also called that night."

"Yeah… He was pretty rattled. He wanted to tell me that Judy had been murdered. He didn't want me to hear it from anyone else."

"Did you ask how he knew she was dead?"

"No. I figured if he was so sure, there wasn't much point in me pressing the issue. He was crying. He was hysterical. I'd never heard him that way. It scared me. I told him I was coming over right away, but he said no. He said he would handle it himself. I tried to talk him out of it—I really felt he needed me there. But he was adamant and said that he would call me after the police left and I could come over then."

"Do you remember exactly what he said that night?"

"Like I said, he was hysterical at first. He kept saying over and over again that Judy'd been murdered. The rest was kind of unintelligible. I told him to call 911 but he said she was already dead. I told him to call the police."

"And a lawyer?"

"Yes. And obviously he called you. I'm glad he did." Nathan withdrew a card and handed it to Sawyer. "Call me anytime. My cell's on the back."

Both men stood and walked out of the coffee shop. Nathan shook Sawyer's hand and walked back to his kayak store.

Sawyer didn't have a son. But he was thinking that if he did he could have done worse than to have a kid like Nathan.

Chapter Fifty-four

Hank Simpson, the detective Wright hired to follow Judy several months ago, was listed in the Yellow Pages under Private Investigator. Sawyer wrote down the address but decided not to call ahead. He knew that private detectives often worked odd hours and that during the holidays business was brisk.

The two-story office building was a couple of blocks down from the Torrance Hospital and housed mostly medical doctors and dentists. Sawyer checked the directory downstairs, saw 202 after Simpson's name, and took the stairs.

The nameplate next to door 202 was empty. He knocked. No one answered. He tried the knob. The door was locked. Just then the elevator opened and a woman carrying a briefcase and a cup of coffee headed his way.

"Excuse me," said Sawyer.

"Yes?" said the woman pleasantly.

"I'm looking for Mr. Simpson."

"Oh, he moved."

"Really? When?"

"Recently. Last week, I think."

"You know where he moved?"

She smiled. "Sorry, no."

"Did you know Mr. Simpson?"

"Not well. But yes, we talked a few times. He was very...'social,' if you know what I mean."

"*Too* social?"

"Let's just say he seemed to enjoy his liquid lunches—oh, I shouldn't have said that."

"No, that's okay. I know Hank from way back," lied Sawyer. "He likes to drink."

"And when he drank, he liked to talk. He seemed to have a lot of spare time on his hands. He said most of his detective work was done at night."

"People do seem to get in more trouble after the sun goes down," said Sawyer amiably. "Before he moved, did he say anything about where he might be going?"

"No. Frankly, I didn't see as much of him the past couple of weeks as usual. He must've been busy."

"You don't happen to know where Mr. Simpson lives, do you?"

"Heavens no." The woman looked at her watch, almost spilling her coffee, and said, "I don't mean to be rude but I've got a patient coming by in ten minutes. I'm a psychologist. The holidays are tough for a lot of people," she said.

"Of course."

Outside in the car Sawyer called Eric Gregg. He wasn't in, but Sawyer left a message and asked him to look up the address for a local PI named Hank Simpson—information didn't have his home phone number or address.

On the way home Veronica called. She asked if Sawyer was free for dinner. He said he had a meeting. He didn't mention that the meeting was with his wife.

As Sawyer drove to Restaurant Christine the question that kept coming back to him was—*Should I tell Rebecca that I had sex with Veronica?*

If he were to "confess" to Rebecca, who would be helped? A wise man had once told Sawyer, "If you want to confess, talk to a priest." Spouses weren't wired for that.

Why should I tell Rebecca about Veronica? She had sex with another man and...my actions were only in response to her actions. Was that true? He thought about that for a moment. Was the only reason he had sex with Veronica because Rebecca had had sex with someone else?

That wasn't the *only* reason, but it *was* the determining one.

Sawyer pulled into the Hillside Village Shopping Center and parked in the underground parking lot.

Restaurant Christine was always worth the price of admission. Sawyer knew that he could go there seven nights a week and get something different and wonderful every night. This was the restaurant he and Rebecca went to for celebrations and special occasions. Tonight was not a celebration. But it was, if not a special occasion, certainly a unique one.

Sawyer checked in with the *Maitre de* and was seated at a booth. He waved to Christine, who was cooking in the kitchen, which was open and visible to patrons. She waved back and smiled.

Sawyer heard the door open. He looked up as Rebecca walked in. She walked over to the booth and sat opposite him.

"Hi," she said.

"Hi."

It was awkward for them both.

"I'm not sure I've got any small talk that's gonna fit," said Sawyer.

Rebecca smiled. "Yeah, I know."

After another awkward silence Sawyer realized that someone had to start. "You called. I imagine there's something you want to say."

"Yes. But I don't know exactly what to say about...the other night."

"You could say you're sorry."

"I'm not. I don't mean to sound callous or cruel. I'm just not sorry. This...this thing that happened is no great love affair. I'm not leaving you for him. It's just something that was...inevitable."

"Inevitable?" said Sawyer incredulously.

"I know that sounds stupid, but it's true. I needed someone."

"I needed someone to be faithful."

"Stop it. Being faithful is not a *goal*. If it were, then couples who can't have sex anymore—for any reason—have got to be the happiest people on earth. You and I can still have sex. I just wanted you to want to have sex with *me*."

"I wasn't out fucking around behind your back."

Rebecca didn't take the bait. "It's not enough to not have sex with someone else. I wanted you to *want* to have sex with *me*."

"Just because you want something, doesn't mean something's missing."

A waitress appeared. Sawyer ordered a bottle of Rombauer Merlot. After the wine had been poured and the waitress had gone, Sawyer said, "I guess the real question is: Where do we go from here?"

"I know."

"You called this meeting."

They both sipped their wine, but neither said a word.

"I still love you," said Rebecca finally.

"What does that mean?"

"I don't know."

"I need to know," said Sawyer. "Do you love me like a friend? Do you love me like my wife? Or do you just feel sorry for me because I walked in on you?"

"I certainly don't feel sorry for you."

"What do you want to happen now? You've got my attention." As soon as the words were out of his mouth, he regretted them. If this were a strategy on her part, or if she had wanted absolution from him, he had just given it to her.

"I don't know what I want. But..." She held up her hand, knowing that was not an acceptable answer and that she would have to bring something to the table. "But I would like to find out if there's anything left in our marriage worth salvaging before we throw it away."

"A lot of things have happened that we can't ignore."

"I don't want to ignore them. Things have to change." Rebecca paused. "Do you realize I'm making an effort here?"

"Do you realize what kind of 'effort' it takes for me to sit across the table from you with those...images playing in my head?"

"I can't erase the past, Sawyer, or apologize it away. It is what it is. If you're interested in trying to work through this, I'm interested. I loved you. I *still* love you. But it takes two to make a marriage work, and if you didn't realize there have been serious problems in our relationship for some time, then you just weren't paying attention."

"What do you want from me?"

"I want to know if you're willing to try to work things out."

"And if I'm not? You're going to go live with your...your 'contractor'?"

"The 'contractor' and I have no future. I never thought we did. But we filled an empty space for each other. For a brief time. I want to know if you want to work things out because I'm fifty years old, not ninety. I think I've still got a third act. I want that. I want that with you. But if you don't, then I need to know so I can make other plans."

"Sounds like a threat."

"Sawyer," said Rebecca, pausing and looking him directly in the eye, "it's the exact opposite. I'm not threatening you. I want you. I love you. If you want to work on our relationship, our marriage, then I'll give it everything I've got. But if you're not willing to try, there's nothing I can do to make it work by myself."

Sawyer processed Rebecca's words. He was now more confused than when he arrived. Did he want Rebecca or did he want Veronica? Or did he just want to be alone for a while? He had loved both women at different times. He knew Veronica wanted him and was willing to fight for him. Now his wife clearly stated that she was willing to work things out...if he wanted to.

"I don't know how I feel anymore, Rebecca. What happened was not some 'theoretical' situation. It hurt me. It hurt me deeply. And it changes things. I look at you and I'm thinking wouldn't it be great if things were back to normal. But you're telling me that normal was the thing that drove you away. I don't know... You can't un-ring a bell."

"I know that. I guess my only point—the reason I phoned you—is that I want to try to save our marriage. I know you're hurt. And if you're so hurt that you can never forgive me, then I need to know that so I can move on."

"You're very narcissistic, you know that?"

"What do you mean?"

"It's all about you. You feel hurt. You feel wronged. You go out and sleep with some guy. And then you come to me and give me this ultimatum that if I can't get over your betrayal quick enough, then you're going to move on. Do you *really* give a damn about how I feel?"

"Calm down," said Rebecca, looking around to make sure that no one was watching them.

"I *am* calm," said Sawyer, but even *he* knew he wasn't.

"I don't need an answer tonight. I just wanted you to know that I'm interested in salvaging our marriage. If you're interested in that too, then we have something to talk about. If you're too hurt, and you can never forgive me, then it really is over. I don't want it to be over, Sawyer," said Rebecca, touching her husband's hand for the first time, picking it up and squeezing it. "I want our marriage to succeed." She paused, still holding his hand in hers, and said, "I'm sorry. Is that what you want me to say?"

"I guess."

The message had been delivered. There was really nothing more to say.

"So, what now?" he said finally.

"I won't say it's all up to you, but a lot of it is. I guess I'll wait to hear from you."

Sawyer took a sip—and then another sip—of his wine and said nothing. In an odd way he felt as though he deserved a moment of non-clarity. His moment to behave badly.

Sawyer was home by nine. As always, his answering machine was blinking when he walked into his office. He hit a button and the messages played. Nothing urgent.

Veronica had called. She said something nice, kind of romantic, kind of sexual—the kind of message she would not have left before last night.

Yesterday his marriage was over. Today Rebecca wanted to make their relationship work.

And Veronica wanted to make *their* relationship work.

Sawyer didn't blame Veronica because she had played by the rules.

He didn't even blame Rebecca... Because he never allowed himself to blame her for anything. Nor did she.

The phone rang. Sawyer saw Noah St. James' name on the Caller ID. "Good evening."

"Hi, Sawyer. Did you speak with Nathan?"

"Yes."

"What did he say about Justin's phone call?"

"He said Justin was really rattled when he called, and that he just wanted Nathan to find out about Judy's murder from him. Did you ask Justin what he said to Nathan?"

"I haven't pressed the issue. Maybe you can bring it up the next time you two talk."

"I will."

"Look, it's not outside the realm of possibility that Justin could be arrested soon. The DA's under a lot of pressure and, even though they don't have anything close to a smoking gun, they've got enough circumstantial evidence to cover their asses even if they have to cut him loose later. It's not my job to solve the case, but I'd sure as hell like to put the media onto another scent. They all seem to be calling for Justin's head. If they had some reasonable doubt, some other suspects, they might stop putting so much pressure on the DA."

"I'm working on it and I'll keep you posted."

"Okay. Talk with you tomorrow."

Sawyer hung up and poured himself a shot of Grey Goose over ice. He opened the Shanghai Tang humidor he kept on top of the half-refrigerator in his office, withdrew a Partagas 160, lighted it, picked up his vodka and went out to the pond.

He didn't smoke cigars regularly. Surprisingly, Rebecca did not object. Of course, she would never allow him to smoke in the house, but she didn't mind him smoking outside. Usually he smoked by the pond in the summer. This time of year it was usually too cold for that. It was chilly tonight, but he didn't care. He petted the fish, then sat on a bench next to the pond, setting his glass on the bench next to him.

As he smoked, he thought. About Rebecca. About Veronica. About Justin and Judy. About his own life.

He thought about calling Veronica, but he didn't know what to say. He didn't know how he felt. He hadn't known exactly how he felt last night when they were in each other's arms. Tonight, after dinner with his wife, he was even less certain how he felt. About either woman.

He finished his cigar and his vodka and went to bed.

Alone.

Chapter Fifty-five

Sawyer awoke around seven, showered, shaved and dosed himself with a cup of coffee. The phone rang and he answered it.

"I've got that information for you," said Eric Gregg.

Sawyer wrote down's Simpson's phone number and home address, thanked his ex-partner, got dressed and hit the road.

Simpson lived in a bungalow on Anza between Pacific Coast Highway and Sepulveda, about two miles from his office. There was no garage and a gray late model Crown Victoria was parked in the driveway. Sawyer parked, walked up the front sidewalk and rang the doorbell. No answer.

"He's not home."

Sawyer turned and saw a Japanese man in boots, a sun hat, overalls, and a sweatshirt with the picture of a cruise ship on the front. He looked to be in his late fifties or early sixties. Sawyer walked over to the man, who was sitting on a garden stool planting agapanthus.

"He hasn't been home for a few days. I'm not sure exactly how many days. His newspapers haven't been picked up for a while. I pick them up and put them in the trash. Don't want people to think you're not home. We do that for each other— look out for each other when we travel."

"That's nice."

"Burglars look for houses where newspapers are left out for more than a day. Did you know that?"

"I heard that," said Sawyer. The man wanted to talk. And Sawyer wanted to encourage him.

"That's what Hank said. He used to be a cop. Private investigator now. He should know about such things. Nice having a cop as a neighbor."

"Yeah, I'll bet. You know how I can reach Hank?"

"No. He didn't tell me he was leaving. Which is odd. We usually tell each other if we're going to be gone for more than a night or two."

"Sounds like you and Hank are good friends."

"I wouldn't say 'good' friends. More than just acquaintances, though. Somewhere in between. I mean, he doesn't confide in me. But we watch a ballgame together now and then. At my place because I have a big screen TV. But he always brings the booze," said the man with a smile.

"Hank ever talk to you about the cases he was working on?"

"Well, not really..."

"Hey, he's not a cop anymore. He can tell his friends whatever he wants about his cases," said Sawyer, trying to make the man feel as though he wasn't betraying his neighbor's trust.

"Sometimes. Nothing confidential. Just general stuff mainly."

"He tell you anything about what he was working on lately?"

"Well..." Suddenly the man said, "Who are you? Maybe I shouldn't be talking to you."

Sawyer smiled amiably. "My name's Sawyer Black. I used to be a homicide detective. Now I write books." It was a calculated risk and he took it. The man wouldn't give him anything else unless he identified himself.

The man's face brightened. "Oh yeah, I know you." He leaned forward conspiratorially. "You thinking of putting Hank in your next book?"

"Something like that. Hank's a very colorful character."

"You can say that again."

"You were saying something about Hank's most recent case..."

"He was very excited about it. Said it was the biggest case he'd ever worked. 'Time to cash out,' he said. I don't know what he meant by that, but he really thought this was 'the big one.' He said he might retire after this case and buy a place somewhere in North Carolina—he's got family there."

"Did he give you any indication at all, even a hint, as to who was involved in this 'big' case or who his client was?"

"No. Hank would never betray a client. All I got from his conversation was that the client was rich and the payoff was big."

"When was the last time you spoke with Hank?"

"Few days ago. I'm not sure exactly."

"How did he seem?"

The man thought about that for a moment and said, "He seemed a little nervous, actually. Not down or depressed, but a little…like I say, nervous."

The two men chatted a few minutes longer, but Sawyer got nothing more.

From his car, Sawyer called Justin and told him he was coming over. Justin said he didn't have time just then.

Sawyer told him to *make* time and hung up.

Chapter Fifty-six

Justin offered Sawyer a Bookers but Sawyer turned it down.
"Tell me about Simpson."

Wright poured himself a half-glass of bourbon on the rocks. Sawyer could see it was not his first of the morning.

"This isn't easy."

"Unless you answer my questions right now, it's going to get a lot harder, Justin."

"Simpson was blackmailing me. As you know I hired him to see if Judy was seeing someone." Wright paused and sipped his drink. "I need to tell you a few other things first. When Judy and I got married one of the conditions in the pre-nup was that I agree to never hire a detective to spy on her or monitor her behavior again. If I did and she caught me, then she had the right to walk away with ten million dollars and there would be nothing I could do about it."

"What if the detective actually discovered she was cheating?"

"Then she gets nothing."

"How does that work? You've been married for fourteen years and you've been making money since then. Isn't she entitled to half of what you've made since you've been married?"

"My lawyers worked it out. Everything I own is in various trusts. Even the dividend income I make on my investments goes directly into those trusts. I have lots of money I made *before* I married Judy and access to a couple of billion dollars if I ever wanted it, but a couple of Century City lawyers spent nearly a million dollars of my money setting up a portfolio of trusts that essentially protect me from Judy's infidelity. As long as she stayed with me, or survived my death, she would live like a queen. But if she ever left me, or cheated on me, then she would leave our marriage with just a little more money than she came in with. As you can see, my worst case scenario was if she discovered I hired a detective to spy on her, when she really wasn't cheating, then having her find out about it."

"Why did you agree to this?"

"You've got to remember, I was about sixty at the time we got married. I interpreted Judy's 'indiscretion' as an act of frustration because I'd told her for years that I would divorce Natasha and did not.

"At the time, she said she was stunned and disappointed in me for having her followed, and that she didn't want to live her life looking over her shoulder trying to appease a jealous husband.

"When I saw those pictures of her with another man, the only thing I could think of was that I didn't want to lose her. Ever.

"So the next day I told Natasha I wanted a divorce and I started proceedings the following week. Judy could have put almost anything in the pre-nup and I would have agreed."

"But you hired Simpson in spite of the fact that Judy might find out and the whole fiasco might end up costing you ten million dollars. And your marriage."

"Ten million dollars to me is pretty meaningless compared to knowing the answer to a question that kept me up night after night. I had to know."

"And if you were wrong, and she found out, she could divorce you and walk away with ten million dollars. You ever think she might be setting you up?"

"I simply couldn't stand not knowing anymore. It was driving me crazy."

"But Simpson found nothing."

"That's what he told me. And I paid him. But then he found out about the pre-nup."

"How?"

"I'm embarrassed to tell you this, but I told him. It didn't occur to me that he would use it against me. I told him in confidence because I wanted him to know that it was crucial to tell no one that I hired him. I didn't want him to get careless and have Judy spot him."

"What exactly did he say?"

"He called me about a week after he finished the job and told me that it would be in my best interest to give him a 'bonus.' He never used the word blackmail, but I knew what he meant. I tried to put him off but he kept pressuring me. Then Judy was murdered and he gave me an ultimatum. Either I give him one million dollars in cash or he would go to the media and tell them that I hired him to follow Judy shortly before she was murdered."

"What did you do?"

"I converted some funds to cash, put the money in a large duffel bag and followed his instructions. Which were to take my boat, alone, to Catalina, walk to the High Hat Grill, go around back and put the money in a green dumpster. He said he would be at the bar, sitting at a booth looking out on the marina so he could watch me. He told me not to acknowledge him, and that he would not acknowledge me. He said that after I made the drop he would immediately pick up the bag. If the money was in there, I'd never see him again. If it wasn't, or if I didn't show, then his next call would be to the media."

"And you haven't heard from or seen Simpson since?"

"No, and I hope to never see him again. It was a tough decision, Sawyer. On the one hand, he didn't have a single piece of evidence that indicated I'd murdered Judy—how could he, because I didn't," said Wright emphatically. "On the other hand, I've seen what the press does with minor details of my life. They add two plus two and come up with twenty-one. If they found out I was having Judy followed... Well, it was worth the money. Even though he might be back. If that happens, I'll deal with it then. Frankly, I was very surprised because I'd used Hank a couple of times before and he'd always been straight with me. I guess for some people certain opportunities are just too tempting to pass up."

"Okay. Next subject... What did you say to Nathan the night of the murder?"

"Sorry?" said Wright.

Sawyer knew that was what some people said when they wanted time to think about their answer. "The night of the murder you called Nathan on your cell phone. What did you say?"

"I don't know… I was pretty out of it. I wasn't thinking clearly."

"You were thinking clearly enough to call me. You were thinking well enough to call Noah. Apparently the only thing you did that wasn't clear and logical was call your son."

"His mother was dead."

"I thought you said he never really thought of Judy that way."

"He didn't. Not in…*that* way. But she was his stepmother and they'd known each other for ten years. I knew they were close enough so that he would be affected by her death. By her *murder*. I didn't want him waking up and hearing about it on the news or having one of his friends calling him and telling him about it. I thought it should come from me."

"That's it?"

"That's it. I just wanted him to hear the news from me."

"Okay, let's move on. What can you tell me about Judy's spending habits?" Sawyer knew from experience that changing the subject unexpectedly sometimes elicited the most honest answers. It caught people off guard.

Wright smiled. It was the first time Sawyer had seen the man smile in some time. "She liked to spend. I've got her credit card receipts and summaries somewhere. Why?"

"What about cash? Did you give her cash?"

"One thousand dollars a week."

"That's a lot of cash to spend per week—on top of credit card purchases—isn't it?"

"Obviously you don't hang out with people like Judy. She could spend a thousand dollars in an afternoon. On lunch with friends, tips, a top she saw while walking past a shop window."

"And you didn't mind?"

"As long as she was loyal to me she had access to hundreds of millions if she wanted it. All she had to do was ask. She had credit cards without limits. One thousand a week cash seemed like nothing, really. And I didn't keep track of it because none of it could be written off and the most it could cost me was fifty-two thousand dollars a year. Like I said, Judy liked her privacy and cash left no paper trail. The important thing was that it made her happy."

Sawyer knew that money didn't *make* anyone happy. He had seen enough life to know that true happiness came from something you couldn't hold in your hand. He knew lots of unhappy people with lots of money. Their wealth simply provided them with more expensive ways to make themselves unhappy. Or worse.

"I'd like to take a look at Judy's financial records for the last year."

"What do you need?"

"Bank statements, credit card statements."

"What are you looking for?"

"I'm not sure. Patterns mainly. Not so much a smoking gun, but a pattern that might provide a glimpse into a part of her life I'm not seeing now. How did she get her one thousand dollars a week?"

"She wrote a check for 'cash' at the local bank, I think. She might have gotten it from ATM machines using her debit card. Our agreement simply was one thousand a week cash, no more. I'm not exactly sure about the mechanics of how she got the money. Let me get you the records."

Wright left the room, returned a few minutes later and handed a file to Sawyer. "That's all her credit card receipts and bank statements for the last year or so."

"Okay," said Sawyer. "I'll look into this and call you. If you hear from Simpson, call me right away."

"I hope I don't, but if I do I'll call you," said Wright and he walked Sawyer to the door.

As Sawyer pulled away from Wright's estate, he had the distinct feeling he would not be speaking to Hank Simpson anytime soon.

Chapter Fifty-seven

Natasha's house was only about two miles away from her ex-husband's—no one on the Hill lived far from anyone else. Sawyer hadn't seen her in a year or two and the last time he saw her they got along rather well. She liked to flirt with men. She also considered herself superior to everyone she met because of her Ivy League schooling—Harvard—and the fact that she had more money than anyone she met—besides her husband, who, since the divorce only had half as much as he used to have.

Sawyer pulled up to the speaker outside the entrance gate and pressed the button. A man's voice said, "Yes?"

"Sawyer Black. I'm here to see Natasha," he said into the microphone/speaker, as though he were ordering a burger and fries.

About thirty seconds passed and then a heavy green wrought iron gate slid open and Sawyer drove his car inside the gates, parked, got out and headed for the front door.

Natasha opened the door and greeted him. "Sawyer," she said, effusively. "How nice to see you. Won't you come in?"

"Thanks," he said and followed her inside.

The foyer, which was three stories high, opened onto a circular staircase that wound to the second and third stories. The first floor entranceway was all white marble and it shimmered from the sunlight coming in from the backyard, which was dominated by a large pool overlooking the Pacific. In the distance, Sawyer saw the two-story bungalow Nathan still used as a second home.

Sawyer followed Natasha out to a cabana next to the pool and they sat in chairs facing the ocean. The woman of the house was tall, just under six feet. She was blonde and her face had been surgically sculpted to preserve naturally high cheekbones and a delicate nose. Sawyer had seen pictures of her when Justin married her. She was a natural beauty. But even natural beauties needed help keeping up after forty-five. Natasha was in her early sixties and she could still stop traffic in her tennis dress.

She tapped her glass, which was almost empty and a man dressed in white shorts, shirt, shoes and socks suddenly appeared. "Can I get you something to drink, sir?"

"Pimm's Cup," said Sawyer, certain that even Natasha's well-stocked bar would not be able to accommodate that order.

"Would you like that with ginger beer and a cucumber, or just lemonade, sir?" said the man.

Despite himself, Sawyer was impressed. "Ginger beer and a cucumber. In a pewter mug," he added.

"Of course, sir," said the man and then he was gone.

"I love this place," said Natasha.

Sawyer wasn't certain whether she was talking about Palos Verdes or her home. He liked both. "Palos Verdes is one of the most beautiful places on earth."

"Whenever I come home from anywhere, I'm always glad I'm here."

"Me too."

"So, what brings you here, Sawyer?"

"Judy's murder."

"Ah, what a pity. I thought that now you were, well, on your own, that maybe this was a 'social' visit."

"This really *is* a small town."

"Big money makes a lot of things small."

Natasha's "man" delivered their drinks on a silver tray and put a napkin under each, then disappeared without saying a word.

"Did you order a Pimm's Cup because you wanted it or just because you didn't think I'd have it?" she said, with a wry smile.

"I love a Pimm's on a hot day," said Sawyer, not answering her question.

"So what do you want to know?"

"You seem to know everything about everyone—including what my wife's been up to. Who do you think killed Judy?"

Natasha didn't answer immediately. She sipped her drink and finally said, "I don't know."

"You can do better than that. I'm sure you've speculated on it dozens of times over the past few days. Everyone has."

"I have."

"And?"

"I still don't know."

"You don't even have a guess?"

"Not really."

"You gotta remember, Natasha, I used to be a cop. And a damned good one. I know you're lying."

She laughed. She didn't intimidate easily.

"So, I'm thinking, who are you protecting?"

"Protecting? Come on, Sawyer. I'm not protecting anyone. I don't know who killed Judy. You're a professional and even you don't know. What the hell do I know? I'm a witness to nothing...except the complete moral collapse of a man I once admired."

"You might be protecting Nathan."

Natasha laughed out loud. "Nathan? You've got to be seriously delusional if you think my son killed Judy."

"I know you're not protecting Justin."

"That's true," she said, taking another pull on her clear liquid drink. "The fact is, I really don't know who killed Judy. But you're right, of course. I have speculated with friends. It seems to be the parlor game everyone's playing. And you know what? Justin's name keeps coming up. I mean, who else would want Judy dead?"

"I don't think Justin did it."

"I know that, Sawyer. I think you're an honorable man. I just think you don't know my ex-husband as well as I do."

"Why didn't you just say you think Justin did it?"

"Is that what you want to hear? I don't think so. You came over here to get some kind of different angle. Something to get the vultures off Justin's back. But I'm afraid you came to the wrong place because, yes, I think he did it."

"You're wrong—I didn't come over here to get a different angle. I came here to get the truth. To flesh out a few details about Justin, Nathan and Judy."

"Like what?"

"How did Nathan handle the divorce? I mean, really."

"Not well. He knew Justin and I split up because of Judy. There wasn't even a decent attempt to cover it up. Which, of course, was humiliating to me. Nathan's perception of his father changed after the divorce. Before, Justin could do no wrong. After, Nathan saw his father's flaws up close and all too personally."

"And you reinforced that perception."

"Yes," said Natasha. "I imagine you expected me to say no. I reinforced that perception because it was true. Justin and I built a life—not from nothing, but not from great wealth. Together we built an empire. Together! And when he decided he wanted a younger model in his bed, he not only traded me in, he humiliated me. Simple as that. If he's in trouble now, it's his own fault."

Sawyer was a little surprised by Natasha's candor. It was clear that she was used to speaking her mind and not being challenged. And not caring if she was.

"I'm a realist, Sawyer. I know people look at me as some kind of parasite who lives on her rich husband's money. I would be as happy as a clam if Justin and I were still married and living in our old house. I loved the bastard. I imagine a therapist might accuse me of still loving him. But I hate him even more."

"Tell me about Nathan," said Sawyer.

"He was a wonderful child. Justin and I had tried to have children for so long… When Nathan came into our lives, it changed everything for the better."

"Nathan was adopted?"

"It's not an affliction, Sawyer."

"I just thought…"

"There was no reason for us to tell everyone we met. Our close friends knew, of course, and we never tried to keep it a secret."

"Does Nathan know?"

"I'm not completely sure. The fact is, he never asked and we never told him. Justin and I talked about telling him and decided we would tell him when he was eighteen. But Nathan was only ten when we were divorced. After we split up, I didn't tell Nathan because Justin had already left me, and I didn't want Nathan leaving me for 'another woman' someday as well."

"What do you mean?"

"You never know how a person will react when he finds out he's adopted. He might have wanted to contact his birth mother. I know it might sound selfish, but I just didn't want to go through that. I suppose I'll tell him someday. When the time is right."

"So he doesn't know."

"Like I said, our friends knew because I obviously wasn't pregnant and then Nathan appeared. We never asked anyone not to say anything. If Nathan knows, he's never said anything to me about it." Natasha took a sip of her drink, set it down and said, "What in the hell does that have to do with Judy's murder?"

"Probably nothing. Like I said, I'm just trying to fill in some holes about Justin, Nathan, Judy and you."

"Well, maybe you better fill them in somewhere else." Natasha stood, indicating that Sawyer was being dismissed.

Sawyer stood. "I understand that Judy and Nathan were here at the same time a few weeks ago when you were having a party. I hear it got pretty wild."

"That's true. It did get a little out of hand. I don't usually have those kinds of parties."

"And I believe you."

"Don't condescend to me, Sawyer. Nobody looks down on me. Not Justin and sure as hell not you."

Sawyer couldn't tell how much of Natasha's bravado was righteous indignation or booze, but he kept going anyhow. "I understand that your son's car and Judy's car were the last two to leave."

"What are you implying?"

"I'm just stating a fact. Maybe you can tell me what it means."

"You should have your mind laundered. My son stays in the back house several nights every month. He rarely tells me when he's coming and he sometimes leaves without saying anything to me. He has a private entrance and doesn't need to come through the main house. He usually comes here to be alone.

"As far as Judy's concerned, we talked that night until everyone was gone. It was a real heart-to-heart. I doubt seriously if she ever even saw Nathan."

"Did you get together often with your ex-husband's wife?"

"We're done here," she said and started walking back inside the main house. Suddenly the man who had served the drinks appeared and stood behind Sawyer, as though herding him toward the front door and out of the house.

When they reached the front door, the man opened it and smiled at Sawyer. As the door closed Sawyer heard Natasha say, "Give my best to your wife." The door closed with a thud.

Sawyer got back in his car, pulled up to the exit gate, which opened after a few seconds, and drove home.

Chapter Fifty-eight

When he walked in he checked his answering machine and there were messages from Veronica, who wanted to have dinner with him; Rebecca, who wanted to have dinner with him; and Zona Day, who said she'd found a photograph of the guy Judy was dating just before she married Justin…and that she was free for dinner.

Sawyer walked out to the pond, took off his shoes and socks, put his feet in the water, and petted the fish as they swam between his ankles. He thought about what Natasha told him. Why was she having a heart-to-heart with Judy, a woman she supposedly despised? How, if at all, did the fact that Nathan was adopted play into things?

Sawyer's oddest feeling was that he actually liked Natasha. She was tough, no doubt about it. No-nonsense. Her husband had betrayed her and she made no bones about the fact that she hated him and would make him pay. She didn't like the replacement trophy wife but apparently had made some kind of peace with her. Sawyer would have liked to have known what the two women had talked about that night. But only two people knew. One was dead and the other knew how to keep a secret.

Sawyer finished his drink, gave a little extra fish food to Ace Junior and walked inside.

He had lots of choices for dinner plans. Too many. He decided not to call anyone back. Except Zona Day.

"Hi Zona. Sawyer here."

"Hi. You got my message."

"Yeah. I'm not free for dinner, but I'd be happy to treat you to a late lunch."

"You're on."

"Misto Caffe, thirty minutes."

"See you there."

Sawyer took a ten-minute power nap, splashed some water on his face, and left for lunch.

Misto Caffe and Bakery was located in the Hillside Village Shopping Center, which also was home to Restaurant Christine. Misto was perfect for lunch, but Sawyer and Rebecca had gone there for dinner several months earlier and Rebecca had raved about their rack of lamb.

Sawyer arrived first and ordered a Blackstone Merlot. Zona Day arrived as his wine was being served and sat down opposite him next to a window in the bakery section of the restaurant. She wore a light green top, low cut to show off, among other things, her spray-on tan. Her white slacks were tight enough so that Sawyer could tell she wore no underwear. A short white jacket tied the outfit together.

"Busy, busy, busy..." she said as she sat down. The waiter came to the table and she told him she would have what the "gentleman" was having.

Sawyer liked *old school*. Partly because he was old enough to remember the rules.

They made small talk until the waiter had delivered her wine. She sipped and said, "Now, that's better." She opened her purse, took out a photograph and handed it to Sawyer. "That's the guy," she said. "That was taken at a Fourth of July party. He and Judy made a nice couple."

Sawyer looked at the photo, which was slightly out of focus. The man had shoulder-length hair and a goatee.

"He sure *looks* like a musician, doesn't he?" said Zona.

"Yes, he does. He looks like every musician I've ever met." Sawyer mentally tried to take away some of the hair and add a few pounds.

"You still can't remember his name?"

"No, like I said, it was one of those one-name kind of things. It came off as a little pretentious, but what the hell... Judy said he was great in bed."

"She said that?"

Zona smiled. "Not in those exact words, but yes, that's what she meant." She sipped her merlot, then said, "So, what did Natasha have to say?"

Sawyer looked at her, surprised.

"Don't worry, I'm not stalking you. I was showing a house down the block from Natasha's place and I saw you drive out the gate."

"I just wanted to clarify a few details. No revelations."

"You wouldn't tell me anyhow, now would you?"

"No."

Zona smiled. "I like that in a man—honesty. Rare these days."

"You said that picture was taken the Fourth of July. What year?"

"The year before Judy married Justin. I know because I'd just met the guy and then he was gone. And then Judy finally married Justin...after all those years. So I guess it was the summer of 1993 because they got married in 1994."

"Is there anything, anything at all you can tell me about this guy?"

"Like I said, he was there and then he was gone. It happened so quickly. Although, it struck me at the time that they didn't seem like 'brand new' lovers."

"What do you mean?"

"You know how it is when you first get together with someone. You go through stages. There's this intense infatuation, then it starts to cool down over time. I could tell Judy and this guy really loved each other, but it seemed a lot like stage two or three, not just something that had begun a few weeks before. They seemed comfortable together."

"Could she have had a relationship with this guy for a long time without you knowing it?"

"That's possible. Frankly, it would have been like Judy to hide something like that from me. She was an intensely private person. The bottom line is that if Judy really did have a long-term relationship with this guy—or any guy—I never knew about it."

"You two were roommates in the mid eighties... What was that like?"

"It was one big party—sometimes we'd go without seeing each other for a week or two at a time. I was very...social. But Justin tried to monopolize as much of Judy's time as he could. In fact, one summer he took her to Europe with him when he opened the Paris office of his company. I was envious as hell. She said he set her up in a beautiful apartment in Paris and they dined in cafes every night, strolled along the Seine, and went to museums. She didn't come back till the following spring. If it were me, I might never have come back."

"Sounds very romantic. Can I keep this?" said Sawyer, tapping the photograph.

"Sure. I don't need it. I wouldn't mind getting it back, though. Maybe you can take me to dinner sometime and we'll call it even."

"Sounds fair," said Sawyer. "I'll make a copy and give you back the original. Where was this taken?"

"On somebody's boat in the Redondo Beach Marina. Actually, I think the guy who owned the boat was a friend of the guy who Judy was with."

"Is this the only picture of that afternoon?"

"No, I've got about another half a roll with pictures of that afternoon. But that's the best picture of the guy."

"The other pictures are on the boat?"

"Most of them, why?"

"Could I see them?"

"Sure. I just searched through a whole box of old photos this morning. The pictures from that afternoon are all together now, right on top."

"Can I come over to your house and see them?"

"I thought you'd never ask," said Zona.

Sawyer and Zona finished their lunch and made small talk, but Sawyer's mind was on the photograph and the others at her house. He paid the check and they were at her house ten minutes later.

"Quite a place," said Sawyer. It was a one-story ranch style home. He estimated it to be about three thousand square feet. She had the obligatory cat, but she also had a beagle whose sad eyes made Sawyer want to give the little guy a pat. Which he did.

"Forgive the mess," said Zona as she disappeared into a room off the living room, where she left Sawyer. Standing in the living room hed could see the ocean. He wasn't looking over a cliff and it wasn't "beachfront," but it was an unobstructed view of the "Queen's Necklace." He knew that on a clear evening the lights that made up the necklace sparkled all the way up the coastline as far as the eye could see.

"Here they are," said Zona as she came back into the room carrying an envelope of photos. She sat down on the sofa and Sawyer sat next to her. She handed him the envelope and he started flipping through the old photos. He was looking for one thing. He didn't find it. Not immediately. About halfway through the photos there was a photograph of two men he didn't recognize. They stood on the dock, each with a bottle of beer in his hand. Right next to the boat.

Which was named *Coltrane's Blues*. "Can I borrow this?"

"It's all yours. But you owe me. Big time."

"You know, you might be right."

Sawyer pocketed the second photo and left.

Before he was in his car he was on his cell to his ex-partner. "Eric, I need you to check something for me."

Chapter Fifty-nine

Coltrane's Blues was not an expensive yacht. It was about half the size of Justin Wright's boat. And it could be a dinghy for Robert Sanchez's yacht. But it was still afloat and looked seaworthy. And according to Eric Gregg, it had been registered to the same owner for the last twenty years.

Sawyer walked up the three steps to the *Coltrane's* deck and said, "Anyone here?"

An indistinct sound came from down below followed by, "I'll be right up."

After a moment, a gray-haired man wearing shorts and a faded Rolling Stones t-shirt appeared. "Can I help you?"

"Maybe. My name's Sawyer Black. I'm a friend of Justin Wright."

The name did something to the man, something that an unfamiliar name would not have done. But he said nothing.

"And you are?" said Sawyer, even though he already knew.

"Bob Mathers."

"Bob, I've got a picture here..." Sawyer withdrew the photograph of Judy and her boyfriend and handed it to the man. "That picture was taken on this boat."

"That was a long time ago."

"So you recognize it," Sawyer said. It was not a question.

The man sighed. He wasn't good at this—hiding things.

"Who is the man?"

Mathers studied the photograph as though he were searching it for a way out. Finally he shook his head. "Don't recognize the guy."

"Really..."

"Sorry," said Mathers, who handed Sawyer the photo as though it were something unclean.

"Because the person who took this photograph told me you were friends with this guy."

Again Mathers shook his head, but he could not bring himself to speak.

"Bob, you're not in trouble here. But I won't lie to you, this might be important. And if you lie to me, well... Then you could be putting yourself in a tough spot."

"Are you threatening me?"

"Absolutely not, Bob. I know you're not involved in any way with Judy's murder. The only way you could jam yourself up is to 'obstruct justice.'"

"You're not a cop."

"No Bob, I'm not. But I used to be one and a lot of my close friends are. I could get a bunch of them down here in about ten minutes and tear your boat apart. Everyone's got something to hide. You, me, the whole world. I'm not here to hassle you. I just want a name."

"It was a long time ago."

Sawyer took a leap. "Did they used to meet here?"

Mathers was silent. "They were in love. Really. I know it sounds stupid, but there wasn't anywhere else they could go without her boyfriend spying on her."

"I'm looking for a name and an address, Bob."

"I haven't seen the guy in years. That's the truth. I swear," said Mathers, trying his best to please. He had the feeling he was in trouble but he wasn't sure how hard it was going to land on him.

"The name?"

"Smith."

"And the first name?"

"That's it. I think he thought it was cool—having only one name. He used to do a song called 'Smith' about everyone being scared of who they really are."

Sawyer recalled Zona saying that the guy in the photo had only one name.

"But I haven't seen the guy in years."

"You look nervous, Bob."

"I'm not used to this kind of thing—being asked questions about someone who's been murdered."

"That's understandable," said Sawyer. "Thing is, Bob, I can't help but think that there's more you're not telling me. Not because you're guilty of anything, but because you think it might make things worse for you. But let me tell you something. As a person who's been around this track a million times, it's the thing you *don't* say that gets you in trouble." Sawyer knew that wasn't true, but it sounded like it could be.

"Smith and Judy..." he said, after a moment. "They had a long-term relationship. They used my boat to get together long before she got married and they even used it every once in a while till about a year ago."

Sawyer knew that was about the time Judy got her studio.

"They thought it was safe here."

"And they paid you...for your inconvenience," added Sawyer quickly.

"It really *was* an inconvenience."

"I can imagine."

"Sometimes they'd take the boat out all day. I had no place to go."

"Friends do for friends."

"Right."

"So, you were about to give me an address for Smith..."

"I was? I don't know where he lives. All I know is that he lives, or used to live, in the South Bay somewhere because he played at clubs down here and ate at restaurants nearby. I never went to his place. He never asked me."

"He ever give you a phone number?"

"No. I asked him for it once and he said it was unlisted and that he never gave it out."

"Doesn't seem fair, him using your boat—your home, actually—and him not even giving you his phone number."

"He was paranoid. It was a dangerous game he and Judy were playing. Justin Wright's a serious guy. Person can get themselves whacked for a few hundred dollars. Some rich guy finds out his wife is fucking some guy, people can get hurt."

"So why did you put yourself in the middle of this? Was it the money?"

"Not originally. In the beginning, I just liked Smith's music. I saw him in some club in Hermosa and I invited him back to the boat one night. He started coming around on weekends and we became friends. He'd bring his guitar and that attracted a lot of women walking by.

"Then he introduced me to Judy. She was beautiful, but I didn't know then about her connection to Justin Wright."

"How did you find out?"

"I suspected something early on because they were so secretive. I figured she was married. There was no ring on her finger, but I figured she took it off when she was with Smith. I never really knew about Justin Wright by name—until I saw the news about Judy's murder. I suspected she was married to somebody who scared them both. I mean, it was like a James Bond movie every time they showed up. They'd never show up together. On the days they'd get together, Smith would meet me for breakfast—he'd always buy—here at the marina. I'd take off for the day and he'd go back to my boat. Judy would come by later. I never knew exactly when."

"But you say they haven't been here for about a year."

"That's right."

"What changed?"

"I don't know. I just figured they had another setup that was easier for them. They never told me."

"When's the last time you saw them?"

"I haven't seen Judy for a few years—Smith would come by, get the keys, and then go to the boat by himself. I just assumed he was meeting Judy."

"The last time you saw Smith was…?"

"I saw him about six months ago at a club he used to play at. He wasn't performing; he was in the audience. We said hello and that was about it."

"The club?"

"The Windjammer in Hermosa," said Mathers. "Am I in trouble?"

"I don't know. I'll keep you posted," said Sawyer and left.

On his way home he called Justin Wright and told him to meet him at the Windjammer at five o'clock.

At home Sawyer logged on to the Internet and went to Justin Wright's company site. He searched for about five minutes and didn't find...exactly what he thought he wouldn't find.

Sawyer unplugged the phone in his bedroom and set the alarm for four o'clock. In five minutes he was dreaming about sailing a yacht down the Seine toward the Eiffel Tower. There was a woman with him. When he awoke he couldn't remember who she was.

Chapter Sixty

The Windjammer had seen better days, but in dim light its age didn't show. Sawyer had heard of the club, which had been around since the seventies and played host to many blues and folk-rock performers, many of whom had autographed photographs on the walls.

"What can I get ya?" said a waitress who wore jeans, high-heeled shoes and a tank top that stopped about three inches above a tattoo that started at her navel and ended someplace Sawyer could only imagine.

He ordered a Grey Goose on the rocks.

Justin Wright arrived as Sawyer was finishing his drink and the two men ordered Grey Goose martinis and a plate of onion rings. When the drinks were delivered, Sawyer and Wright clinked glasses and sipped their martinis. In the background a guy with long hair and a muscle shirt was singing Dave Mason's "Feelin' Alright."

"You said we needed to talk," said Wright.

"Your company doesn't have offices in Paris, does it?"

"No. Why? Is that important?"

"Never did, right?"

"No. What are you talking about?"

"How old is Nathan?"

"What does that—"

"How old?" said Sawyer, cutting him off. He wasn't in the mood.

"Twenty-two."

"Does Natasha know that the child she adopted was Judy's baby?"

Wright's face did some emotional gymnastics. In an instant he donned masks of indignation, denial and, finally, acceptance. "No," he said finally. "And I hope it stays that way. She's loved Nathan from the time he was five days old. The whole thing seemed like a perfect fit. Judy didn't want to be a mother. I didn't want to have a child out of wedlock—especially with what Natasha would make of it. And Natasha couldn't have children. We tried for years."

"Why at that exact time? You're rich. Why didn't you buy a baby before?"

"Like I say, it all seemed perfect. Natasha and I were trying to have a baby for several years. When we finally accepted the fact that it wasn't going to happen, Natasha was crushed. We started looking into adoption and we got on a couple of waiting lists. Naturally, I greased the skids with some cash here and there, but we still didn't have a baby.

"Within months of finding out that Natasha couldn't have children, Judy became pregnant. I told Natasha that I had located a child and made arrangements for us to adopt the child immediately after its birth. I told Natasha that the mother would prefer not to meet with us, but that the child came from 'good genes'—whatever the hell that means.

"I sent Judy to Paris, got her an apartment there and visited her every weekend—I was setting up my London office at the time, so it was easy to work out. I arranged for her to have the best medical care and she gave birth to Nathan in November of 1986. I flew back with Nathan on the corporate jet and literally put him in Natasha's arms. I think it was the happiest day of her life," said Wright, suddenly lost in a memory that seemed to surprise him.

"Did Judy come back with you?"

"She stayed in Paris for a few months to recuperate and get back in shape. A week or so after I gave Nathan to Natasha I went back to be with Judy. We both returned to California in early March."

"And Natasha never suspected anything?"

"No. Nor does Nathan. There was no point in telling either one of them the truth. Natasha loves Nathan so much. And he loves her. Judy was Nathan's biological mother, but Natasha is his *real* mother."

"How did Judy feel about that?"

"She understood what she had done. What she had given up. When she found out she was pregnant she wanted to have an abortion. Being pregnant was not part of her plan. Had I not intervened Nathan would never have been born."

"But she must have felt something for her son over the years as she got to know him."

"Of course. But she knew that revealing the truth would hurt and confuse a lot of people. She made an agreement and was willing to honor it."

"You sure?"

"I'm positive. What was she going to say? 'Hi, Nathan. I'm your mother and I gave you up because I was banging your father when he was married to your mom and now I want to be a part of your life'? I don't think so."

"So Nathan never had a clue he was adopted?"

"I don't think so."

"You're not sure?"

"I can't be completely sure, but I'm pretty sure. Even if he would have, he certainly would have no idea that Judy was his biological mother. Natasha and I were going to tell him he was adopted when he was eighteen. She reasoned that by that time he would be mature enough to handle it, and would be permanently bonded to her. By the time Nathan was eighteen Natasha and I were divorced. So we never had that talk. The reason I'm not one hundred percent sure is because I don't know if Natasha ever told him. If she did, I don't know about it."

"Didn't you think it would ever come out? I mean, Justin, you put your 'love child' into your own home! Didn't you think there were going to be consequences down the road?"

"To be honest with you, no. Like I said, Judy didn't want the baby and Natasha wanted a baby desperately. It seemed like a perfect fit."

"After you and Judy were married for a number of years, and she was around Nathan... Are you sure she didn't have second thoughts about your arrangement?"

"She was okay with it. She and I talked about the situation every once in a while and she realized that Nathan had a great life the way things were, and that he would never have been born had Judy chosen his fate."

"And she never thought about breaking down, in a moment of guilt or a drunken stupor, and telling him that she was his mother?"

"No. Definitely not. I knew Judy better than anyone. Her overwhelming emotion about Nathan was guilt. And she was not the kind of person to confess in order to receive absolution."

"So you're sure that Judy never talked to Nathan about being his mother?"

"Yes, I'm sure. Not that it didn't trouble her."

"I thought you said Judy was okay with it."

"She *accepted* it. Judy and I talked about having our own child, but I couldn't father a child anymore. When it became obvious that Judy and I weren't going to have any children of our own, the more obvious it became to Judy that we already *had* a child—Nathan. I think it weighed on her now and then."

"Was she more upset about it recently?"

"Not that I noticed. She knew that telling Nathan wouldn't do anyone any good. She was resigned to be close to him. I think she held out some kind of romantic fantasy about maybe telling Nathan on her deathbed, thirty years from now, that she was his real mother."

Sawyer withdrew the photograph of Smith and slid it across the table. "Recognize this guy?"

"Yes. That's the man Judy was seeing before we got married. Can't say he's changed much."

"The photo was taken about that time."

Wright nodded and slid the photo back to Sawyer, who pocketed it.

"Do you have a reason for showing me that picture?"

"You haven't seen that man since then?"

"Certainly not. Judy promised me that she would never see him again and I believed her."

"But you still hired a private detective just to make sure."

"Not because of that particular guy. Besides, Simpson came back with a report that indicated Judy was not seeing any other men, including the guy in the photo. Look Sawyer," said

Wright glancing at his watch, then back at Sawyer, "I've got to meet Noah in about twenty minutes. You need to ask me anything else?"

"No, that's about it."

Wright took out his wallet, withdrew a fifty and tossed it on the table. "Cheers," he said as he finished his drink and then left.

The guitar player on stage was finishing a stripped down version of the Who's "Won't Get Fooled Again." No one was listening, except Sawyer.

He didn't stick around for the ending.

Chapter Sixty-one

There was a football game on the TV at Admiral Risty and Michael was between sets, sitting at a corner table. He spotted Sawyer and waved him over.

"Long time, no see."

"Two days," said Sawyer.

"Lot can happen in two days."

"I need more to happen." Sawyer withdrew the photograph Zona Day had given him and slid it across the table. "You know this guy? He used to play here in the South Bay a few years back. Went by the single name of 'Smith.'"

Hall held the photo so the light from the candle on the table illuminated it better. Finally there was a glimmer of recognition. "Yeah, I know this guy. I don't really *know* him, but I know who he is."

"You're kidding!" said Sawyer. Most hunches didn't pan out. But it always felt good when one did. Sawyer had reasoned that since Hall and the man in the photograph both played various South Bay venues for years, it was possible their paths had crossed.

"His name's Barry Key—he thought the 'Smith' thing was a conversation starter. I didn't recognize him right off because he's bald now. Shaved his head, I think. But that's him."

Sawyer recalled that the man in the studio next to Judy's said he saw a bald man go into her studio. "You're sure?"

"Definitely. We both used to play at a coffeehouse in San Pedro—Cathedral of the Senses. That was about 2000 or 2001. We were on the same bill at those places pretty often for a year or two. I haven't seen him for two or three years, though. Why?"

"If I told you I'd have to kill you."

Hall's eyes got wide. "Does this have to do with Judy's murder?"

"Look, we're friends, right?"

"Right."

"As a favor to me, don't tell anyone—and I mean *anyone*—about this for two days." Sawyer knew that if he was right, by then everyone would know Key's name. "I need your word on that, Michael."

"You got it." Hall looked at his watch and said, "I gotta start playing. Any requests?"

"How about 'Bonfire of Broken Dreams'?"

"I always like it when people request songs I wrote."

Sawyer waited till Michael had finished, then he left.

But not before putting a twenty in Michael's tip jar.

As he walked to his car Sawyer was thinking about one thing. Barry Key and the initials in Judy's diary: B.K.

Sawyer called information and tried to get a number for Barry Key in several South Bay cities but came up empty. It was five-thirty. Eric Gregg would have left the office. He called anyway and was told that Gregg would be in the office at nine the next morning. Sawyer called Gregg's cell but it was turned off. He left a message saying that he needed an address for Barry Key, and that the person he was looking for would probably be in the San Pedro area. He finished by asking Gregg to call him the next morning as soon as he had the information.

Sawyer got home about six, took a shower, fed the fish, and had a cup of coffee.

He went into his office and checked the answering machine. There were calls from Veronica and Rebecca about having dinner tonight. Sawyer called Rebecca and told her he had to work tonight and that he would call her tomorrow and that, perhaps, they could have dinner tomorrow night. He called Veronica and arranged to meet her at *La Rive Gauche* in an hour.

Sawyer searched the Internet for any information about Barry Key and didn't come up with much. Apparently he had played on a few of albums in the late eighties and early nineties for a singer whose name Sawyer didn't recognize. There were no photographs of the guy and there wasn't much else. He had access to St. James' LexisNexis tomorrow, but by then he figured he would have Key's address from Gregg.

Sawyer opened the file Wright had given him that contained Judy's financial records. It looked as though she cashed a check for one thousand dollars every Friday, with only a couple of exceptions. She didn't write that many checks. She used credit cards for most things.

Her credit cards had dozens of restaurant charges every month, easily averaging one restaurant charge a day. He could see that she was not eating alone, but hardly anyone ate alone at a restaurant. By itself, it meant nothing. Most of the other charges were for clothes.

After about a half hour he noticed that almost every Friday she ate lunch at a restaurant in San Pedro. The restaurant varied, from a place in Ports O Call, to Whale and Ale, to Marcello's, to the San Pedro Brewing Company. But almost every Friday she cashed a check for one thousand dollars and went to lunch somewhere in San Pedro.

Sawyer changed into jeans, a bright white shirt—starched and just removed from the dry cleaner's plastic wrap—casual shoes and a blue herringbone jacket.

Chapter Sixty-two

Sawyer and Veronica arrived at the same time and parked next to each other just outside *La Rive Gauche*. Veronica had never been there and was charmed by the quaint yet elegant atmosphere. Sawyer ordered a one-hundred-seventy-five-dollar bottle of Bordeaux he remembered from a tasting at one of the local wine shops. What the hell, he thought. He would bill Wright. He wasn't taking a fee. The billionaire could afford his meals. Especially now that Wright had an extra one thousand dollars a week.

Sawyer and Veronica made small talk while the waiter delivered and uncorked the *Chateau Quinault L'Enclos Bordeaux*, then poured it, waiting for Sawyer's blessing, which was given immediately.

At *La Rive Gauche* Sawyer always got the same thing: rack of lamb and onion soup. Since Veronica had never eaten there before, she duplicated Sawyer's order.

Over salad, Veronica raised her glass and clinked it against Sawyer's. "To us."

Sawyer didn't know exactly what to say.

"Just say it," she said playfully.

"To us," he said and they drank.

"No matter what happens, I'm glad we're back..." She was going to say "together," but she said, "...in touch. I don't know what's going to happen with you and Rebecca and you don't either. I'm just grateful for what *is*. That's all. And if you and Rebecca work things out, that's okay too. At least we have one helluva good working relationship."

"That we do," said Sawyer. "Speaking of work, I might have something for you. Ever hear of a guy named Barry Key?"

"No, but I can guess where you're going with this. He's Judy's lover. The guy everyone's looking for but has never seen."

"It's just a lead now. I'll know more tomorrow morning and I'll call you. See, I play fair with you."

"Come on, Sawyer. You're not playing fair with me—about anything. But I'm a big girl and I know what I'm doing."

"You're so cynical," he said with a smile. "I'm just telling you what I know when I know it."

"Right," said Veronica. She didn't believe it for a minute.

"Okay, let's change the subject. You got anything for me?"

"Not much. I'm hearing some rumblings about one of Justin and Judy's 'sex club' members. I don't know what he wants to say, but apparently he's willing to talk—I'm getting this from a 'friend of a friend.' Could be something, could be nothing. I'll let you know."

The food was delivered and it was as good as Sawyer said it was. Veronica said it was the best rack of lamb she ever had. Sawyer poured the last of the Bordeaux into their glasses and sighed. "Rebecca called tonight and wanted to have dinner. I told her I was busy."

"With me."

"I didn't mention your name."

"You know, I can keep you *very* busy."

"Yeah, I remember. What I don't know is what's happening with Rebecca and me. If it were one of my books, I'd have the protagonist reconcile with his wife and live happily ever after." He paused. "But I'm not sure I want that."

"You're not sure you want 'happily ever after' with me either."

"The only thing I am sure about is that I don't know what I want."

"I love decisive men." She paused. "Don't worry, I love you too."

"You do?"

"What?"

"You love me?"

Veronica smiled and took Sawyer's hand in hers. "I do love you, Sawyer. Is that what you want to hear? I love you," she said landing hard on each word.

"It's nice to hear someone say it and mean it. But I'm not sure that's enough."

"It's never enough. Rebecca used to love you and you used to love her. People have to work at a relationship or it ceases to exist. If you and I love each other today—and I believe we do—memories of how we used to feel won't be enough to keep us together ten years from now. I think that's one reason it helps to actually *like* the person you love."

"What do you mean?"

"I mean, I've felt very passionate, lustful, romantic love for a couple men in my life who I really didn't like that much. They were wonderful to be *in* love with but terrible to love. I like you. I always have. I enjoy hanging out with you even when we don't hit the sack. You make me laugh—not too much in the past few days," she joked. "But on the whole, I feel relaxed around you. Comfortable. Sex can go away. It might be no one's fault. What do you do then? If you don't like the other person, and the sex is gone—no matter how terrific it used to be—you're stranded on an emotional island for the rest of your life."

"Sounds like this hits close to home."

"All I'm saying is that you and I have it all: We like each other and we make each other laugh."

Sawyer smiled. He almost said, "I love you," but he didn't. Some things were hard to take back. Especially when they could wind up hurting people you liked. He looked at his watch. "I think I'm going to call it a night."

"Yeah, me too."

"You staying down here tonight?"

"No. I've got to feed my cat and do some paperwork at home."

"Look, Veronica... I know you're not asking me for an explanation, and I'm sure this doesn't come close to one, but here goes. I don't know what's going to happen with Rebecca, and I don't want to put you in the emotional crossfire. But if this sounds like some kind of 'kiss off,' it's not. I'm interested in pursuing something with you—a 'relationship' with you. It's just that it's not fair to you—or to Rebecca—to move forward until she and I have things resolved."

"Okay," she said and took the last sip of her wine.

"We talked last night. She said she wants to work things out—if I want to. I don't know what I want to do. I've got lots of years invested in our relationship, but I'm tired of going through the motions with someone who doesn't love me anymore. All I know is that if I were to choose tonight, between you and Rebecca, I'd choose you. But that isn't the way real life works. I'm still married to Rebecca and she and I will figure out what we want to do soon. Very soon."

"I'll be here, Sawyer. Not forever, but for a little while."

"Or until a better offer comes along."

"Don't flatter yourself, Sawyer. A better offer than you comes along more often than a bus."

She said it so sincerely that he couldn't help but laugh out loud.

Chapter Sixty-three

Sawyer got home about 10:30. The pond lights were off. Otherwise he would have petted the fish. He checked the answering machine and Rebecca had called again. She said it was okay to call late. Till midnight. He checked the clock again. There was time. For what, he thought? What did he want to do?

Sawyer thought about having yet another drink and calling Rebecca. He had called people late at night after he'd been drinking. In the morning he often wished he had simply gone to bed. Tonight he made the phone call.

And poured himself a drink.

"Thanks for calling me back," said Rebecca.

"You're still my wife. You call me, I call you back. That's the way it works."

"This isn't an easy time for us. I know that."

"I imagine it's a little easier for you than it is for me," he said.

"If you really think that then you still have no idea what I'm talking about. I'm not some 'desperate housewife' jumping into bed with the first guy who tells me I don't look my age."

"I never said you were."

"I know you're hurt. Do you really want to know why I did what I did?"

"I'm not sure." After a moment he said, "Yes."

"It wasn't because you were too busy. Even when you weren't busy, you didn't seem interested in me. And it wasn't because our sex life started slowing down. It was because you no longer showed me any affection. You remember how you used to hold my hand or offer me your arm when we went out? Remember how you used to touch my forehead and kiss me on the nose every night before we turned off the lights?

Remember how you always made sure at least one part of your body was touching mine all night? You remember all that?"

"Yes."

"Where did it go?"

"I don't know." Sawyer thought about saying something like, "Things change," but he knew there was more to it than that.

"I know a relationship goes through stages and I know things aren't always white-hot. But people who like each other show affection. Not all people, I guess, but you do—at least you used to. I'd much rather have you touch me on my forehead and kiss me on my nose every night than spend the night fucking."

"Really?"

"Not really," she said, and they both laughed a little. "But seriously, I would. You know why?"

"Why?"

"Because it lets me know you still care. If you screw me every weekend, all that really tells me is that you care that you still have a sex life. When you touch me—really take the time to touch me in a way that you touch no one else—that makes me feel loved."

"So what's all this talk about sex?"

"Sex is not that important to me. Being appreciated makes me feel good. Being loved is what lasts. If I know you love me, then all the rest is gravy. I mean, how many positions are there anyhow?"

"I don't know. I'll have to ask Michael. He wrote the book on sex, you know."

"You know what I mean."

"I do." Sawyer paused. "Was it really all that bad?"

"It wasn't that it was so bad. It was just that I knew how good it could be."

"Wasn't there some other way to get my attention?"

"I tried. You just didn't seem to notice. I got to the point that I didn't care anymore. And when you walked in on me that night, you looked more wounded than angry. I was honestly surprised to see that you still cared that much." After a moment Rebecca said, "I know things have changed. But that doesn't mean they have to change for the worse. You know what they say: 'What doesn't kill you makes you stronger.'"

"I don't know… This is a tough one."

"I know. I don't expect a miracle." After a brief pause, she said, "Then again, maybe I do."

Sawyer just sighed.

"I'm not going to push you," said Rebecca. "I just thought you deserved an explanation."

"I appreciate that." Sawyer sighed again. "Look, I've really got to get some sleep. But I'm glad you told me."

"Yeah, me too. Goodnight."

"Goodnight," said Sawyer and he hung up. As he curled up in bed, he felt cold. It was winter. But the chill he felt was not from the weather.

He felt alone.

He fell asleep quickly.

And dreamed about having his lifeline cut from a spacecraft and floating out into space. He awoke an hour later in a cold sweat gasping for air.

Chapter Sixty-four

The phone rang and Sawyer answered it. "Yes?"

"Sawyer?" said Eric Gregg.

"Good guess," said Sawyer groggily.

"I've got an address for Barry Key."

"San Pedro?"

"Your talents are wasted in police work. You should work in a circus."

"I've got a pencil," said Sawyer and he wrote down the address as Gregg read it to him. "And Eric…"

"Yes?"

"I think it would be a good idea if you met me there."

Gregg knew his partner well enough to know that Sawyer knew something he wasn't telling him and that it would be in his best interest to do what Sawyer said.

"What time is it?" asked Sawyer.

"Eight-thirty."

"I'll meet you there at ten," said Sawyer and hung up.

He called Veronica and told her that if she wanted the "story of a lifetime" she should jump in her car and head south. He gave her the address.

Sawyer was there before Veronica or Gregg. Gregg arrived five minutes after Sawyer arrived and Veronica ten minutes after that. The three of them stood in front of an old three-story building on Sixth Street in San Pedro.

"Looks like a converted bank building," said Gregg.

"That'd be my guess," said Sawyer as he walked into the building's small lobby. Lots of marble and oak and a black wrought iron elevator that led to the second and third floors. There were four names on the mailboxes. Three of them had condo numbers beginning with the number two. Key's was the only condo number beginning with the number three. Apparently he had the entire top floor. That didn't come cheap, even in San Pedro.

"This is where you get off," said Gregg to Veronica. It sounded more official coming from a guy with a badge. She gave Sawyer a look, but he gave her a what-can-I-do kind of look and then followed his old partner into the elevator.

Upstairs, Sawyer knocked, then tried the door handle. It didn't open. Gregg walked to the end of the hall and checked out the view.

While Sawyer picked the lock and opened the door.

All it took was a single whiff to realize someone was dead in Barry Key's apartment. Gregg walked in first and Sawyer followed.

Key was dead, his head on a table next to a spilled bottle of Scotch. An empty bottle of over-the-counter sleeping pills lay just beyond his outstretched and lifeless right hand. From the condition of the body it was clear to Sawyer and Gregg that the man had been dead a few days. While Gregg gravitated toward the body, Sawyer moved around the room cautiously, careful not to disturb anything. On the table there was a note that was barely legible because it was soaked in Scotch.

Judy was my true love
But she betrayed me
That was a pain I could not bear
Now we will both be together
In a better place
May God forgive me

In an instant Sawyer realized everything had changed.

"Looks like your buddy just got a get-out-jail-free card," said Gregg.

Chapter Sixty-five

The story didn't hit the news for about an hour. No other media showed up till after eleven. Partly because Veronica did her best to keep a lid on things and partly because local media didn't connect the suicide of some guy in San Pedro to Judy Wright's murder.

At least not until Veronica connected the dots with a live exclusive from outside Key's apartment about 10:45.

Sawyer had immediately turned things over to Eric Gregg, who called Riley Gaines and the local cops. Sawyer was nowhere to be seen when the black-and-whites arrived. He told Veronica he would call her later.

As he pulled away from the scene Sawyer called St. James and told him he was on his way over and to cancel any appointments.

Sawyer parked in front of the Neptune statue, hit the lock button on his remote and walked up a flight of stairs to St. James' place.

The lawyer waved Sawyer into his office and closed the door.

"Hope this is good news."

"The cops are at Barry Key's apartment in San Pedro. Ever heard of him?"

"No. Should I?"

"Actually, yes. He killed himself a few days ago and left a suicide note. Said he killed Judy Wright."

"What the fuck!"

Sawyer had never seen St. James surprised. He was a guy who was always three or four moves ahead of everyone.

"Looks like Justin's lucky day."

"This is unbelievable," said the lawyer, genuinely stunned. "Is it on the news yet?"

"If it isn't, it will be soon."

"Unbelievable," repeated St. James. "Have you told Justin?"

"No. I'll leave that to you."

St. James did a few mental calculations. "How do you know about this before the media?"

"Let's just say I've got a knack for being in the right place at the right time."

"I owe you. But Justin owes you more. Hell, he could have been in jail in a couple of days without this. I have to tell you, things weren't breaking our way."

"Yeah, I know."

"You don't look happy. I'd think you'd be happy for Justin."

"I am. I've just got other things on my mind. And I'm tired. Really tired. So, give Justin a heads-up and remind him to keep his mouth shut. He's grieving for his wife and relieved that her killer has been..." Sawyer was going to say caught, but instead he said, "...identified."

"This is terrific! You got dinner plans?"

"I don't know."

"You do now. Pacific Edge. Tonight. Seven o'clock. And you're at the head table with Justin and me. I won't take no for an answer."

"Okay. I'm going home to get some sleep," said Sawyer.

He went home, unplugged the phone and collapsed in bed. He knew Veronica was busy and if he wanted to see her all he'd have to do is turn on the TV. As he fell asleep he was thinking about whom to ask to dinner—Veronica or Rebecca? Maybe he would just go alone. He was thinking that when he fell asleep.

It was nearly 4:30 in the afternoon when he awoke. It had been a number of long days in a row and tonight would probably be another long night. He also knew that his answering machine was probably full by now—he had a vague recollection of hearing the phone in his office ring while he was dreaming about Barry Key playing music at The Windjammer. Sawyer was in the audience with Judy and Danny Rosenberg. He awoke with a jolt thinking that everyone in his dream was dead. Except him.

The messages were mainly of the can-you-believe-it variety. Zona called. She recognized Key's picture on TV. He called her and told her she was invited to the celebration dinner that night. Not as his "date," but as his guest. She had earned it.

Veronica had called. She sounded excited and wanted him to call her. Rebecca had left a message. She sensed that Sawyer had something to do with what she was watching on TV. She wanted him to call her. Justin Wright had called. The message was simple: "Thanks. I owe you."

Sawyer made himself a Grey Goose martini and went out to the pond. He put his feet in the water and felt the fish swim between his ankles.

Koi had a good sense of hearing and whenever Sawyer opened one of the back doors that opened onto the pond, the fish, led by Ace Junior, would school to the side of the pond. Ace Junior would stick his head above the water in anticipation of being petted. Sawyer always petted him first. It was odd to bond with a fish, thought Sawyer. Sometimes he felt closer to this fish than to most people.

Sawyer's cell rang. He saw that it was Veronica and he answered it.

"I'm a star. Again. Thanks, Sawyer."

"I'm glad you still remember my number. And you're welcome. But you owe me."

"Big, big, big time. I'm probably going to have to be your slave for a while. Got any ideas?"

"None that I'd like to describe over a cell phone."

"You're reading my mind."

"St. James is having a celebration dinner tonight at Pacific Edge. You busy?"

"Very. But for you…"

"You and I will be at the head table with Noah and Justin."

"I'll be there. What time?"

"Seven."

"See you at seven. Anything you'd like me to wear?"

"I can think of something I'd like you *not* to wear."

Veronica laughed. "See you at seven."

Sawyer pushed the End Button on his phone and set it down next to him. Ace Junior was sticking his big head out of the water again. Sawyer went inside and got some fish food, returned and tossed the shrimp pellets into the water. He made sure Ace Junior got the most.

Chapter Sixty-six

Tatiana saw Sawyer as soon as he walked into Pacific Edge and offered him a glass of champagne, which he took. Justin Wright was seated at the head table. Veronica was seated next to him and they appeared to be deep in conversation. There were probably fifty people in the restaurant. Sawyer recognized about a dozen, including Zona Day, who was surrounded by several men in suits giving her their full attention. The rest, he figured, were media types Noah wanted to spin and employees from St. James' three offices.

For a moment, Sawyer watched, with begrudging admiration, as St. James held court, at least a dozen people gathered around him, hanging on his every word. Sawyer knew that people were intimidated by "the system." No one was quite sure how the system worked, but they knew that beating it had something to do with money. Watching St. James bend the system to his—or his client's—will was like watching a surgeon perform brain surgery: It seemed like a miracle when it worked because so much could go wrong.

The way most people looked at it, St. James had just performed another miracle.

As Sawyer passed by Zona Day, the real estate agent was regaling her admirers with stories of her Native American heritage and he thought he heard Rock Hudson's name mentioned. She saw Sawyer and excused herself, dispatching one of the men to fetch another glass of something clear that had an olive in it.

"Sawyer, I can't thank you enough," she gushed. "I've got one guy who wants to sell his house and two who want to buy two-million-dollar second homes. Cash. I told them I'd work with them."

"Sounds like you could work them over pretty good."

"A girl's gotta make a living. Besides, no one gets hurt. Unless they want to," she said with a smile that Sawyer figured was an indication she was getting a little drunk. "Did that picture I gave you help? That's the man who killed himself, right?"

"Yes. And it did help. Thanks."

"Least it's good to know Justin's off the hook. We're not friends and I know he doesn't like me. But he seems like a nice old guy. Nice *rich* old guy. And he really seemed to love Judy."

"And don't forget... He *is* single now."

"That's true. Actually, I feel a little sorry for him. I heard on the news that Barry Key killed himself because he found out about 'the club.' I thought about that and I realized that Judy actually betrayed her lover *and* Justin. I can imagine how Justin felt and I can even understand how her lover felt. I mean, to be with someone that long, you'd think you'd know someone."

The man Zona sent for her drink returned, handed her a glass and tilted his head to indicate that when she was done, he would be waiting.

Just then Sawyer saw Veronica waving him over to her table. He said goodbye to Zona and made his way through the crowd to the head table. Wright stood when Sawyer arrived at the table, embraced him, then the two men sat down, Veronica between them.

"Justin was telling me how much he owes you," said Veronica.

"It's good to have a rich person owe you."

They all laughed politely.

"Thanks again, Sawyer. I can hardly believe it's over."

"The media frenzy isn't quite over—ask Veronica," said Sawyer. "But it'll die down. A month from now, you can focus exclusively on grieving for Judy. You won't have to worry about going to jail or proving your innocence."

"Thank God," said Wright. He sighed and took a sip of champagne.

"I've got to go to the little girl's room," said Veronica. She stood and was gone.

"I really do want to thank you, Sawyer. I know it was you who figured this whole thing out. Fucking cops… They just wanted my scalp on the wall from day one."

"It wasn't that easy to figure out. Judy was very careful."

"I know. I think maybe that's the hardest thing to take: That I didn't know. A husband should know, don't you think?"

"A spouse is often the last to know."

"You live with a person three hundred and sixty-five days a year, for years, and you still don't know them… It feels weird. It makes you think—*re*-think—everything about your past together. Did she *ever* mean what she said, or was she just playing me? Did she…"

"Don't do that to yourself, Justin. No good can come from it. Trust me. Just let it go."

"I know, but—"

"Let it go," said Sawyer, this time more forcefully.

Veronica returned and sat down next to Sawyer. He felt her hand on his knee and then it moved to his crotch. There was something in her hand. She opened her hand and Sawyer took her offering. He looked at her and smiled. She wanted to kiss him but this was a very public function and they were both very public figures at the moment.

Sawyer pocketed Veronica's panties and tried his best to focus on what Justin was saying. It wasn't easy.

Just then St. James, who had returned to his seat beside Wright, repeatedly tapped a spoon on his water glass

"I'd like to make a toast," said Noah.

Everyone stood.

"To the truth. To an appreciation of freedom and liberty. And to Justin," said the lawyer, turning to Wright. He purposely left out Sawyer. He didn't want the media buzzing around Sawyer any more than they already were.

The rest of the room raised their glasses in Wright's direction and he nodded. And everyone drank.

Wright stood and said, "I'd like to thank you all for being here to share this bittersweet moment with me. I'm happy that people now realize that I didn't murder my wife, but I'm greatly saddened by her death. I especially want to thank Noah—and I hope he's not billing me for this dinner."

Laughter.

"And I want to thank my friend, Sawyer, for believing in me. He was one of the first people I called when this happened. I knew I could count on him to find the truth. I can honestly say that I wouldn't be sitting here with you all tonight, had it not been for my old friend." Wright raised his glass toward Sawyer. "To Sawyer Black," he said.

Everyone toasted Sawyer, who nodded to Wright and finished what was left of his champagne. St. James wished he had spoken to Wright about not mentioning Sawyer to the media, but it was too late.

The party went on till about 10:30. The bill came to about five thousand dollars, including the tip. The lawyer paid the check with his credit card. It didn't really matter. Justin was paying for everything, one way or the other. But he didn't care. He had just saved a few million dollars he would have been on the hook for had he been arrested and gone to trial.

Veronica was enjoying herself. She was being interviewed by her colleagues. She was back in the game.

Justin refused to be interviewed, but Noah took all comers. He held forth about truth, justice and the American way—he looked and sounded a lot like Superman.

St. James, Wright, Sawyer and Veronica were the last to leave. They lingered in the parking lot next to St. James' car, a black Rolls Royce Corniche, which had been pulled up to the restaurant entrance by a chauffeur.

"This is all good," said Noah, as his chauffeur held open the back door and waited for the lawyer to get in. "But let's all keep a low profile. We've got our story out there and everyone knows Justin is innocent. Let's just let things run their course. No TV interviews—sorry Veronica," said Noah, looking at the reporter. "Let's take 'yes' for an answer."

With that, St. James got in the car. The chauffeur closed the door without acknowledging anyone else, walked around to the other side of the car, got in and drove away.

"Thanks again, Sawyer," said Wright, shaking Sawyer's hand, nodding at Veronica, and then walking to his car.

"So, it's just you and me, kid," said Veronica. "And I can't go anywhere without my panties. I've got goose bumps. You wanna see?"

"Actually, I do."

"You're bad."

"I hear it's good to be bad."

"So, are you going to finish what you started?"

"You staying down here tonight?"

"Pacific Blue Inn. Room 228."

"I'll follow you."

Chapter Sixty-seven

As Sawyer followed Veronica to the hotel, his cell phone rang. He checked the Caller ID. It was Tony Arquette. He flipped opened his phone and said, "Sawyer."

"You alone?"

"I'm in my car. Yeah, I'm alone."

"We need to talk."

"When?"

"How about tonight?"

Sawyer thought about saying that it was too late—it was almost eleven. But his curiosity was piqued. Arquette was a heavy hitter. He didn't call Sawyer after ten in the evening just to shoot the breeze.

"Does this have something to do with Judy's murder?"

"Maybe."

"So talk to Riley Gaines. He's running the show."

"I want to talk to you."

Sawyer considered his options. "Meet me in the bar of the Pacific Blue Inn in twenty minutes."

"Okay," said Arquette and he hung up.

Sawyer flipped his phone closed. And drove on through the night. The fog had settled in and he could barely see fifty feet in any direction. He cautiously followed Veronica's taillights.

Sawyer pulled in next to Veronica's car in the parking lot, and walked her inside. As they walked he told her he was going to meet someone in the bar and that he would be up in about a half hour or so. She kissed him and went up to her room.

Sawyer got back in his car and waited until he saw another car pull in. He watched as Tony Arquette got out of his car and headed for the hotel entrance. Sawyer got out of his car and Arquette turned toward the sound.

"Sawyer. Thanks for meeting me."

"You're welcome," he said, shaking Arquette's hand. They walked inside and took seats at a table in the bar.

They each ordered a brandy and made small talk until the bartender turned his attention toward the TV. They were the only patrons in the bar.

"I'll get to the point, Sawyer. As you know, I was a member of Judy's 'club.' There's something I didn't tell you. I spoke with Sanchez and Woodbridge and they told me they didn't tell you either."

"Tell me what?"

"Judy was blackmailing us. Or at least she was planning to."

"That's a pretty significant detail to leave out."

"Consider our situation. We were already on the radar for Judy's murder. If Gaines would have found out Judy was planning to blackmail us… Well, let's just say we all thought it was in our best interest to leave that part out."

"Okay."

Arquette sighed deeply. "You know what they say—'there's no fool like an old fool'? Well, the members of the club were old fools. The only things we had in common were that we were senior citizens, rich and vulnerable to blackmail. In the beginning it seemed like everyone had something to lose and it was kind of like 'mutually assured destruction' if anything came out about the club. But Judy didn't care. It wasn't like her husband didn't know. Justin was there every night. He saw what she was doing and liked it.

"Anyhow, one by one, over the past few weeks, she approached us and hinted that she might 'need some money.'"

"She hadn't done that before?"

"No. The Club has been going on for almost a year and her wanting money was a new wrinkle. But my take was that this was what she had in mind all along. Gain our confidence over time, get us to tell her things we didn't want made public and… Well, we all feel like idiots. I think something happened recently and it triggered her end game."

"Any idea what happened?"

"No."

"So why would she do this?"

"The only reason people blackmail other people is for money."

"So why are you telling me this now? Looks like everyone's off the hook."

"Maybe."

"What do you mean?"

"I mean, if this guy, Key, who committed suicide was really her great love, then it makes sense that she might have been leaving Justin for him. If that's true, then Key probably was aware of the blackmail plot."

"But they're both dead."

"Exactly. If she was leaving Justin for Key, and Key knew about the blackmail plot, why did he kill himself when he already knew what was going on and the blackmail money was their ticket out?"

Sawyer thought about that a moment. That was true. If Key knew Judy was setting up the members of the club, it followed that he probably—but not *necessarily*—knew how she was doing it. If he knew, then what the hell was he referring to in his note when he said Judy betrayed him? Was she betraying him in some other way? Maybe she was going to run away with someone else. Maybe she was just going to take the money and leave him, too. Sawyer had immediately assumed that the betrayal to which Key referred was her sex with other men.

"Judy had other things on us besides the fact we were having sex with her. She drew us out over time. She would occasionally meet with each of us privately—even though it was against the rules—and she would get us talking about things. About our companies, our careers...things we should have never told anyone. Things we *still* would not like made public."

"Did she keep a record?"

"I never saw it, of course, but she very well could have. I started feeling uncomfortable with her questions and I spoke with Rosenberg. He told me that he had 'inadvertently' told her about some 'clever' thing he did for a rich client on the Hill, which wasn't exactly kosher. A few weeks later Judy told him that she needed some money and that if he couldn't 'help her out,' then she would call the IRS. It really freaked him out."

"Enough to commit suicide?"

"Maybe. His career and reputation would be ruined if she went public."

"But she was dead when he 'killed himself.'"

"Yeah, I know. Cop to cop, I'm telling you that something's not right here. I don't know what it is, but I know you know what's going on more than anyone."

"I'm not sure about that."

"I just thought you should know what was *really* going on. And...if you come across something..."

"Like any records Judy kept that could be...embarrassing?"

"Exactly. I'd appreciate anything you could do to make sure that information never sees the light of day."

Sawyer didn't ask Arquette what Judy had on him. It wasn't important. As long as he didn't kill her.

"We were stupid, Sawyer. Most guys our age don't get propositioned by a beautiful woman. And her husband didn't mind. Hell, he even provided the booze and helped us lie to our wives. It was absolutely perfect."

"Until Judy turned up dead."

"Yeah, the world fell apart that day," said Arquette, taking a sip of brandy.

"How could you let this happen, Tony? I can understand Rosenberg, but you?"

"Vanity. My ego got the best of me. Anyhow, that's about it. If you happen to come across any...anything that would be better off kept private... Well, it would just be better you coming across it than anyone else. And we would all be very...'grateful.'"

Arquette was silent for a moment. "Look Sawyer, I know that no one in the group killed Judy, Key or Rosenberg. We were scared and we were stupid, but we all know the difference between humiliation and murder." Arquette took a twenty and a ten out of his wallet and tossed them on the table. "Thanks for meeting me." He stood, shook Sawyer's hand and left.

Sawyer took his drink out onto a small veranda and looked out onto the ocean. The fog had inexplicably cleared and he could see the moon glistening across the Pacific. He didn't enjoy seeing Arquette humbled before him.

But that wasn't why he suddenly felt uncomfortable.

Chapter Sixty-eight

When he knocked on the door, Veronica greeted him wearing only a t-shirt she had apparently brought along for the occasion.

"I was getting cold without my panties," she whispered.

Sawyer smiled, kissed her, withdrew her panties from his pocket and handed them to her. She tossed them on the bed.

Sawyer reached around Veronica and grasped her smooth buttocks in his hands. She pressed herself against him and started breathing faster, but Sawyer didn't respond and she pulled away.

"You're not going to like this," said Sawyer.

"Bad news?"

"I'm not sure yet."

"Does it have something to do with the person you met in the bar? It wasn't Rebecca, was it?"

"No. I can't explain it to you right now, but I promise I will and soon. Probably by tomorrow. But I can't stay. I've got to work this out. My mind's going a million miles a second."

Veronica sighed. She was disappointed but she knew Sawyer well enough to know that there was no point in pushing it.

"Thanks for bringing back my panties," she said and kissed him on the lips.

"I'm always a gentleman," he said.

"Not always," she said, kissing him again. "Okay, you better go before I attack you."

He smiled and kissed her one last time. "I'll call you tomorrow."

Veronica just nodded and closed the door behind him.

As he drove back up the Hill, Sawyer couldn't shake the feeling that he was missing something obvious. He was a very logical person, which was one reason he loved doing the Sudoku puzzle every morning. It was a game of logic and there was a finite solution.

Sawyer knew that the key to solving a Sudoku was to make sure you never made an incorrect assumption early on. If you did, no matter how clever you were the rest of the way, the puzzle would turn out wrong.

The solution to the puzzle of Judy's murder seemed out of whack. In most people's eyes the case was over. Solved. A couple of unimportant loose ends didn't seem to bother anyone. *There were always loose ends.*

What most novices didn't understand about Sudoku puzzles, thought Sawyer, was that when people got to the end and "just a couple of numbers" didn't fit, they thought it was a minor error and that they had *almost* solved the puzzle. The truth was that when they went back and compared their work with the solution, they weren't even close.

Because they had made an incorrect assumption.

Chapter Sixty-nine

The clock on the cable box read 11:31 when he got home and tossed his keys onto the kitchen island. He poured himself a snifter of Hennessy XO and went into his office. He ignored the answering machine.

He put his feet up on his desk, leaned back in his chair and sipped his XO. It went down like liquid velvet. He took a deep breath, closed his eyes and tried to clear his mind.

After about fifteen minutes, he picked up the file Wright had given him that contained Judy's financial records for the past year. He started paging through it again, looking for... He didn't know what he was looking for, but he didn't know where else to start. He had correctly deduced that Judy was cashing a check and probably giving the money to Barry Key every Friday, while paying for lunch for the two of them at one of several San Pedro restaurants.

Sawyer knew what was bothering him. If what Arquette told him was true—that Judy was blackmailing the club members—then the dominos started falling in one direction. Sawyer didn't want to believe it and he would need more than logic if he planned to do anything about it.

He picked up the diary again and leafed through it. It all seemed in order. The "BK" references were the only thing incriminating in the entire document. The rest could all be explained away as artistic musings. The "erotic verses" could have been written about Justin, one of the members of the swing club, Key, or a fantasy lover. He searched the forty or so pages for any capital B's or K's in the diary's main text. He found no capital K's and two capital B's. They both looked like the B's in the BK references. Judy often didn't capitalize words—even the first word of a sentence.

Sawyer sifted through Judy's cancelled checks. Lots of checks made out to "cash." It was amazing, thought Sawyer, how many business names *didn't* start with the letters B or K. He figured that any check made out to anyone other than "cash" took money out of Key's pocket, so there weren't many of those.

He was almost at the bottom of the pile of checks when he came across a check made out to the "Boy's Club of America" for one hundred dollars. The B in "Boy's" didn't look anything like the B in the diary.

From an envelope on his desk Sawyer retrieved the day planner pages he had shown to the handwriting expert. On October 8th there was a list that included the notation "stop at Bank of America and cash check." He compared the B from the Bank of America notation to the B on the Boy's Club of America check. They didn't match. Yet the B on the day planner list matched the B from the BK references in the diary.

Sawyer searched through the clutter on his desk and found the handwritten note Justin had given him to get him past the landlord at Judy's studio. There were no capital K's in the note... but there was a capital B.

"Dammit!" said Sawyer. He sighed deeply and leaned back in his chair. He was thinking about how complicated things seemed so simple when you knew the answer.

It was almost 12:30 but Sawyer realized there was somewhere he needed to be.

Chapter Seventy

Sawyer pulled up to the gate in front of Wright's house. He pressed a button. Thirty seconds later, after a second buzz, Justin answered, "Yes?"

"It's Sawyer."

"Sawyer, what the hell... What time is it?"

"It's time for us to talk."

About ten seconds later, the gate swung open and Sawyer parked in the underground garage.

A moment later, Sawyer stood in Wright's foyer opposite Justin who wore a robe and pajamas.

"Sawyer? What are you doing here?"

"I need to talk to you about something."

"Tonight?"

"You owe me, remember?"

"You're right." And with that, Wright led Sawyer into the library.

"Can I get you anything?"

"No, I'm good."

The two men sat down, Wright behind his desk, Sawyer in a chair opposite him.

"So, what can't wait till the morning?"

"I know what you did, Justin. I know you killed Judy. And I know you killed Key or had him killed."

"What in the hell are you talking about? Key killed Judy, then he killed himself."

"That's what you want people to think. That's what you wanted *me* to prove. That's why you pointed me to the diary before anyone else."

"It was Judy's diary. Your handwriting expert said so."

"All he said was the diary and the day planner pages you gave me were written by the same person. That person was you."

"That's ridiculous."

"Maybe, but it was also pretty clever. You created a diary, probably based on Judy's real one, but you made one major addition: Barry Key's initials scattered throughout."

"You're scaring me, Sawyer."

"You ought to be scared. I'm not guessing here, Justin. I know. The B's don't match Judy's handwriting—I compared them to Judy's cancelled checks. But they match yours. The letter you gave me to get into Judy's studio had a B that matched the BK notes in the diary. It's *your* handwriting, not Judy's."

After a moment, Wright said, "In case you don't read the newspapers, Sawyer, this case is closed. My wife's lover killed himself when he found out she was sleeping with four other men every week."

"Key knew about the 'Club' all along. It was his and Judy's ticket out. You found out about her affair—my guess is that Simpson told you about Key. So, if she left you or if you threw her out, either way she'd be broke. And Key had no money. At least not the kind of money Judy was accustomed to."

"This is madness, Sawyer. It's just not true."

"There's more. She was planning to blackmail your friends. The Club was her insurance policy for the future. Four rich men, with big egos and a lot to lose if their infidelity and other secrets were ever disclosed. Key wasn't upset because she was having sex with those guys. He'd shared her for years with you."

Wright opened a desk drawer and Sawyer went stiff. Wright pulled out a bottle of Bookers and poured some bourbon in a mug in front of him. He didn't offer Sawyer any.

"Handsome boy, Nathan," said Sawyer tilting his head toward a large photograph on the wall of father and son smiling on Wright's yacht.

Wright sipped his bourbon and said nothing.

"You know, he doesn't look much like you."

Wright looked Sawyer in the eye.

"He looks a lot like Barry Key."

Silence.

"Is that what Judy went to see Natasha about the night they had their little heart-to-heart? To tell her that Nathan was *her* child?"

Wright sighed wearily, but still said nothing.

"Is that why Judy called Nathan the night she died? Was she getting nervous because she thought you found out about her 'exit plan'? Was she going to tell Nathan at lunch the next day that you weren't his father?"

"That night I overheard her talking with Nathan," said Wright with a sad smile. "She told him that she wanted to take him to lunch. She said there was something significant she wanted to tell him and that it was important they meet the next day. I knew what she was planning to tell him. It was merely another in a long line of betrayals. You know how old I am, Sawyer?" Wright didn't wait for an answer. "I'm seventy-two. I have more money than a dozen lawyers could pry from me if they worked overtime for the rest of my life. All my companies run without me. I just show up to shake hands and tell stories. The guys who run things don't need me and, truth be told, really don't want me around. I don't play golf well. I don't play tennis at all and I drink too much.

"Two things made life worth living: Judy and Nathan. Until about a month ago, I still thought Judy loved me. Not passionately like in the beginning, but I thought she still cared for me and stayed with me because she loved me. I didn't care about her flirting with other men or this whole thing with the Club. It was her idea and I thought it would make her happy and make up for the discrepancy in our sex drives. I realize now that the Club was just Judy's way to cash out of a loveless relationship with some old geezer she never loved in the first place."

"How did you find out she was seeing Key?"

"It took me a while to catch on. Within a week of my retirement, a year ago, Judy rented her studio. Before I retired, she came and went as she pleased without any questions from me. With me around the house every day, she needed an all-purpose excuse to go out anytime she wished. Renting a studio in San Pedro was perfect for her. She could say she felt inspired to work on her paintings anytime night or day. And because the studio was in San Pedro, if I ever looked at her credit card receipts and saw all the San Pedro restaurant charges, she had an answer."

"Do you think she was using the studio to meet Key?"

"Maybe, but I doubt it. I found out from Simpson that Key had been living in his place for years. I think the studio was just her excuse for being in San Pedro. My guess is that they met at his apartment. I have to hand it to her, though. The studio was a perfect ruse.

"I bought into it till about a month ago. Judy started acting more distant than usual and spending more time out of the house. That's when I hired Simpson. He tailed her and it didn't take long for him to catch her with Key at his place. I could tell from the photographs that it was the same guy. Even though he was bald now, I recognized him.

"At first, I didn't know what to do. I realized, however, that I'd been betrayed all these years and that she had never been faithful to me. I started to put two and two together and I wondered if she and Key had been seeing each other even before I caught them in 1993. And if that were true...

"Nathan is diabetic and has regular checkups with a doctor who's not only my personal physician, he's also a very close friend. Nathan was scheduled to have a regular checkup the week I found out about Key. I asked my friend to take some blood from Nathan and check it against my blood for paternity." Wright sighed and sipped some bourbon. "The tests confirmed that Nathan is not my biological son."

"And that's why you killed her?"

"No. In fact, I thought that maybe we could still come to some kind of face-saving mutual understanding. I knew she needed and wanted the money. Why else had she stayed with me all these years? And I knew that the pre-nup didn't allow her to walk away with anything—despite what I told you."

"You two had been married for about fourteen years. A good lawyer might have found a way to get her a large settlement regardless of the pre-nup."

"As I explained before, my lawyers set up my financial affairs so that she couldn't get to my money. Besides, I have a dozen lawyers on retainer who would keep her in court for ten years. And I was sure that Judy wouldn't want to wait that long."

"So you confronted her."

"Yes. I told her I knew Nathan was not my son and that she was seeing another man. She laughed at me. I'll never forget that moment. It was the first time I'd ever seen my wife without her mask. It was the real Judy. She had such contempt for me. She hated me. She said she didn't need my money. She told me about the Club and how she was ready to 'ring the cash register.' She had intended on playing things out a little more with Arquette, Woodbridge, Sanchez and Rosenberg, but now that I knew, she was going to take action."

"So that was the triggering event. When was this?"

"A few weeks ago. I did my best to regain my composure because I knew that my relationship with Nathan depended on how I resolved things with Judy. I asked her for a week or two so that I could tell Nathan face to face, in my own way. I pleaded with her, telling her she owed me at least that much. She didn't agree until I told her I'd sweeten the pot with an extra million dollars—as long as I could speak with Nathan first. I told her she had nothing to lose—she'd waited more than twenty years to be with her lover, what was another week or two. She agreed.

"By the next morning I had formulated a plan. I would kill Judy and have Simpson kill Key the same night, after I'd killed Judy. I didn't think I could deal with Key—he was more than twenty years my junior. Simpson agreed to do the job for a quarter of a million dollars, wired to an offshore account."

"I'm surprised an ex-cop like Simpson would have done a murder for hire."

"Simpson had the feeling life owed him something. Guys like him always have their price. It wasn't hard to find."

"But this is murder," said Sawyer, shaking his head.

"I know. I'd never killed anyone before. Never even *thought* about killing anyone. But I felt completely justified in killing Judy and Key. They had done worse to me. For nearly a quarter of a century my life has been a complete lie. My marriage to Judy was a lie. I divorced Natasha because I loved Judy and then built my life around her. I raised Nathan believing he was my own flesh and blood. That was a lie too. I'm seventy-two years old. My marriage and my son were everything to me. And Judy was taking them both away.

"She also took something else that I hadn't realized was so valuable until they were gone: she took my memories. Everything I believed to be good about my relationship with her never really happened. While I raised another man's child, Judy and Key laughed behind my back and spent my money.

"I couldn't let Judy take Nathan. If I lost my son, there would be nothing for me in this life except reminders that I was no longer needed...and no longer loved. If my plan worked, then I could still have my son. How could Judy and this...this asshole take Nathan away from me?" said Wright, looking at Sawyer as though waiting for an answer. "They never did anything for him. I've been there for him every day of his life."

"It wasn't like they were going to kidnap Nathan and make him live with them, Justin. The kid's in his twenties."

"But they were going to tell him I wasn't his father," he said, as though that explained everything.

Maybe it did, thought Sawyer.

"Even if I got caught... It wouldn't be worse than losing my son."

"How did it actually go down?"

"The plan was that I would kill Judy after one of the Club nights. The day of the murder Simpson waited outside Key's building and went inside when Key left. He picked the lock and waited for Key to return. He knew Key wouldn't come back to the apartment that night with Judy because of the Club. When Key came back, Simpson surprised him from behind and used something to render him unconscious. I want to say chloroform, but I'm not sure if that's it. Something like that. Simpson knew what to do.

"Early the next morning when Simpson saw on the news that Judy was dead, he woke up Key and poured a bottle of sleeping pills and half a bottle of Scotch down his throat."

"And he wrote the note."

"Yes. While Key was unconscious, Simpson searched the place for samples of Key's handwriting—the note was only a few lines and spilling the Scotch on the note made Simpson's version hard to analyze. While he was looking for handwriting samples, Simpson found Judy's diaries."

"There's more than one?"

"They were embarrassing to me and incriminating. She had written about me confronting her about Nathan not being my son and that she feared I might do something to harm her and Key."

"What if something went wrong on Simpson's end or your end?"

"If something went wrong on Simpson's end, he was supposed to call me on our home phone at twelve-thirty exactly, let it ring twice, then hang up. I wouldn't answer, but no one else would call at that hour and hang up after two rings."

"What if Judy answered?"

"She never answers our home phone. I do. She has a private number and a cell phone. Anyhow, Simpson would be calling on a disposable cell phone so there was no way to trace the call back to him.

"If something went wrong on my end, I would call Simpson's disposable cell. If he received a call from me on that phone he planned to toss it off the Vincent Thomas Bridge. I was to let it ring three times, and then hang up. Since no one actually answered the phone, I could always say that I knew nothing about it and that Judy must have made the call."

"So where is Simpson?"

"I really don't know."

"I think you do."

"What I mean is that I couldn't find him now even if I wanted to. Part of what I told you about Simpson and Catalina was true. I owed him his final payment. I told him I wanted to make sure we weren't seen together and that meeting on my boat was the best thing. He took the hydrofoil to Catalina and I took my boat.

"Simpson arrived before I did. He had instructed me to anchor my boat in the mooring I lease in Avalon Bay. He told me to take my dinghy to shore, go to the High Hat Grill and stay there until he checked out the boat and came to get me. He told me to put the money in a suitcase that would be in plain sight when he boarded the boat. He said he would be armed and would search the boat for hidden assailants or weapons before he allowed me back on board. When he knew the money was there and the boat was clean, he would come back to shore and meet me at the High Hat Grill, which is located on the main street in Avalon. You can see the whole bay from there, including my boat. We would then return to the boat and he would tell me where he wanted to be dropped off—he wouldn't tell me where that was, but it could have been Long Beach, Redondo Beach, Marina Del Rey, or somewhere else.

"Everything went according to plan. When he met me in the restaurant, he took me into the restroom and patted me down for weapons or a recording device.

"To show there were no hard feelings, I went into a liquor store across the street and purchased a bottle of Simpson's favorite Scotch. We went back to the boat and I went down in the galley with the bottle. I returned with the Scotch and two glasses. However, I'd switched the bottles of Scotch—I had put poison in a different bottle of the same brand of Scotch that I'd purchased before I left Redondo Beach. When he saw what was apparently the same bottle I just purchased, he didn't think anything of it.

"About a half hour later we were out in the middle of the Pacific and Simpson was dead. I had ten dumbbells on the boat, each about fifty pounds. I attached them to a heavy chain, spacing them each about two feet apart, and then wrapped the chain around Simpson's neck. I pushed his body over the side and then I tossed the weights over one by one."

"You really planned this out."

"You forget that that's what I do—not murder, but plan. I built an empire and when I focus on something, it gets done."

Wright sipped his Bookers. "Simpson was a greedy bastard. Last thing he said was he wasn't sure this was going to be the last payment—what with the media playing the case up so big."

"What about Rosenberg?"

"Danny was a frightened little man. His murder was completely his own fault. Well, mostly his own fault. When he realized that Judy was going to blackmail him and possibly destroy his life, he decided to take matters into his own hands. He tried to get something on Judy to use against *her*. To get her to back off. He couldn't very well hire a detective—he didn't want to explain the whole situation to someone else—so he did the next best thing. He followed her obsessively for about ten days. He even took time off work."

"How did that get him killed?"

"Unfortunately for Danny, he happened to spot Simpson, who was also following Judy during this time. Danny even photographed him with a digital camera.

"The morning after Judy's murder, Danny called me and told me he knew who killed Judy. He said that he had seen some guy hanging around her, staking out her place, taking pictures of her. He described Simpson and he told me he had photographs of the guy and even his license plate number."

"Why didn't he take the information to the police himself?"

"You know Danny. He's very timid, very naïve, really. The last thing he wanted to do is put himself in the middle of a high-profile murder case and explain how he got there. I asked him if he made any copies of the digital photos and he said no. I asked him if he had written down any of the information about Judy and Simpson and he said just in the notebook he kept when he followed her. He asked me if I could present the information to the police myself. Of course, I said I would. I immediately arranged a meeting with Simpson and he arranged…everything else."

"Danny's murder."

"Simpson said he tried to make it look like suicide, but he had to act quickly. The police could pull Danny in any time and if that happened, it was over for us. Simpson thought about leaving a note to wrap it up nice and neat, but he didn't have time to make it work."

"You were lucky."

"Maybe. Some of it was luck, some of it was the fact that I simply executed my plan. I've done that all my life. I'm not afraid to take action. I've found that taking no action will usually hurt you more than taking action.

"And the way I see it, Sawyer, you're the only one standing in my way now. No one else figured it out."

"I don't think you've totally convinced Riley Gaines. I think he'll catch on. Eventually."

"All that matters is what he can prove."

"It's over, Justin. I can't—I *won't*—protect you."

"You don't have to. Just don't do anything. Can you do that?"

"No, I can't."

"How does a hundred million dollars sound? I've got almost three billion. I don't need the money. I need the time and I need my freedom. Hell, make it five hundred million wired to an offshore account. That's serious fuck-you money, Sawyer."

"Last guy you made that kind of deal with is fish food off Catalina."

"Simpson was a schmuck. He sold himself cheap. And even when I paid him I knew I couldn't trust him. Everyone's got his price, Sawyer. Everyone. Including you."

"You're right. But sometimes that price isn't measured in money."

"I could hire someone to kill you."

"You'd better do it fast because I've got Riley Gaines on speed dial."

Again Wright reached into the drawer from which he had removed the bourbon. This time he pulled out a gun. He didn't point it directly at Sawyer. He didn't have to.

"Don't do this, Justin. It's over. Don't make it worse."

"Worse? I'm going to jail for the rest of my life. My life is just about to be reduced to a punch line by a bunch of late-night comedians. And my son is just about to realize that not only am I not his father, I also killed his *real* mother and father. Make it worse? I don't think that's possible."

Sawyer crossed his legs and felt for the gun in his ankle holster—old habits died hard. He had come prepared. No man was more desperate than one who had nothing left to lose and Sawyer knew the position in which he was putting his old friend.

Wright tried to smile, but the muscles didn't seem to work anymore. To Sawyer it seemed the saddest smile he had ever seen.

"You can't get away with killing me, Justin. A successful murder is something you've got to plan. You know that. This is spur of the moment. Besides, Veronica and Eric Gregg know I came here to meet with you in the middle of the night." It wasn't true but Sawyer figured that when someone pointed a gun at you the boundaries of ethical behavior expanded rapidly. "You can't possibly get rid of all the blood in here if you shoot me. And how would you dispose of the body? What are you going to do with my car? You've got to leave it far away from your house. And if you do, how do you get back home without help? And if you get help, you're right back where you started from with me—someone knows your secret and you'll have to kill them too."

"I'm not going to kill you, Sawyer. So you can leave your gun holstered. I've got a deal for you. I know my life is over. And let me make one thing very, very clear: I won't let you take me in. I'll kill myself first."

"Don't do it, Justin..."

"I've got a hundred thousand dollars in cash in my safe. It's yours. Just walk out that door and let me turn myself in."

"Bullshit. You won't turn yourself in."

"You're right. But I just want to see Nathan one more time. I *need* the opportunity to explain to him a few things face to face. Once I'm arrested and the media knows what happened, I'll never get a chance to explain. When Nathan's gone... I'll tell him I'm turning myself into the police and I'll...finish things."

"What if you run?"

"I won't run."

"You'll excuse me if I don't believe you. You're a little short on credibility with me."

"I'll give you my passport."

"You could have a dozen others. You could have prepared for this moment."

"Where could I go, Sawyer? What would I do? I'm seventy-two years old. The police will soon know all the details of my involvement in the murder of four people. Details you will tell them. I'm tired, Sawyer. I don't want to go to jail and I don't want to go to trial. I just want it to be over. But not without having the chance to explain what I did and why to Nathan. Unless I get that opportunity, he'll hate me for the rest of his life."

"Okay, so how would this work? The clock is ticking."

"Nathan's coming over for brunch. That would be about eleven. Give me till one."

"Give me some kind of guarantee that you won't run."

"I'll give you the murder weapon." Again Wright reached into the drawer and this time withdrew a knife wrapped in a white cloth, in a large plastic bag. Sawyer could tell the stains on the cloth were dried blood. Wright set the bag on the desk.

"That couldn't have been in the drawer," said Sawyer. "The cops scoured this place."

"I have a hollow-wall safe in my bedroom. In fact, I have three safes in the house. Most people have one. The police usually don't suspect that you have two safes, let alone three. And the hollow-wall safe isn't metal. It opens only with a remote control—built into my bedroom TV remote—and it only works with a ten-digit password. The only way the cops could have found it was to tear down the house and search the rubble."

"That could be any knife and it could be anyone's blood."

"Okay, how about the knife *and* a handwritten confession? You can tell me what to write. I'll do it in my own handwriting and sign and date it. You can take it and the knife with you. If I renege on the deal, you'll have a signed confession and the murder weapon."

"Plus, you don't leave this house. In case you think about skipping out, I'll have Gregg station a man outside to make sure you don't run. I'll tell him to stop and search Nathan's car or any other car that leaves this house. And no other visitors. That includes Noah."

"Fine. All I want is my last face-to-face with Nathan. Then I'm done."

While Wright wrote his confession, Sawyer tried to think about what else could go wrong. Of course, there were a number of clever ways Wright could skip out. But the old man was right. Where could he go and what would be the point? Sawyer would have the signed confession, the murder weapon, and a step-by-step explanation of the crime that fit the facts.

Even more important, Sawyer could tell that Wright was beaten. It was over.

Sawyer called Eric Gregg at home—he only used that number in an emergency—and asked that a man be stationed outside the Wright residence for twenty-four hours, starting in about thirty minutes, no sooner. Sawyer also told him to tell his man to stop anyone but Nathan from going in and to search any car that left, including Nathan's. Sawyer asked Gregg to trust him. Which was easy for Gregg to do because he did.

When he was done talking with Gregg, Sawyer asked Wright, "Do you use a local courier service?"

"Taylor's. Why?"

"Call them and tell them to come by immediately because you're leaving town and don't want to leave the package outside the front gate very long. Tell them you want the package delivered between noon and one o'clock because there's something important you need the recipient to sign and that he will not be home until noon." Sawyer didn't want to be carrying around evidence in a murder investigation. The fact that Wright had sent the confession and the murder weapon to Sawyer and then committed suicide made some sense. And if Wright actually committed suicide, then no one would look that closely at the details. On the other hand, if Wright skipped out and Sawyer was withholding evidence at the time... The ex-cop knew he would be in trouble.

According to Sawyer's plan, he would receive the package between noon and one. Then he would call Gregg, who would call Gaines, and they would all meet at Sawyer's place. By two o'clock half the LAPD would descend on Wright's mansion.

And it would finally be over.

Sawyer watched as Wright filled out the shipping label and addressed it to Sawyer, who told him to check the box indicating that the package cannot be left without a signature. This created a verifiable alibi for Sawyer—he could say that the first he knew of any of this was when he received the package, which would be sometime between noon and one.

Wright stuffed the confession and the knife into the large, bubble-wrap envelope and sealed it, placing the shipping label on the front of the envelope. He called the delivery service and then he put the package outside his front gate.

A few minutes later, Sawyer saw the Taylor truck pull up and a delivery guy walk to the front gate, pick up the package and leave.

"Aren't you forgetting something?" said Wright.

"What?"

"The hundred grand."

"I think the less money I get from you the better, Justin. You owe me about a thousand dollars in expenses."

Wright walked to a wall safe, took out a stack of money and counted out five thousand dollars. "Untraceable. No checks. It's honest money. I owe you the expense money and I'm giving you a reasonable bonus. Take it, Sawyer."

"I'll take the thousand," he said. "I've got receipts for most of that." He looked at his watch. "I'm going now. Good luck, Justin."

"Thanks for everything. I really appreciate it. And Sawyer?"

"Yes?"

"Look in on Nathan now and then, okay? I don't expect you to take care of him or anything like that. Just... I don't know. He's going to be alone now."

"Sure."

Sawyer pocketed the money and started for the door. Over his shoulder he said, "Make sure Nathan's out of here by one."

Sawyer parked up the block so that he could see any car entering or leaving Wright's home. Just in case. A few minutes later a police car pulled up in front of Justin's house and parked.

As he drove back to his place, Sawyer was thinking that a twenty-two-year-old kid worth three billion dollars would never be alone.

****

Sawyer would later learn that Nathan came for brunch and that he and his father talked till just before one. Wright had told him everything—most of it anyhow. The young man then returned home, believing his father planned to turn himself into the police.

Immediately after his son left Wright had put on a Frank Sinatra CD that included two of Wright's favorites, both of which he programmed to repeat: "It Was a Very Good Year," and "My Way."

An empty bottle of Bookers was found next to the body along with a note admitting that he had killed his wife and paid for the murder of her lover, Barry Key, who was also Nathan's father. His note didn't reference Simpson or Rosenberg, but the confession Sawyer had did. Wright's note also said that he had sent a package to Sawyer and directed him to give the contents to the police.

Sawyer felt a mixture of feelings about how things eventually played out. He felt sad for a man who was so cruelly betrayed. He felt anger toward a man who had murdered his wife. One feeling that totally surprised him was that he felt glad that Wright had finally told him the truth.

Chapter Seventy-one

It was a strange and sad day. Sawyer let the answering machine pick up every call. He knew who was calling and why.

Late in the afternoon he called Rebecca and invited her to dinner at Fu Yuan Low, their favorite Chinese restaurant in the South Bay.

Sawyer arrived about fifteen minutes early and ordered a Grey Goose martini.

Rebecca arrived exactly on time and she was dressed provocatively. Not in a mini-skirt or low-rider jeans, but she looked good. She always looked good when she wanted to, thought Sawyer. He stood, Rebecca kissed him on the lips and they sat down opposite each other in a booth next to the window, far from anyone else.

"I didn't hear your name or see your picture on the news. So, why do I get the feeling you ran the whole show?"

"I didn't. I missed a lot. More than I should have. I just got the opportunity to make up for it in the end."

A waitress took an order from Rebecca for a glass of merlot and left.

"I've been thinking about our talk the other night," said Sawyer. "I feel kind of adrift… I don't know how I feel about a lot of things right now."

"You mean me?"

"I mean a lot of things. I'm supposed to be a hotshot cop and one of my 'friends' almost used me to get away with murder. My wife is so unhappy that she takes a lover—and I had no idea things were that desperate. It's like I don't trust my instincts anymore. It's like the life I thought I was living doesn't really exist."

"It exists. Maybe it's just different from what you thought it would be."

"I don't know… I just feel lost. And this is not just about you having sex with another man—although that's part of it. I realize that I haven't become the person you thought I would be." Sawyer held up his hand, anticipating her reply. "I'm not saying you expected too much. All I'm saying is that you believe I'm not the person you married. And maybe you're right. *Undoubtedly* you're right. Each of us expected that the other would live up to at least a certain amount of expectations. I think you believe I've failed you. And maybe I have."

"Those are your words, not mine."

"Sometimes people just change."

"People change in every marriage. It's just that in the marriages that work, people change together or make room for the differences because their love for each other is big enough to accommodate them." She paused and said, "I don't need you to be the person I married. I just need you to be the person who really wants to be married to me."

Sawyer said nothing.

"You really don't love me anymore?" asked Rebecca sincerely.

"I didn't say that. All I know is that we don't love each other the way we used to. We feel *obligated* to each other. We *have* to do things, *have* to feel things… That's not us. We don't *have* to stay together. We both have other options."

"You're talking about your old girlfriend, Veronica." It was not a question.

Sawyer thought about saying that wasn't true, but instead he said, "Actually, yes. And I never would have even thought about getting together with her had things not reached this point with us."

"So you *are* involved with her."

"Not really. I could never be 'involved' with anyone unless things were over between us. And they're not."

"Are you saying you would never have been with her had I not acted the way I did?"

"I'm not 'blaming' you. You made a choice and I made a choice. It's that simple."

"That may be what happened, but it's not simple."

"You moving out and everything that's happened since just got me to re-think things," said Sawyer. "I realize now that you weren't happy and I was so out of touch with you that I didn't even notice."

"Did you ask me to dinner tonight to officially end our marriage?"

Sawyer didn't answer immediately. "No. But I've got to find out how I feel about things before we re-commit to each other."

"Which allows you to go out and fool around with Veronica, or anyone else, guilt free."

"I don't look at it that way."

Rebecca thought about saying something, but she simply took a drink of her wine, which had just been served.

"It's funny..." said Sawyer. "If people had 'adjustable rate marriages'—marriages that needed to be re-evaluated every seven years—I think people would treat each other differently."

"That's a novel idea. It's also stupid."

"Think about it. If people had to renew their vows every seven years they would be more conscious of what the other person wanted, they wouldn't let themselves get so out of shape, they wouldn't take each other for granted. What's wrong with that?"

"Even if that happened, most men would still end up screwing their secretaries."

Sawyer sipped his martini and said, "You're probably right." He always liked Rebecca's sense of humor and her intelligence. And her legs. There was a lot he liked about her and he was starting to see those things again in a new light.

"So, what's the next step here?" she said finally.

"You've got your place—for a few more weeks—and I've got mine. We're not divorced. Let's just take a break. I need to get my instincts back."

"Don't fool yourself into thinking Veronica's the answer."

"I won't."

This was not the way Rebecca had thought things would play out. She had a new teddy in a bag in the car. She had planned to follow Sawyer home and show him her new purchase. "You know I love you, don't you?"

"And I love you," said Sawyer. "But it's different now."

"Passion changes in every marriage."

"I know that. I just want us to love each other enough to make it worth the work our marriage needs to survive."

"I hope we do," said Rebecca, reaching across the table and taking Sawyer's hand.

"Me too," he said sincerely. "Me too."

They talked and ate. Both recalled memories of cherished pets, holidays and vacations—memory was the thread that stitched together the quilt of life.

An hour later they embraced in the parking lot. They were not husband and wife like they were before. They were not lovers who couldn't keep their hands off each other like they had been years ago.

But they were closer than they had been in a long time.

Chapter Seventy-two

Sawyer went home and parked in the driveway. The angels were still lit. He walked over and touched one for luck.

When he was inside he went to the pantry, scooped up a cup of fish food and walked outside to the pond. The lights were still on.

He removed his shoes and socks, sat on the edge of the pond and tossed a handful of pellets toward Ace Junior.

Sawyer had no idea what all this meant. He had been cuckolded, lied to and used by someone he thought was his friend, and made love to by an ex-lover.

He figured that, at the end of the day, it all had something to do with love, money and growing old...in one of the most beautiful and privileged neighborhoods on the planet.

It was hard to figure out life's grand design. No amount of money could keep death away if it had your name on it. Sawyer saw wealthy vegetarians die prematurely of breast cancer...while George Burns smoked and drank till he keeled over at one hundred years old.

Sawyer realized that if there was such a thing as karma it wasn't something that balanced things out in a single lifetime. Clearly, evil men prospered while good men suffered. And if karma could not be explained in a single lifetime, then did karma need to be understood in the context of a "thousand act play," in which we were simply watching a single act and, therefore, could not tell the heroes from the villains? If so, Sawyer figured that the answers to how things worked were well beyond him. Greater minds than his had tried and failed to figure it out. And maybe that was all he needed to know—that life was more about living it than figuring it out.

Maybe life was to be enjoyed as much as you can for as long as you can, thought Sawyer. Maybe that sounded selfish. Maybe it was. That didn't mean it wasn't true.

Maybe it wasn't much more complex than that. All he knew was that he hadn't been enjoying life much these days and that that was no one's "fault" but his own.

And whether he was going to live another forty minutes or forty years, life wouldn't be worth much unless he learned how to enjoy it.

He also realized that that was not as selfish as it sounded. When he was happy, those around him were happier. When he was happy, he got more done and his positive attitude rubbed off on others. Sawyer had realized long ago that no one could make him happy but himself.

Somewhere along the line he had lost the sense of gratitude he used to feel for the short life he was living. He thought of Justin Wright, one of the richest men in the world, lying dead in his twenty-seven million dollar mansion. Suddenly Sawyer felt embarrassed by his own riches that he had overlooked for so long. Would not Justin Wright have traded his entire fortune for Sawyer's life—a chance to wash away all the sins and all the pain? To live a life that had promise and a future? To live a life where he could love and be loved?

Sawyer's thoughts drifted back to an evening last summer when he had met Judy Wright for dinner at the Palos Verdes Inn. She had told him she wanted to discuss something with him in private. She said that Nathan had been arrested for DUI and she needed some advice on how to proceed. But it became clear to Sawyer during their meeting that that was not the real reason Judy had asked him for a drink.

They had talked and laughed a lot. And flirted a little. They were having a good time.

She said that Justin was out of town and asked if it would be okay if she called him again. Soon. Sawyer had a pretty good idea how that story would end and, while flattered, had politely declined. Even though things hadn't been great recently between him and Rebecca, he was certain that hanging out with Judy when Justin was out of town would only make things worse. Besides, Justin was his friend.

Sawyer wondered how he would have answered Judy if she had asked him the same question a few days ago. Timing was something you either had or you didn't. Was it fate?

Or just plain luck.

Whatever it was, Sawyer could feel the momentum shifting and it was going his way. And while he felt lucky, he knew he was not invincible.

He was not the King of the World.

Merely the Prince of Palos Verdes.

About the Author

Stephen Smoke is the author of 18 novels, including *Black Butterfly*, *Pacific Coast Highway*, and *Pacific Blues*, under his own and other names. He has also written eight non-fiction books. Mr. Smoke has written and directed feature films, including *Street Crimes* (starring Dennis Farina) and *Final Impact*, and has written screenplays for others, including *Magic Kid*.

He founded and published *Mystery Magazine*, and published the first online mystery magazine (*Hamilton Caine's Mystery Digest*, on CompuServe) in 1984.

Mr. Smoke is also a published songwriter and in 1989 recorded an album (in support of his novel, *Trick of the Light*) on which several well-known musicians, including Rock and Roll Hall of Fame member, Garth Hudson (the keyboard player in Bob Dylan's backup band, The Band), played on various tracks. He is also a member of ASCAP and regularly collects royalties for music he has written. He occasionally plays at local coffeehouses and other small venues.

In 1997, his company, Onlineseminars, produced one of the first continuing education for-credit online courses. Later, with a partner, he published the first Standards for Online Learning.

In the mid 90s Mr. Smoke started working on his *Bill of Responsibilities* series and in 2002 finished work on the *Teen Bill of Responsibilities Course*, which is now taught in several Southern California schools. The author is actively involved with various corporate entities, teachers groups and community organizations in order to bring the FREE program to schools around the country. His book, the *Corporate Bill of Responsibilities,* also has a companion Workshop.

The author is currently working on his next novel, *Cathedral of the Senses*, which is the follow-up to *Trick of the Light.*

You can contact Stephen Smoke at
stephen@stephensmoke.com.

Made in the USA
Las Vegas, NV
27 November 2022